The WAITING

Books by Suzanne Woods Fisher

Amish Peace: Simple Wisdom for a Complicated World
Amish Proverbs: Words of Wisdom from the Simple Life

ॐ LANCASTER COUNTY SECRETS ॐ

The Choice
The Waiting

൦ Lancaster County Secrets ൦

Book 2

The WAITING

A NOVEL

Suzanne Woods Fisher

Revell

a division of Baker Publishing Group
Grand Rapids, Michigan

Published by Revell
a division of Baker Publishing Group
P.O. Box 6287, Grand Rapids, MI 49516-6287
www.revellbooks.com

Printed in the United States of America

Library of Congress Cataloging-in-Publication Data
Fisher, Suzanne Woods.
    The waiting : a novel / Suzanne Woods Fisher.
        p.   cm. — (Lancaster County secrets ; bk. 2)
    ISBN 978-0-8007-3386-5 (pbk.)
    1. Amish women—Fiction. 2. Amish—Pennsylvania—Fiction. 3. Lancaster County (Pa.)—Fiction. I. Title.
PS3606.I78W35 2010
813'.6—dc22   2010021026

Scripture used in this book, whether quoted or paraphrased by the characters, is taken from the King James Version of the Bible.

Published in association with Joyce Hart of the Hartline Literary Agency, LLC.

10   11   12   13   14   15   16   7   6   5   4   3   2

Love and thanks to all my family,
near and far.

1

$\mathcal{M}$orning dew shimmered in the warm summer sun as Jorie King led the last horse to a paddock by the road. She unhitched the halter and gave the horse a swat on his hindquarters to hustle him into the pasture. She couldn't help but smile. A stubborn one, he was. Must be part mule.

As she swung the gate closed, she noticed a car at the end of the driveway. A stranger leaned against the hood of the car, his arms crossed against his chest. When the man spotted Jorie, he waved to her and called out, "Hey there! Ma'am! Any idea how far to a gasoline station?"

Jorie latched the paddock gate and walked over to him. "About two miles," she said, pointing up the road.

The man regarded Jorie with mild curiosity, tilting his head as he appraised her prayer cap and Plain clothes. "My car ran out of gas."

Jorie spotted her neighbor across the street, leading some cows to their pasture to graze. "Ephraim!" she called out, waving to the boy. "Ephraim, would you bring a can of gasoline down here?"

Ephraim did a double take when he noticed the stranger. Jorie

The Waiting

swallowed a smile at the boy's reaction—not many men in Stoney Ridge had skin the color of chocolate. A few cows split off and wandered into the cornfield before Ephraim suddenly remembered them and rounded them up. He guided them through the pasture gate, locked it, and waved to Jorie as he ran up the long drive to the barn.

Jorie waited for the tall dark man to speak again. The stranger seemed at ease with silence. His gaze followed Ephraim until he disappeared into the barn, and then the man's eyes swept across the countryside in front of them. "I think that might just be the most beautiful place I've ever seen."

Jorie looked over to take in the sight of the farm: the two-story white frame house nestled against a hill. A gray-topped buggy leaning on its traces by the large barn. About halfway up the drive, a ribbon of a creek wove parallel to the house. On the banks of the creek sat an enormous willow tree that provided shelter to a handful of sheep. And surrounding the house were acres and acres of fields, straight and even rows of corn and wheat. The only sound punctuating the stillness was a distant neighbor calling for his cows. "That's Beacon Hollow. It belongs to my neighbors, the Zooks."

"Clear to see they're good farmers," he said as his eyes scanned the farm.

They stood silently, waiting for Ephraim, listening to the husky whisper of the dry August corn in the fields. "The Zooks have always been farmers," she finally said, breaking the quiet. "They were some of the first settlers around here. Now the land is farmed by four brothers." She looked up the drive to see Ephraim on his way down the hill, lugging a red can of gasoline with two hands. "Ephraim is one of the brothers."

"Don't tell me they're all as young as him, managing a big farm like that!"

8

Jorie smiled. "No. He's the youngest. The oldest brother is Caleb. He and his wife Mary Ann are really running the farm. Matthew—he's eighteen—he does quite a bit of work."

"Where's the third brother?"

Jorie hesitated. "That would be Ben. He's in Vietnam."

The man looked at her curiously. "Pardon me for asking, ma'am, but I thought the Amish didn't fight in wars."

Jorie's chin lifted a notch. "He's *not* fighting. He's a conscientious objector."

Ephraim crossed the road with the full gas can and gave a shy nod to the stranger. The man poured the gasoline into his tank and tightened the cap, then handed the can back to Ephraim. He reached into his back pocket and pulled out a wallet, opened it, and took out a few dollars to hand to Ephraim. "Let me pay you for the gasoline."

Ephraim shook his head. "No n-need."

The man offered the money to Jorie, but she waved it away.

"I'm beholden to you. And I like to pay my debts." He peered into his wallet. "Say, do you like wild animals?" When Ephraim's eyebrows shot up with interest, the man smiled and held out two tickets. "These are tickets to the Mezzo Brothers' Circus & Menagerie that just came to Lancaster. Most of the animals are on the shady side of retirement, but there's a young cougar. The trainer said he just bought it off of a trapper in West Virginia last week."

Ephraim shot a sideways glance to Jorie before accepting the tickets. She smiled and gave a brief nod. If Cal and Mary Ann objected, she would explain the circumstances, maybe even offer to take Ephraim to the circus. Everybody knew how he loved animals.

He put down the gasoline can to study the tickets, a look of wonder on his face. "They r-really have a c-cougar?"

"They used to roam free in Pennsylvania," the man said. "The last one was killed in the 1930s." He put a hand on his car door, but his gaze had settled on the horses behind Jorie, as if watching them eat was the most fascinating thing in the world. "Are those Belgian drafts?"

"Percherons," Jorie said.

Ephraim pointed to Jorie's driveway. "That l-leads to S-Stoney Creek, the K-Kings' farm. They b-breed Percherons." He looked back at the man. "Most every P-Percheron around here is f-from the K-Kings. N-No one knows horses l-like Atlee K-King." He gave Jorie a shy smile.

She was surprised and pleased that Ephraim spoke to the man. He didn't talk much, especially around strangers, self-conscious of his stutter.

"They sure are beautiful creatures," the man said. A colt peered over the pasture fence at them for a moment, then tossed his dark mane and trotted off down a dirt trail to join his mother.

The clang of a dinner bell floated down on the wind. Ephraim's head jerked toward the farmhouse at Beacon Hollow. "Friehschtick!" *Breakfast!* He gave a quick nod to Jorie and the man, grabbed the empty gasoline can, and set off at a sprint up the long drive to the farmhouse.

Jorie shrugged, lifting her palms. "When you're thirteen years old and growing like a weed, mealtimes are serious business."

The man got into his car, turned on the ignition, leaned his head out the window, and grinned. "Meals are serious business at any age." As he drove off, he called out, "Thank you, ma'am, for your help."

Ma'am? Wasn't that a term the English used to address older women? Jorie put her hands up to her cheeks. She knew it seemed vain, but being called ma'am made her feel older than her twenty-four years. A horse leaned his heavy head over the fence, sniffing for grass, and pushed his nose at her, making her stumble a step. She caught herself and whirled around, laughing. "Leave it to you, Big John, to remind me not to take myself too seriously." She stroked his forelock. "Especially on a beautiful Sunday morning like today." She gave him a pat and went up to the farmhouse to get ready for church.

As soon as Caleb Zook tucked his beard to his chest, a signal for silent prayer before breakfast, Ephraim bowed his head slightly and watched for Cal to close his eyes. Then he quietly stretched out his hand so that it rested on the handle of the syrup pitcher, ready to make his move as soon as the prayer ended. He closed his eyes, and halfway through the prayer, he felt Cal gently place his hand over Ephraim's and squeeze hard, really hard, until Ephraim released his grip and slipped his hand into his lap.

"What do you think we should do tomorrow?" Cal asked as soon as prayer ended, reaching out for the syrup pitcher.

Ephraim settled for the bowl that held steaming scrambled eggs. "C-cut hay," he said, dishing out a spoonful of eggs onto his plate before taking a mammoth bite.

The sound of footsteps thundering up the wooden porch stairs, two at a time, interrupted the discussion as the door swung open and warm air swooped in. "Sorry to be late," Matthew said, scraping his boots on the mat. He gave Ephraim a sideways glance. "Thought you were coming back to the barn to help me sterilize those milk cans."

Ephraim shrugged. He had gotten distracted when Jorie called him down to help the man who needed gas, then completely forgot about Matthew waiting on him for help.

As Matthew pulled out a chair and sat down, he picked up the bowl of scrambled eggs and started to dish them onto his plate.

"First, wash up," Cal said. "Then, prayers. Then, eat."

Matthew pushed himself away from the table and went to the sink to wash his hands. "Where's Mary Ann and Maggie?"

"Upstairs," Cal said. "Maggie's having trouble with her hair. We can't be running late today for meeting."

Ephraim's eyes followed the syrup pitcher as Cal set it down, and Matthew grabbed it as he sat down at the table. Ephraim sighed as he watched his brother pour a small river of syrup on his scrapple, dripping down the edges, pooling on his plate.

"I think cutting hay sounds like a good plan, Ephraim," Cal said. "The front that came through last night left us a beautiful day. Maybe it'll stay clear for a while." He smiled as he handed the pitcher to Ephraim. "Though I always have to laugh at myself when I try to plan for the week. Weather is God's way of keeping a farmer humble."

Ephraim tried pouring the few remaining drips of syrup onto his scrapple, gave up, and reached past Matthew to grab a piece of toast before that, too, was gone.

"Did Jorie King say yes to teaching?" Matthew asked.

"She did," Cal said, looking pleased. "Took a month of convincing but she finally agreed. How'd you guess that?"

Between bites, Matthew said, "Ephraim said he saw her in the schoolhouse yesterday."

"She was s-sweeping it out," Ephraim answered in a mournful tone.

"Getting it ready for next week's start," Cal said. "Did you offer to help her?"

Ephraim stopped chewing his toast. The thought hadn't occurred to him. Cal rolled his eyes.

"Ha! Our Ephraim keeps as far a distance as possible from a schoolhouse when he doesn't have to be there," Matthew said.

Ephraim tried to kick him under the table, but Matthew, expecting it, quickly moved his legs out of reach.

Seven-year-old Maggie galloped down the stairs with her hair firmly pinned into a tight bun, covered by a freshly starched prayer cap. Her mother, Mary Ann, followed behind her. They sat down at the kitchen table, bowed their heads for a moment, then Mary Ann jumped up. The toast was burning and she hurried to yank the toast tray from the oven.

Mary Ann seemed flustered today. Ephraim thought it might have something to do with lots getting drawn today for the ministers for the new district. He had heard plenty of neighbors say they were hoping and praying Caleb Zook would draw the lot.

"So Jorie King is going to be the teacher?" Maggie asked, poking her glasses higher on the bridge of her small nose.

"Maggie, sometimes I think you've got ears like an Indian scout," Cal said. "Yes, Jorie will be your teacher this year."

Maggie dusted her oatmeal with brown sugar. "Why is she called Jorie?"

"Her grandmother is Marge and her mother is Marjorie, so Jorie's name is shortened to avoid confusion," Cal explained.

"Why ain't Jorie married?" Maggie asked, using a fork to saw her scrapple into tiny bite-size pieces. "She ain't *that* old. And she's awful pretty."

"Isn't. She *isn't* that old," Cal said. "And whom a teacher courts is none of our concern." He pointed to her plate to keep eating.

"Matthew said she's been asked a dozen times." Maggie took the smallest possible bite of her scrapple. "Matthew said she always says no."

"Matthew needs to remember that careless words are a displeasure to the Lord," Cal said, as he gave Matthew "the look"—one eyebrow raised over a stern face.

Ephraim grinned. He could tell Cal's heart wasn't in it. He saw Cal cast a glance at Mary Ann, at the sink scraping burnt edges off the toast, before leaning over to whisper to Maggie. "Jorie and your Uncle Ben have an understanding. As soon as he gets back from Vietnam, they'll get married. She's just waiting on him."

"Ephraim's hoping Jorie will hang on a few years and wait till he can grow some whiskers," Matthew interrupted, elbowing Ephraim. "If I were you, little brother, and had a schoolteacher who looked like Jorie King, I'd be offering to sweep that school-house morning and night." He turned his head toward Mary Ann, whose back was to him while she stood at the counter, buttering toast. Satisfied she was preoccupied, he whistled two notes, one up, one down, while outlining an hourglass shape with his two hands.

Ephraim blushed furiously, made a grab for the milk pitcher, and knocked it over.

Cal jumped up and tried to mop up the milk before it spilled onto his lap. "Matthew, you fulfilled your teasing quota for the day and it's only seven in the morning."

"Will you teach me how to whistle, Matthew?" Maggie asked.

"Can't, Magpie," Matthew answered. "Not until your front teeth grow in." He peered into her mouth. "I declare, all of your teeth are falling out and nothing's coming in. I'm starting to think you're going to be toothless, like ol' Amos Esh." He sucked in his lips and chomped down on them, trying to look toothless. "Don't worry, though. I'll get you a pair of store-bought choppers for your birthday."

Maggie looked to her father with saucer eyes.

"Matthew is trying to upset you, Maggie," Cal assured her. "Your teeth will come in when they're good and ready. Finish up so we won't be late. It's a big day."

Leaning against the sink, wiping her hands with a towel, Mary Ann said, "I'm worried you're going to end up in the lot."

Cal got up to refill his coffee cup. "Now, Mary Ann, the Lord didn't intend for his people to worry."

As Ephraim inspected the remaining quarter of his toast, butter on the edges, red raspberry jam heaped on top, Cal's thought forever struck him as odd. Cal worried almost as much as Mary Ann.

Cal put down the coffee cup and placed a hand on Mary Ann's shoulder. "I have more faith in our people than you do. They have better judgment than to vote for me as a minister."

She covered Cal's hand with hers, but Ephraim could tell she had a different idea of how folks would vote.

Twenty minutes later, after Ephraim's and Maggie's faces were scrubbed so they shone, Cal herded everyone into the buggy and slapped the reins on the horse's hind end to set off down the long drive to the road. At the end of the drive, he stopped the horse and let Matthew jump out to get yesterday's forgotten mail from the mailbox. Matthew walked back to the buggy, sifting through the mail, then stopped abruptly. He tore open a thin gray envelope.

"Shall I get a rocking chair for you, Matthew, so you can read in comfort?" Cal asked.

Matthew held up the envelope and its contents. "It's from the U.S. Selective Service. 'You have been reclassified from 1A to 1W and must report to the Armed Forces recruitment office in Philadelphia, Pennsylvania, for a physical exam on September 1st, 1965.'"

His news had an impact on the family of a thunderclap out of a clear blue sky. Mary Ann shot Cal a look of alarm. Ephraim felt the breakfast in his stomach do a flip-flop. Even Maggie stopped humming, and she was always humming to herself. She opened her mouth to ask a question, but Ephraim nudged her.

"Not n-now," he whispered in her ear.

Quietly, Cal said, "I'll go with you for that meeting."

"No, you won't," Matthew said firmly. "I can handle this myself." He tucked the letter in his coat pocket and climbed onto the back of the buggy.

"How long has Ben been gone now?" Maggie asked.

Mary Ann turned her head to look at her daughter in the backseat. "Nearly two years."

Matthew leaned toward Ephraim. "How many times do you think we're going to get asked today if we've heard from Ben? Last time, I counted thirteen." It was a question that confronted them every time they went to church or to town or to any gathering.

"Will Matthew be sent to Vietnam too?" Maggie asked.

"No," Cal said in a tone that meant the discussion was over. He slapped the reins on the back of the horse to get it moving.

Ephraim elbowed her as an awkward silence covered the buggy.

"What?" Maggie whispered to him, palms raised.

"He's worried M-Matthew will get s-signed up t-to g-go," Ephraim whispered to Maggie.

"I don't get it," Maggie whispered loudly.

"Me n-neither."

"There's two types of conscientious objectors," Matthew explained in a longsuffering voice. "There's the conscientious objector who won't serve. And then there's the C.O. who will serve.

16

That's what Ben got signed up for. He got tricked. So that's why he was sent to Vietnam."

"Why didn't Ben just tell the government he was tricked?" Maggie asked. "That he didn't want to kill anyone?"

"He's *not* killing anyone," Cal said sharply.

Mary Ann turned and placed a hand over Maggie's small hands. "What's done is done. But we pray every day that Ben is safe and well and coming home to us."

"But why couldn't he just explain—"

Ephraim covered Maggie's mouth with his hand. Maggie was too young to realize that those unanswerable questions about Ben grieved everyone. But Ephraim knew.

"That's enough talk about war and killing," Cal said. "It's a beautiful Sunday morning and our thoughts should turn to the Lord."

They *should*, Ephraim thought, but thoughts were hard to control. Sometimes his thoughts bounced around like a game of ping-pong. Mostly, his ping-pongy thoughts had to do with getting his chores done as fast as he could so he could sneak off to the Deep Woods. But anytime Ben's name was brought up, which was often, his thoughts hung there, suspended. He couldn't stop thinking and worrying about him. Where was he? Was he in danger? Could he be captured and tortured as a prisoner of war, like stories he overheard when he went to town with Cal?

After meeting ended that morning, the children and non-members went outside while the members remained in the house to choose two new ministers for the newly split district. The bishop, Isaac Stoltzfus, would oversee both districts.

"It always gives me the chills, this lot choosing," Jorie said to Mary Ann, as they stood in line to whisper their choice of a minister to the bishop. "All that separates one man from the other is a slip of paper and the will of God."

Mary Ann turned to her. "I'd forgotten that your father was a minister too. Then you understand how hard it can be—adding those duties on top of a busy farmer's life."

Jorie nodded. "The day Dad drew the lot, Mom cried all afternoon."

"How are your folks?" Mary Ann asked.

"It's taken awhile, but they feel as if Canada is home now," Jorie answered. Three years ago, her parents and siblings had moved, with four other families, to start a new settlement. She had chosen to stay behind to help her grandparents with their horse breeding farm. She never regretted her decision. She loved those Percheron horses as much as her grandfather did. And, of course, there was Ben. He had asked her to stay.

Jorie glanced across the room at her grandfather. With his thick head of snow white hair and bushy eyebrows, he reminded her of a white polar bear, big and strong. He winked when she caught his eye. His familiar deep-lined face was dear to her heart, and she knew there were more lines etched into his face this year than last. Atlee King was doing all he could to keep the farm solvent. Their best broodmare, Penny, died while trying to deliver twin foals. Penny was an older horse, but she'd always been a sweet, gentle mother, producing strong and healthy babies. There were always problems with the horses, but that particular setback—losing Penny and her foals—was an enormous loss.

When Caleb Zook asked if Jorie would teach, at first she said no, but he kept asking and she kept thinking about it. The extra income could help her grandfather and she wouldn't have to go far from home. Still, the thought of what she had agreed to made Jorie's stomach churn. It wasn't the teaching part—it was that blasted state exam the eighth graders needed to pass in late May. Mr. Whitehall, the superintendent of public schools, was not shy in sharing his opinion that one-room schoolhouses were an antiquated system. He was only making concessions to the governor of Pennsylvania, he pointed out, to allow for them. But if those eighth graders didn't pass that state exam in late May, she knew it could have repercussions for all of the Amish schools.

When she admitted to Cal her concerns, he insisted that if anyone could help those scholars pass that test, he knew it would be Jorie. "Our district needs you," he told her. "It's an unusually big eighth grade class this year, and either they are woefully behind in their studies from the school they've been attending, or they might—not all, mind you—be a little . . . slow to learn. Either way, you're the only one I can think of who can bring them up to standard."

Oh, she hoped he was right. She was starting to wake up regularly in a panic, dreaming it was already May and the scholars all failed the test. She shook her head to clear it of that thought, and suddenly realized that she was next in line and the bishop was waiting for her.

She quickly whispered her choice to him and found a seat next to Mary Ann. "Folks are praying the lot will fall to Cal."

Mary Ann smoothed out her apron as if sweeping away her concern. "There are plenty of other good candidates."

Sylvia, Mary Ann's sister, seated on her other side, slipped an arm around her sister and gently squeezed her shoulder. "Caleb is far too young," Sylvia said, giving Jorie a thin smile. "We need ministers who are old and wise."

Cal may be young, but Jorie knew there weren't many men who had the effect on others like he did. When Cal spoke, others always listened. If he walked into a room, everyone in it seemed to breathe a little sigh of relief. As if all would be well.

But Sylvia obviously disagreed. The way Sylvia was staring at Jorie right now, with those piercing dark eyes, reminded her of a Cooper's hawk, arms out wide like wings stretched protectively around Mary Ann. She knew it wasn't right to let her mind meander down such lanes, comparing people she knew to birds and animals. The images just popped, unbidden, into her mind. Silently, she asked the Lord to forgive her for such foolishness and managed a smile in return for Sylvia.

The bishop announced that five men had been recommended by the members. Caleb Zook's name was indeed on the list. Jorie felt torn between relief for the church and empathy for Mary Ann. Isaac reminded everyone that each nominated man would choose a hymnal, the *Ausbund*, and in two would be a slip of paper. From those lots would come God's choices to lead his flock.

A library hush fell over the room as the hymnbooks were placed on the tabletop. A prayer was offered, then the nominees stood, one by one, to claim a hymnal. "Please not Cal, Lord, please not Cal," Mary Ann whispered, unaware that others could hear her.

Samuel Riehl was the first to open the hymnal. He held up a slip of paper and his wife, Rachel, gasped. Then two more men opened empty hymnals. It had come down to Cal and Henry Glick. As Cal opened his hymnal, his shoulders slumped. He turned around, looked at his wife, raised his eyebrows, and held up the hymnal for all of the church members to see the white slip of paper.

Henry Glick grabbed Cal's hand and pumped it enthusiastically. "May God be with you, Caleb."

Jorie had to bite her lip to keep from laughing at the look of relief on Henry's face. She felt Mary Ann lean into her shoulder, and she shifted to look at her—as Mary Ann slumped over into Jorie's lap in a dead faint.

2

When Mary Ann came to, people were standing above her like nurses puzzling over a patient. As her vision came into focus, she recognized her husband's light blue eyes, filled with worry. Then she realized that Jorie was the one cradling her head in her lap.

"She didn't expect Cal would be chosen," she heard her sister Sylvia say. "None of us did. She's just plain overcome."

Marge King, Jorie's grandmother, put a cool hand on Mary Ann's forehead. "Any fever?" Marge demanded. She fancied herself a healer, but everyone steered clear of her remedies.

Slowly, Mary Ann shook her head.

Marge looked unconvinced. "Still feeling dizzy and light-headed?"

Mary Ann tried to wave Marge off. How could she possibly put into words all that she felt right now? She had dreaded this morning, knowing in her heart what was to come. As soon as she saw that slip in Cal's hymnal, a deep foreboding settled over her, a portent that life would never be the same. She pulled herself up to her elbows and insisted she was fine.

"I'll stay close by," Marge said, clearly disappointed.

As Cal helped her to her feet, Mary Ann was glad Maggie was outside with Ephraim and Matthew and hadn't seen her faint. Deeply embarrassed, she wondered if her sister was right. Maybe she had been overcome by the news of Cal drawing the lot. Being a servant of God was a burden and a responsibility, she knew that to be true. It was an unpaid position without any training, and a man was appointed for his lifetime. On top of an already heavy workload, Cal would be called upon to drop everything for the needs of the church members. The duties would follow Cal like a shadow. He would be a fine minister for the new district, she had no doubt. But at what cost?

"That's twice you've fainted in one week," Cal said quietly as he helped her stand. "Two days ago, in the kitchen, when you were canning tomatoes, and now today. Maybe you should see the doctor."

She shook her head. "Drawing the lot just . . . shook me up, is all."

"I can't blame you," Cal said. "I wanted to faint dead away, too, when I saw that slip. Sure you're feeling all right? You still look a little pale."

"I might be fighting a virus," she answered, slipping her hand through the crook of his elbow. "I've been a little tired lately."

After a time of lunch and fellowship, Cal pulled Maggie and Ephraim out of a softball game to return to Beacon Hollow for the afternoon milking.

"Dad?" Maggie asked, as she climbed up into the buggy. "Will you be marrying and burying folks now?"

Mary Ann turned in the buggy to look at Maggie, seated next to Matthew. Once Maggie got started with her questions, there was no end in sight. And the comments she could make! Mary Ann never knew what would come out of her daughter's mouth.

"So maybe you can marry off Matthew to Fat Lizzie before he leaves!" Maggie puckered her mouth and made kissing sounds. "I caught her making googly eyes at Matthew during meetin'."

"Maggie Zook!" Mary Ann waved a finger at her daughter. "Lizzie Glick is a fine girl. She's . . . she's just big boned." She turned to face forward. "Besides, only a bishop does the marrying."

"M-Matthew's s-sweet on Wall-Eyed Wanda," Ephraim said quietly to Maggie.

Whipping her head around to glare at Ephraim, Mary Ann said firmly, "Wanda Graber can't help having a lazy eye."

"I'm not ready to be tied to any woman's capstrings quite yet, little brother." Matthew doffed Ephraim's straw hat and sent it spinning into the back of the buggy.

As Ephraim scrambled over the back of the bench to retrieve his hat, Mary Ann noticed how much he had grown this summer. He was slight and gangling, with a freckled complexion and straight, blond hair—nothing like Cal, who was tall and broad shouldered, with thick dark hair and skin that was tanned by the sun. Ephraim wasn't a boy any longer, nor was he a man. He was at that difficult in-between stage.

Cal, uncharacteristically solemn, hardly noticed the teasing. Mary Ann knew he was thoroughly preoccupied with the changes being a minister would bring for the family. And he was losing Matthew's help on the farm just as he would be so busy with new duties. They would all grieve over losing Matthew—and it wasn't just the help he gave. Matthew was the heart of their family. She had raised him like her own since he was ten years old—he had been a beautiful, golden-haired boy, and now he was a handsome young man, sturdy and bold, with laughing eyes. What would their home be like without his rascal's smile and teasing ways? She didn't even want to imagine it.

Cal went to bed early that night, worn out by the day's events. Mary Ann tiptoed into the bedroom to get ready for bed. The moon was coming up full over the sloped roof of the barn, casting its light through the window. She listened to her husband's steady breathing and stood by the bed for a moment, watching him. Even though it was vain to think it, she loved his looks. He had such a remarkable face, a truly breath-catching face: strong-boned but refined, with a hint of a Roman nose. It still caught her by surprise, to be Cal's wife, even after eight years of marriage.

She had wanted to marry Cal from the first time he had taken her home from youth group. There were plenty of other girls who had a hope pinned on Caleb Zook. He was handsome, intelligent, kind, all of those things, but what set Cal apart—what had always set him apart—was that he had been given more than his share of wisdom. Even when he first took over Beacon Hollow, after his folks' accident, neighbors would watch for the day when Caleb Zook bought his seed and then they would start planting. They knew Cal could call the weather like no one else. It ran in the family with those Zooks, her father used to say. They were just known for having more than their share of common sense. Except for that Ben, her father would add. It might have skipped a generation with Benjamin Zook.

Once or twice, Cal stopped by her farm on a summer evening for a long walk. She had assumed she wasn't really his kind of girl. She was attractive enough, but there were prettier girls. She was flat where she should have been flounced out, thick where she should be thin. And she was two years older than him.

Then the Armed Forces started conscripting men for the Korean War and Cal was called to serve two years in a hospital in Philadelphia. She never heard from him, not a single letter, the entire time he was away. He came home every so often for a weekend, but he never stopped by her farm. She started to think he wasn't planning to return after his duty was served. But then his folks were in a terrible accident. A truck sailed through a stop sign and crashed into his parents' buggy, killing them instantly. The government released Cal from duty and he was suddenly back again, stepping into the gaping hole of his parents' absence. He cared for his younger brothers and managed every aspect of Beacon Hollow.

Cal was far more serious than when he left, far more grown up. He asked to take Mary Ann home from a Singing one evening, and five months later, asked if she would marry him. She was so surprised that eager words tumbled out of her mouth before she could stop them: "Oh yes! Oh yes, yes, yes!" And then, to her great embarrassment came the words, "But . . . why?"

Then it was his turn to look surprised. It was her heart, he told her. That was what made a woman beautiful.

Cal was a kind and good husband to her. He never expressed disappointment that their family was so small, though she was sure he must have felt it. Most of her friends had four or five children by now. She had given him Maggie. And a beautiful little boy, Sammy, who never took a breath.

She said her evening prayers in silence while she changed. As she unpinned her dress to change into her nightgown, something caught her eye in the moonlight. She went over to the window and held out her arm. A large bruise ran from her shoulder to her elbow. She couldn't remember banging herself to cause such a mark, but life on a farm was filled with heavy work. It probably happened when she was helping the boys pour a milk can into the bulk tank.

She promptly put the bruise out of her mind and slipped into bed next to her husband.

In late August, on the first day of school, Jorie arrived before 7:00 a.m., though school took up at nine. Cal was already there, opening up windows to air out the heavy smell of linseed oil he had used to seal the wooden floors and keep down dust. The schoolhouse sat on a corner of Beacon Hollow's farmland, donated to the new district. Cal had organized a work frolic in late July to build the schoolhouse in one day. The aromas of raw wood and fresh paint mingled with the linseed oil, permeating the room.

Cal smiled when he saw her. "I missed all of this. We didn't have parochial schools when I was young." He turned in a slow circle, admiring the building. "I was bused to a public high school about an hour away. We spent so much time on that bus my father used to call it a dormitory on wheels."

"I'd forgotten that you finished high school," Jorie said. "You have a diploma, don't you?" She raised her eyebrows. "Maybe *you* should be teaching."

He was grandly dismissive of that notion. "Oh no. A public school education only gave me a headful of useless information about the kings and queens of England, and how the human being evolved from a one-celled organism." He lifted open another window. "This little room, all that goes on within these four walls—this is where our scholars will be prepared for our way of life." He spun around and pointed to her. "And you're just the one who can do that."

He laughed when he saw the look of panic on her face. "You'll do fine, Jorie King. The Lord will not fail you."

"It's not the Lord I'm worried about. It's those eighth grade boys." At the front of the classroom, she crossed her arms across her chest and walked a tight little turn, back and forth. "It's such a large amount of eighth graders. And all boys! Out of a classroom of twenty-five scholars, I only have six girls. I noticed those eighth grade boys in church yesterday." She stopped to look at him. "Some of them *must* be fifteen!"

"Two are sixteen. They still haven't passed the test. This will be the year, though, that we will clear that logjam of boys. They've spent the better part of ten years on a long journey through eight grades."

She clapped her hands against her cheeks. "Cal, you are expecting me to be a miracle worker. Seven scholars have to pass that test come May or the superintendent is threatening to close our school. I don't know what I've let you talk me into."

Cal winced. "Eight. Ray Smucker is coming today too."

She shuddered. Those Smuckers were legendary for contrariness.

"I have confidence in you, Jorie," he said kindly. "But . . . there is a big stick up on the wall, just in case you need it." He pointed to a large ruler, hanging by the blackboard. He put on his straw hat and tipped it. "Looks to be another hot day today. Good for the hay."

She scowled at him. "Bad for the scholars."

He grinned. "Don't forget. School lets out at four."

Forget? How could she forget when school let out? She was already counting the hours.

Jorie spent the first hour taking enrollment and reassigning seats. The front row was the first graders, the populous eighth grade took up the last three rows. When she got to the sixth grade, she saw a hand waving, frantically reaching to the sky to catch her attention. "Esther Swartzentruber?"

Esther sprang up. "I just thought you should know that Ray Smucker is eating an apple." She spoke with great authority and jerked her pointed chin in Ray's direction. "In class."

"Oh?" Jorie said. "Thank you, Esther. Please sit down."

Esther sat down, pleased with herself. She had her mother Sylvia's fragile elegance, with sharp brown eyes and finely cut features. Jorie knew Esther also had Sylvia's capability to slice peoples' hearts to ribbons.

Jorie looked at Ray. The chair was too small beneath his bottom and his knees did not fit under the desk, so he stretched out his long legs into the aisle and crossed his ankles. On his face was a look of defiance. "Ray, please put your apple in the trash."

Ray didn't budge.

"Ray, didn't you hear me?" Her voice was steady but forced.

Ray met her gaze. "Soon as I'm finished with it," he said, letting a broad smile escape. "Don't want to be wasting it." He took another bite of the apple.

Jorie hesitated on the edge of a decision. She knew this was her make-or-break moment to earn the scholars' respect. She walked down the aisle toward Ray, who sat there, defiantly eating his apple. "You must not have had enough for breakfast today." She spun around. "Does anyone else have any apples in their lunch?"

Twenty hands shot up. "Please get them." The scholars rummaged in their lunches and handed Jorie the apples. She walked up and down the aisles, collecting the apples in her apron. "Here you go, Ray. Eat up." She put the apples on his desk and went back to the front of the class to resume roll call.

Ray looked victorious. At least, until the eleventh apple. By then, he was looking a little sick of apples. By the fifteenth, he was barely chewing, and by the twentieth, he grew still and his face was pale.

"Whoa, pal," Eli Graber said, seated next to Ray. "You're looking a little green there. You're not going to puke, are you?"

"No," Ray answered, clearly annoyed.

Suddenly, his eyes went wide. A wrenching heave rolled up from his stomach and he vomited in the direction of Esther, seated in front of him. Esther froze, her shoulders hunched up by her ears, then she screamed as if an arrow had pierced her back. Ray wiped his mouth with his sleeve, glared at Jorie, staggered outside, and took off down the road.

Jorie came to herself with a start. "Ephraim, go get a bucket of water and a rag." She turned to Esther. "Stand still, Esther, so I can clean you up. Really, he hardly got anything on you. In fact, take off your apron and you'll be as good as new." The rest of the children started to gag from the smell and clumped by the windows, trying to breath in great gasps of fresh air.

"Er is sich alles verblut!" Esther shouted, pointing at a first grader. *He is all bloody!* "Er is am Schtarewe!" *He is dying!*

Jorie looked to see Tommy Fisher, standing against the wall, start to cry. A red rivulet ran down his chin from one nostril, dripping blood onto his light blue shirt.

Maggie came up to Jorie and quietly whispered, "Aw, he was just picking his nose."

Jorie grabbed a tissue from the box on her desk and slid down onto one knee in front of Tommy, working fast. She rolled the tissue tight and stuffed it up into his bleeding nostril, trying to staunch the flow. "You're not going to die, Tommy. Now hold this," she said, putting his hand up on his nose and leaning his head back.

Breathing a little hard, with sweat dripping down her back from either the excitement or the heat of the morning or both, Jorie closed up the enrollment book. "Grab your tablets and pencils and let's go outside."

The class poured out behind her.

Jorie supposed, with such a day as she was having, it was inevitable that she would get a visit from Sylvia Swartzentruber. She always found herself surprised by the fact that Sylvia and Mary Ann were sisters. They were as opposite as two women could be.

Ben used to say that Sylvia looked as if she had a popcorn kernel stuck in a back tooth. "I would bet money on the fact," he had said more than once, "that Sylvia has never once had a laughing jag. Not once in her life."

Jorie would scold him for saying such a thing, but she wouldn't deny it.

Sylvia wrinkled her nose at the lingering smell when she stepped into the main room of the schoolhouse. Then her eyes went wide at the sight of the window that had been shattered by a fly ball during a lunchtime softball game. "Caleb Zook donated the land and built this school," she said, her voice as sharp as a pinch, "and within one day, you have already let this building fall into disrepair." She huffed. "According to Esther, today was a complete and total disaster."

"Not entirely, Sylvia," Jorie said. "I admit there were a few . . . unexpected twists and turns . . . but by four o'clock, things were pretty well organized." All in all, she felt rather satisfied. The books were taken out of the cupboards and distributed, letters and numbers were written on the blackboard, and no other injuries had occurred.

Sylvia cocked her head like a wary sparrow. "Esther told me you are planning to have a Christmas program. That's the most ridiculous thing I've ever heard. Those things end up just filling their heads with nonsense and taking away time that ought to be put on lessons." She crossed her arms against her chest. "Plus, it makes them vain and forward."

Jorie heartily disagreed, but she kept that opinion to herself. How could learning—any learning—be thought of as nonsense?

"And the next time someone loses their breakfast on my Esther, I expect you to have the good sense to send her home to change her clothes. She came straight home, took a long bath, and is lying down with a frightful headache."

"I'll keep that in mind," Jorie said.

She breathed a sigh of relief as Sylvia, finally exhausted of scoldings, turned and left for home. She knew God loved each and every soul, but she wondered if even the Almighty Lord found it took a little more effort with Sylvia Swartzentruber.

Matthew was almost done sawing up a large tree branch that had fallen during a heavy rainstorm so it could be split, seasoned, and used for firewood. He stopped to wipe his brow and noticed Jorie King drive a buggy up the long lane that led to the farmhouse and barn. He dropped the saw and took a few strides to the water pump. He quickly pumped some water and washed off his face, then smoothed his blond hair back under his black felt hat. He ran his hand over his chin, checking to see that he had shaved his whiskers properly. He wiped his hands on his pants and hurried to meet her, hoping she had time for a talk. Jorie King might be his brother's girl, but his heart beat faster when he saw her. He knew it wasn't the Plain way to believe in luck, but sometimes he thought Ben was such a lucky dog. He was always lucky. Lucky in life, lucky in love.

Matthew had never seen such a color of hair as Jorie's. When the sun hit it just right, like it did in church yesterday, it looked like it was nearly on fire. For a moment, his mind wandered to a daydream of liberating her hair from that starched bonnet and those nasty-looking pins, then his vision was interrupted when Jorie said, "Mary Ann told me your news, Matthew." In a flash, she hopped down from the buggy. "What do you think about leaving us behind and living in the big scary city of Lebanon?"

Matthew grinned and squared his shoulders, trying to look like a man. "Truth be told, Jorie, I think the federal government isn't a bit interested in what I think about it." He wouldn't admit it to her, but he was disappointed he ended up getting sent to the Veterans Hospital in Lebanon, just an hour away by bus, to work in the psychiatric rehabilitation ward. He was worried Cal would ask him to live at home, but his brother never said a word about it. That was Cal, though. He believed a man had to make his own decisions in life.

Matthew had his heart set on New York City. Once, while he was in town, he heard a song on the radio at the hardware store about New York City being a place where people never slept. Imagine that!

"I'm hoping you'll be able to return for our Christmas program in December," Jorie was saying, jolting him back to the present. "Ephraim will be the angel Gabriel, announcing the coming birth of the Christ child. We've already started to work on it."

Matthew's heart soared. Jorie King wanted to see him again! "Well, I'll be sure to—"

"If you're looking for Mary Ann, she's in her garden," Cal said, coming toward them from the barn.

Matthew tried not to scowl at Cal for interrupting.

"It's you I'm looking for, Cal, if you have a moment to spare," Jorie answered.

"What is it?" Cal asked, leaning against the fence. He shot his brother a look to give them a little privacy, so Matthew went back to the woodcutting. He used the hatchet to hack twigs off of the branch so he could keep one ear on the conversation.

"It's about one of the boys at school."

"Someone giving you a hard time? I hope it's not Ephraim."

"No, nothing like that. In fact, it's just the opposite."

"How so?"

"Did you mean what you said in your sermon yesterday? About how husbands should be listening to their wives? That a wife's opinion should be considered a gift of wisdom to the husband?"

"Of course I meant it. What are you getting at?"

"Ray Smucker came for an hour on the first day of school, just long enough to get on the attendance roll, and left."

"So I heard," Cal said, eyes laughing. "He had a hankering for an apple. Or two. Ephraim said you handled it as calm as a summer day."

"Ray hasn't been back since. I stopped by the farm and spoke to Lyddie." She tilted her head. "Gideon told her that Ray doesn't need any more schooling."

"Gid has never set much store in book learning. He only went through the fourth grade himself. He raised his older boys the same way, letting them miss months at a time when he needed them on the farm. Guess he feels they turned out all right."

"That was a different time," Jorie said. "The school districts had a more lenient eye toward farming families. And Gid had a different wife for those boys. I know this is a late-in-life child for him, but Lyddie is young. She wants Ray to get some schooling. He's older than Ephraim and hardly knows any English. How's . . . ," she glanced at Matthew, who ducked his head down, "will he get along in life without knowing English?"

Matthew covered a grin. Those Smuckers weren't known for being the brightest lanterns in the barn. They were a difficult bunch to deal with. They hardly knew any English, so they had to depend on others for dealings outside the Amish community. And they were always borrowing money from others and forgetting to pay back the loan. Cal loaned Gideon Smucker hundreds of dollars to buy tools and start up a blacksmithing business. Gideon started the business, then soon lost interest. Once or twice, he overheard Mary Ann gently chide Cal to remind Gid to pay back the loan, but Cal refused. He said their money belonged to the Lord, and it was the Lord's business to remind Gid to pay back his debts. Mary Ann wasn't inclined to challenge her husband, but after Cal left the kitchen, Matthew heard her muttering to herself that the Lord probably had better things to do with his time than be a debt collector.

Matthew was surprised that Jorie even bothered worrying about Ray; other teachers sure didn't waste any time worrying about a Smucker. Maybe it was because she was new to teaching this year and there'd been so much controversy about the Amish having their own schools. Cal felt Stoney Ridge had an example to make for other Amish communities who were having terrible times with the Department of Education.

Just last week, Matthew saw some letters in the *Sugarcreek Budget* about fathers in Indiana and Ohio who were getting tossed into jail for not wanting their children to be bused to large public schools. Over a decade ago, the same thing had happened in Pennsylvania. Matthew's father was one of those men who had been tossed in jail and fined, repeatedly, for not letting Cal go to high school. Finally, a superior court ordered Cal to go. He remembered how mad his mother was, banging pots and pans in the kitchen and telling his father they should up and move to

Canada or Mexico. His father worked in a different way, much like Cal, moving calmly toward a goal. He started a letter-writing campaign to the governor. He wrote a letter every day and encouraged others to write too. The governor finally agreed to a compromise—Amish children over the age of fourteen went to a vocational school until they were sixteen. Cal said he was hoping the Pennsylvania Compromise would be so successful that it would clear the way for Amish brethren in other states.

Cal had just set the date for the work frolic to build the schoolhouse and was heading home from town when he nearly ran his buggy into Jorie, walking down the middle of the street on her way home from town. She was reading a book and didn't even hear his buggy. Cal said he pulled over to see what the Sam Hill was the matter with her, noticed the book she was reading was *Silent Spring* by Rachel Carson, and offered her the teaching job, right on the spot. She didn't accept at first, but Cal had made up his mind and, once decided, nothing could budge it loose. He kept on asking her until she said yes. Matthew wasn't really sure why Cal was so all-fired determined to hire Jorie, especially since she didn't really want to teach. There were at least three other girls he knew of who wanted the job, but Cal didn't think they would inspire the scholars.

"Matthew," Cal said, jolting him out of his reverie. He pointed to the fallen tree limb. "The branch isn't going to trim itself." Then he turned back to Jorie. "Seems like this is a job for the deacon."

"I agree." She crossed her arms over her chest. "So before coming here, I went and spoke to Jonas. He said he agreed with Gideon."

Cal kicked at the ground. "Aw, Jorie, I can't go over there and start telling a man how to raise his son."

At Cal's hesitation, Matthew noticed Jorie's back stiffen a notch. She was exasperated, Matthew realized, and it looked like steam trying hard not to rise from a kettle. He thought being mad made her look especially beautiful. A stain spread up her cheeks and her eyes got all wide and fiery. Passion, he thought. She was a woman with passion. Not like most girls he knew. Girls like Fat Lizzie, whose large eyes followed him around during meetings. He was looking forward to meeting more girls like Jorie King while he was living in Lebanon. There was a big world to explore and the United States Government was going to help him do it.

"But you're a minister now," Jorie told Cal.

Cal took off his hat and raked a hand through his hair. "My job is to take care of our members' spiritual needs."

She put her hands on her hips. "Why shouldn't you be teaching a man how to be a good father? Maybe then you won't *have* to worry so much about spiritual needs."

Matthew stopped hacking off twigs and glanced at Jorie and Cal. He got a kick out of watching her speak her mind to Cal. With her hands hooked on her hips, Matthew couldn't help noticing how small her waist was. His gaze drifted to her face. He wondered what it would be like to kiss those lips—they were so full. He had tried to kiss Cindy Yoder once, but she started giggling and couldn't stop. He had been looking forward to kissing since he was Ephraim's age, but kissing Cindy was a dire disappointment. She was too young, only sixteen. He was pretty sure kissing a mature woman like Jorie would be different. He shook his head. His thoughts were going down twisted, dangerous paths.

Matthew's gaze shifted to Cal, who held his hat in his hands and was turning it around, fingering the brim. That meant his brother was thinking about what to do. He was thinking hard. The more times he turned his hat around, the stickier the problem. Jorie's head was tilted up to look at Cal, much taller than she was, waiting patiently for him to respond. For a split second, he thought he saw something else in Jorie's eyes. Some kind of feeling for Cal that made Matthew uneasy. Then the look in her eyes passed, and she turned her gaze to the setting sun.

Maybe it was just a look of admiration. People often looked at Cal like that, as if they expected him to spout forth wisdom with a Solomonic flair. Yet Cal would be the first to say he was just a man, like any other man.

Softly, Jorie added, "In the English system, a truant officer could arrest Gideon Smucker."

Cal bristled.

She gripped her elbows and looked past him to the willow tree hanging its limbs over the little creek. "How many times have you said that the new superintendent is watching our school? You said we need to comply with what he's asking of us or we may end up having to bus our scholars to that big public school."

Cal raised an eyebrow. "That's pretty ironic coming from a teacher who seems to be spending most of her time outside of the classroom with those scholars."

"That classroom is stifling hot. Besides, we *are* studying. We're studying nature. Making observations."

"And when the time comes for that year-end state exam, you'll end up spending the month of May cramming those eighth grade heads with book learning."

"They'll pass," she said, drawing her five-foot-three self up tall. "They'll all pass."

"I'm sure they will." Cal smiled down at her, obviously enjoying her indignation.

She waved her hand away. "Those state tests don't tell everything. They don't test a child's curiosity, or intuition, or sensitivity . . ." She looked down at the ground. "I just don't believe in letting the classroom interfere with an education."

He gave a short laugh, amused. "A sentiment best kept to yourself."

"Maybe you could talk to Gideon and remind him that he's got a boy who needs to be educated. And he should've stayed awake during your sermon yesterday. He could've learned something."

Cal put his hat back on and adjusted the brim, a matter decided. "Well, now you've pointed out something that is a serious grievance. If a man is sleeping through one of my sermons, well, that's something that's got to be dealt with."

"Oh, you!" She threw up her hands in mock despair and started walking to her buggy, but Matthew could see she was smiling.

Cal followed behind and helped her climb up. "I'll talk to Gid."

"When?" she asked him.

"Jorie King, you are more free with your opinions than—"

"Than a new minister?" she asked with a sly grin. "Soon, Cal. Please pay a call on Gideon Smucker soon." She slapped the reins on her mare and drove down the lane.

Matthew threw down the hatchet and joined his brother, watching Jorie's buggy drive down the long lane.

Cal glanced at him. "Heard everything, I suppose."

"Yup," Matthew answered. He folded his arms across his chest. "I like her. She's got spunk."

"I'll say," Cal said, shaking his head. "Go tell Mary Ann I had to run an errand."

"Shall I tell her the minister is off on his first mission of mercy?" Matthew grinned.

Cal bent down, picked up the big axe, and thrust its handle against Matthew's chest with his two hands. "Might be gone awhile, so you'll need to finish up that branch by yourself."

Matthew's smile faded.

When Cal went to speak to Gideon about sending Ray to school, he heard an earful about Jorie's teaching style. "That Jorie King don't teach nuthin' worth learnin'! Those kids spend half their time up in trees. I seen 'em with my own two eyes." Gideon poked two fingers at his eyes to emphasize the point. "Ain't it true, Lyddie?"

Lydia, a quiet, defeated-looking woman, refilled the cups of coffee. "Ray might like going to school, Gid. Jorie makes learning real interesting."

Gideon snorted. "She's encouragin' them kids to have a early death! It makes my blood run cold to see the boys climbin' to the very tops of those big trees at Blue Lake Pond last Friday."

"Oh *that*," Cal said. "Ephraim told us they needed a crow's nest for nature study. Fridays are their field afternoons. Then they have to write compositions on what they've observed in nature."

Gid snorted again.

Cal saw the hunting guns lined up in a wall shelf and tried a different tack. "Did you hear that pesky bobcat got into Amos Esh's sheep pasture?"

"Yeah, I heard."

"Jorie had the scholars memorize a quote by Ernest Thompson Seton: 'Animal tracks are the oldest known writing on earth.'"

Gideon looked bored. "Book learnin' don't make a hill of beans of difference."

Cal took a sip of coffee. "Now hold on, Gid. That quote got Ephraim thinking. It was Ephraim who tracked down that bobcat. He laid a trap for it."

Gideon raised an eyebrow. "That Ephraim always was a boy for the woods."

"Maybe so, but Jorie gave him the idea of how to trap him. She had told Ephraim, just the day before, that bobcats have insatiable curiosities. Almost everything attracts their attention. So he put out a trap with a little bit of catnip oil. He learned that from school."

"Humph." Gideon stroked his gray beard, listening to Cal. "That's an old trapper's trick."

From behind Gid's back, Lyddie lifted her eyebrows at Cal, a small gesture of appreciation. Gideon leaned back in his chair.

Cal looked out at the fields. "Looks like you've finished your second hay cutting."

Gideon followed his gaze, then let out a deep sigh. "I suppose I could spare Ray for a little while. Since the harvest is near done."

"I think that's a wise decision, Gid." Cal stood up. "Well, Mary Ann will be wondering what's happened to me. Thank you, Lyddie, for the good-tasting coffee."

Gideon walked him to the door. "Just so's you know, I didn't vote for you for minister."

Cal turned to him and gripped Gid's shoulder with one hand. "Now that just tells me how wise you really are, Gid. I didn't vote for myself, either."

"But I did!" Lyddie called out. "I voted for you, Caleb!"

Cal turned around to wave and heard Gideon scold his wife, "A woman ought not to contradict her man in public."

Before heading into the hardware store late one afternoon, Cal handed Ephraim two dimes. "One for you and one for Maggie too. But no Tootsie Rolls for her. Too chewy. Not till those front teeth make their grand appearance."

Ephraim grinned and went inside to the racks that held the candy bars. His mouth watered at the sight. He loved candy.

Cal walked down the center aisle until he came to the nail bins. As he searched for the type of nails he wanted, Ron Harding, the owner of the hardware store, walked out of the back room. "Hello there, Cal. Sure has been a dry spell we've been having." He looked out the window at the dark clouds. "Those clouds look threatening, though. Always threatening, never delivering. Weather can sure be aggravating."

"It has been dry lately," Cal said agreeably. Ephraim knew he was just being kind. He was always amazed at how much the English carried on about the weather. What was the point? Weather belonged to God.

Ron arched an eyebrow at Ephraim, who was closely following this back-and-forthing. "Say, would you have time for a word?" he asked Cal. "Outside?"

"Give me a minute," Cal said.

"What's your favorite?" Ephraim heard someone ask.

When Ephraim jerked around, he saw the friendly face of Fat Lizzie, the girl whom everyone knew was sweet on Matthew.

Ephraim pointed to the Tootsie Rolls.

"Mine too," she said.

Cal came up to them and handed a bag of nails to Fat Lizzie to weigh so he knew what he owed.

"How's the new school doing?" Lizzie asked him. "I think you were awful smart to hire Jorie King as the teacher." She leaned over the counter and whispered to Cal, "She knows more than most folks about all kinds of things, especially those horses. It makes Ron mad when folks ask Jorie's advice before they buy his harnesses."

Cal grinned. "She's got her work cut out for her, making sure those eighth graders pass that state test next May." He motioned to Ephraim. "Every single scholar needs to pass that test, including our Ephraim."

Ephraim put a Tootsie Roll and a package of Life Savers on the counter and hunted for his dimes as Cal went outside to talk to Ron Harding. Ephraim searched the ground, still couldn't find the dimes, and looked at Fat Lizzie in a panic.

She just waved it off. "My treat today," she told him, with a finger to her lips like they were sharing a secret.

Ephraim didn't know why Matthew was always making fun of Fat Lizzie. He liked her. She was always doing stuff like that for him and Maggie, buying them candy and gum. Matthew said it was only because she was trying to make a good impression. She *was* making a good impression, Ephraim told him. A fine impression. He thanked Fat Lizzie with a grateful nod and walked outside to join Cal.

"I hear you're the head honcho now," Ron Harding was telling his brother.

"Just a minister," Cal corrected.

"Well, I'm just a hardware store owner. But I know that citizens look to us leaders to guide them." He leaned against the porch pole and crossed his arms. "Cal, I was hoping you might use your influence on the Amish folks."

"I would never do that," Cal said. "I only take care of my people's spiritual needs."

"Sure you do! Remember how your people weren't going to take that polio vaccine? Then you gave them a talk, and next thing we knew, your people were taking part in the national vaccine, lined up getting their sugar cubes just like real Americans."

Cal crossed his arms. "What's on your mind, Ron?"

"Seems to me that when you live in this country, you need to be a good citizen."

"We pay our taxes and volunteer as firefighters."

From behind Cal came a drawling voice. "And your people chew up our roads with those danged horses. You won't fight in our wars, but you benefit from being safe in this country."

Cal spun around to face Jerry Gingerich, who worked at the gas station across the street from the hardware store. Cal didn't say anything, he just held Jerry's gaze. Jerry dropped his eyes first and looked over at Ephraim.

Jerry had a neck thicker than any Ephraim had ever seen. His arms and hands were also massive, but what scared Ephraim were his eyes. He thought they were blank and stupid most of the time, but when Jerry looked him up and down, they narrowed into tiny slits. Ben, like Cal, had gone to public schools and had been friendly with Jerry. Ephraim didn't have many memories about his folks—he was only four when they passed—but he did remember the look on his mother's face when Ben hung around with Jerry. Even now, Jerry had a reputation for being a troublemaker. Everybody knew he played gambling card games in the back room of the gas station.

The only thing good about Jerry Gingerich, Ephraim had always thought, was his hunting dog, Rex, a black mutt. Ephraim held out his hand and Rex trotted over to investigate, sniffing tentatively. Satisfied, Rex backed up a few feet and sat down by

Jerry's side, like a sentry guard. If Rex could pump gas, Ephraim was pretty sure he could outwork Jerry.

"Now Jerry," Ron said in a calming voice. "Cal's brother Ben is serving as a conscientious objector. He's over in Vietnam." He looked at Cal. "And I heard that your brother Matthew just got called up too. That right?"

Jerry spat on the ground. "Those C.O.'s are safe and sound and cozy, while my brother is serving active duty in the Marines."

"Jerry!" Ron said, clearly exasperated. "Your brother is stationed down in North Carolina." He frowned at Jerry before turning to Cal. "Alls I'm saying, Cal, is that it would be a good thing for this county if you would help us in a sensitive matter."

Cal glanced at Ephraim. "Speak your mind."

"If you want to keep living the way you're living, then you need to do what we tell you to do," Jerry added with a sneer.

"That's enough, Jerry!" Ron looked across the street at the gas station. "You've got a customer." He waited until Jerry ambled back across the street. "All that I wanted to say is that you folks have enjoyed your way of living out here, set apart, and able to mind your own business. We want to keep things that way. But there's a fellow trying to buy a house in this town. He's not our kind of man. If he buys in Stoney Ridge, we'll all lose. Others will be coming in right behind him. That's the way it works with those people. I've seen it with my own eyes. Our land value drops and before you know it, we're looking like Philly or Camden. No townsfolk will sell to him, I made sure of that. So I'm thinking he might try next to find something out in the country. So I'd like you to talk to your people and make sure no one sells to him."

Cal looked at Ron Harding as if he was speaking in Chinese.

"A fellow named James Robinson."

"The veterinarian that's buying Doc Williams's practice?" Cal asked. "We need a good vet. Doc Williams said he's never seen a young vet as capable as James Robinson."

Ron snorted. "Well, we don't need this one."

Cal looked at him, puzzled.

"This one is a colored man."

3

On the morning of September 7, after Maggie and Ephraim went to school, Cal and Mary Ann waited at the bus stop with Matthew to say goodbye. "Well, Matthew," Cal said. "Just as well to get it over with and not have it hanging over your head. The time will fly like a flock of birds. Soon, you'll be back home with us. Ben too. Then we'll see to splitting up Beacon Hollow or buying you both a farm, just like we always said we would."

Mary Ann listened to the two, talking in low voices. *Oh Cal, don't you see? Leaving isn't hanging over Matthew's head. He can't wait to go.* There was a glint in Matthew's eyes that was hard to miss. She always worried he was like Ben in that way. Matthew had a bent toward English things. Worldly temptations.

Yes, two years will fly by. But then would he really come back?

As soon as they saw Matthew off on the bus, Cal and Mary Ann drove the buggy to town for an appointment with their family doctor. More inexplicable bruises had been popping up on her arms and legs, heavy and purple. She finally went to the doctor earlier in the week and he arranged some tests for her right after the visit. She wasn't too concerned about the results; Marge thought she was just anemic. But now she noticed that Dr. Lachman—whom she had known all her life—avoided her eyes, and her heart started to pound as if it was clubbing her chest.

Seated across from them at his desk in his office, Dr. Lachman said the bruising was caused by acute myeloid leukemia. She couldn't understand all that the doctor was trying to explain, that a rapid increase of immature blood cells was crowding out her bone marrow, making it unable to produce healthy blood cells. But she did understand that leukemia meant blood cancer.

"How long, Mary Ann?" Cal asked her, all color drained from his face. "When did you first notice the bruising?"

She looked down at her hands and noticed they were trembling. It was suddenly so hot in the office. She could feel a trickle of sweat roll down her back, but strangely, her hands were ice cold, so she wrapped them in her apron. "A few weeks ago," she answered quietly.

"Why didn't you say something?" Cal said.

"I thought it was the flu," she said, fumbling for the words. "There was just so much going on . . . Matthew's news, you became minister, school started up . . ." She started to cry but bit her lip to stop. She didn't want to cry. Once she started, she wasn't sure she could stop.

Cal crouched down beside his wife. "Oh Mary Ann, please don't cry. I can't bear it if you cry." He covered her hands with his.

Mary Ann looked down at her husband's large, calloused hands. How she loved those strong hands. She tried to draw in a breath, but it caught in her throat. "How long?" she asked the doctor in a quiet voice. "How long do I have?"

"No, no. We're not going to be thinking like that," Cal said, rising to his feet. "You can do something, can't you, Dr. Lachman?"

"This is a rare cancer, Mr. Zook, and a very aggressive one."

Mary Ann flinched as if the doctor had reached across his desk to strike her. Cancer. *Slap.* Aggressive. *Slap.*

"There's got to be *something* you can do," Cal insisted.

The doctor kept his eyes on his desktop.

"What are you saying?" Cal asked, his face ashen. "You can't be telling me she only has a short time to live. She's only thirty-two years old!"

"How long?" Mary Ann repeated. She had a hard time talking around the knot in her throat, a knot made of tangled threads of fear, worry, and unbearable sadness. "A year? Six months? Just tell me the truth."

Dr. Lachman took a deep breath. "Not months. A matter of weeks and days."

"Lieber Gott." Cal leaned forward, palms on the doctor's desk. *Dear God.* After a long moment, he spoke in a hard, desperate whisper. "Please, Dr. Lachman, there's *got* to be something."

Dr. Lachman rubbed his forehead. "I suppose we could try some treatments, but—"

"See, Mary Ann?" Cal jumped on that, his eyes filled with hope. "See? I knew there could be something to try." He looked at the doctor. "I've read there are all kinds of new medical discoveries going on, all the time."

"That's true enough," Dr. Lachman said. "Breakthroughs in research are going on all the time. Why, just last year, the Surgeon General announced that smoking can cause cancer."

"I don't smoke," Mary Ann said sharply. She didn't mean to sound so harsh; it just seemed like such a ridiculous comment to make.

Dr. Lachman looked away. "What I meant was that scientists are on the brink of discovery."

"Do I have time to wait?" she asked, but the doctor had no answer for her.

The first thing Matthew did after getting off the bus in Lebanon was to find a place to live. Lottie, the supervisor at the Veterans Hospital where he had been hired to work, gave him the address of a lady named Mrs. Flanagan, who lived close to the hospital and had a room to rent. Lottie must have tipped Mrs. Flanagan off that Matthew would be a good tenant because the older lady seemed to be expecting him. The front door opened as he approached it and a heavyset woman with dyed orange hair, penciled eyebrows, and a thick, doughy face lumbered out to meet him. She showed him the room to rent and within minutes, he had a new home. If you could call the tiny room a home; he thought of it more like a shoe box. Still, he was grateful.

After unpacking, he retraced his steps back to the bus stop, certain he had passed a barbershop on the way. He had never been in a barbershop before. His mother, and then Mary Ann, had always cut his hair out on the back porch. The barber, a short man with a round belly, pointed to a pedestal chair bolted to the cracked linoleum floor, then flung a plastic apron over Matthew's chest and spun him around, peering at his longish hair. "We don't get too many hippies coming in here."

"But I'm not a hippie," Matthew said. "I'm starting a new job tomorrow at the Veterans Hospital."

"Well, then, how 'bout a buzz?" he asked Matthew with a glint in his eye.

Matthew nodded, not quite sure what to say, nor what a buzz meant. Just a few minutes later, he was educated.

He paid for the haircut, mumbled a thank-you, and looked for a shop where he could buy a baseball cap to cover his conspicuously bare head.

Dr. Lachman scheduled Mary Ann to start chemotherapy immediately—the side effects were so intense that she was nauseous, fought fever and chills, and was exhausted. Her sister, Sylvia, organized a steady stream of helpers from the church so that Mary Ann was never alone. She tried telling Sylvia that all she really wanted was to be alone, but Sylvia was not convinced. Her sister came every day, right after school, and brought eleven-year-old Esther to play with Maggie, which meant Ephraim disappeared into the woods and Maggie was in a bad mood for the rest of the evening. Mary Ann empathized. Esther bossed Maggie and Ephraim around just like Sylvia used to boss Mary Ann. As much as she loved her sister, Sylvia had an effect on others like a dark cloud on a beautiful day.

Shortly after breakfast on Saturday, Marge King came to pay a visit at Beacon Hollow. Mary Ann was resting in her room when Marge burst in, Jorie trailing behind with an apologetic look on her face. Marge went right up to Mary Ann, took her pulse, and rested her palm against her forehead. Mary Ann knew that Marge was happiest when she was playing doctor, and she had a feeling she was about to get the full treatment.

Marge peered into her eyes and said, "I've got just the thing for you. I'll go downstairs and whip it up."

"She's been itching to come," Jorie whispered to Mary Ann after Marge went downstairs. "She's been working on a curative since she heard your news. I recommend tossing it out the window when her back is turned."

Mary Ann smiled at her friend. Being around Jorie was like a breath of fresh air. She found she even felt a little more energetic. "Would you help me get dressed so I can go downstairs? I'm tired of being in this room."

Sylvia swept in as Jorie was brushing Mary Ann's hair to pin it into a bun. She walked up to Jorie and snatched the brush from her hand. "You are *not* her sister."

Mary Ann blanched as Jorie backed away with a hurt look on her face. Sylvia meant well, but she only knew one way of helping others, and that meant total control. It had been that way since they were children. Their mother had passed when the sisters were young, and even though Sylvia wasn't much older than Mary Ann, she assumed the role of mother and big sister, rolled into one. Mary Ann even thought Sylvia intimidated their father. He had tried courting a few women, but Sylvia found serious character flaws in each prospective bride. He didn't take a second wife until Sylvia married Noah Swartzentruber. And as soon as Mary Ann married Cal, he sold his farm to Noah and Sylvia and moved with his new wife to Sarasota, Florida. When Noah died, unexpectedly, Mary Ann thought Sylvia and Esther might go live with their father, but Sylvia didn't have any reason to leave Stoney Ridge. Though it wasn't spoken of, everyone knew Noah Swartzentruber had been a wealthy man.

"Not so hard, Sylvia," Mary Ann said, wincing, as Sylvia pulled a brush through her long hair.

But it was too late. Sylvia suddenly dropped the brush on the floor. The three women stood there, staring at it. Clumps of long hair were on the brush, fallen from Mary Ann's head.

It was too hot to sleep. Ephraim tried to dwell on thoughts of winter: sledding down Eagle Hill, ice-skating on Blue Lake Pond. But in the middle of September, cold weather was a distant dream.

Lying in bed, listening to the crickets, Ephraim found himself swirling in worries. In just a week's time, Mary Ann had gone from feeling a little poorly to barely able to get out of bed. Her sister, Sylvia, had taken over their home and dished out chores like she owned the place. Cal assured him that it was only for a short while, that Mary Ann would be as good as new soon. But what if Mary Ann didn't get well?

He let his thoughts drift to Vietnam, a place that seemed about as foreign as a place could be. What if Ben didn't come home? It was a question he tortured himself with on nights like tonight, when he couldn't sleep. The worrisome thoughts came too fast. He wanted Ben at Beacon Hollow, to throw softballs against the barn and to teach Maggie to swim at Blue Lake Pond. He'd tried to help her swim a couple of times this summer, but she sunk like a stone.

Ben had taught Ephraim a few cuss words that he tried to practice when he was alone. He tried them out today, when he was hiding from Esther, but found he didn't have the heart for cussing, and he didn't know what the words meant, anyway. Ben said he would teach him the meanings of the insults when he came back home. So Ephraim quit trying, prayed for forgiveness, and went home for dinner.

Early Sunday morning, Cal took a cup of tea upstairs to Mary

Ann and was surprised to find her getting dressed. "Just what do you think you're doing?"

She pinned the top part of her dress together. "Going to meeting."

He set the teacup down on the nightstand. "You must be out of your mind. You're not strong enough."

"Going to meeting gives me strength. There's no place I'd rather be today than at church with my family, hearing you preach."

Cal sat on the bed. "You shouldn't even be around so many people coughing and sneezing. You could get sick and . . ."

"And what, Cal? Catch cold and die?"

As soon as the words tumbled from her mouth, she wished them back. Cal's shoulders drew back as if he'd been hit. She hadn't meant to sound mean. Harsh words were not said in their home. But something needed to be said. They both needed to face the truth of how sick she really was.

She saw Cal's glance shift toward the door. Maggie was peeking around the open door, overhearing their conversation. Mary Ann reached out her arms for her daughter, who rushed into them.

"I'm feeling fine, Maggie. Truly, I am." Mary Ann smoothed her daughter's soft cheek. Her heart ached in a sweet way as she watched the relief ease Maggie's small face.

Rehearsing for the Christmas program had gone so badly during Monday's practice that Ephraim told Maggie to go home without him, and he darted past her before she could start up with any of her endless questions. He hurried through the pasture field, crossed the creek and several fences and fields, and reached his favorite place on earth: the Deep Woods. The Deep Woods belonged to Bud Schultz, their English neighbor to the north. Bud didn't mind people traipsing through the woods, as long as they left it unspoiled. Ephraim knew there were folks—both English and Plain—who borrowed Bud's woods without a care. Sometimes, Ephraim would bring a sack to carry out empty bottles of beer and spirits he came across. He couldn't let garbage remain in that beautiful place. The Deep Woods was a remnant of virgin woods, bordered by a stream and a marsh. It was impossible to log by horses, and somehow, over the last three centuries, those majestic trees had slipped by unnoticed and been spared the axe.

His father had taught all of his sons from an early age to love the Deep Woods. He remembered his father saying, in a voice of reverence, that these woods were what the country looked like when the first settlers arrived from across the Appalachians.

Ephraim knew these woods like he knew Beacon Hollow. Even in the deep shadows of the setting sun, the place was familiar to him, filled with landmarks of childhood memories: an enormous old oak where he had once taken refuge from a skunk passing by; a makeshift blind where he could watch white-tailed deer; a stream where he had been able to catch fat fish in no time. He found his favorite spot—a felled beech tree, covered with a cushion of moss. On the tree was carved his father's initials: "SZ, 4/8/26, caught 3 cottontails." He sat down and became utterly still. Soon, the woods came alive with creatures. Around Ephraim's neck hung his binoculars. He slept with them nightly and polished them weekly, and nothing was as dear to his soul.

High above Ephraim's head came a *peck-peck-peck* sound. He slowly lifted the binoculars to his eyes and followed a branch until he saw a redheaded woodpecker drilling for insects in a nearby tree. Two squirrels raced through the treetops. Then the woods became silent, like a curtain had been drawn. He heard the steps of someone approaching and jumped up.

"Ephraim!" Jorie reached him, panting. "I was just about to give up looking!"

"W-what's w-wrong?" His first thought was of Mary Ann.

She held up a hand to catch her breath, then plopped down on a fallen log. "I just wanted to give something to you, but you lit out of school so fast!" She handed him a sketch pad, along with a charcoal pencil. "It's for you. To make observations of nature. When I graduated eighth grade, my teacher gave me a set of paints and a sketch pad, so that I would keep painting. I guess I had thought it would end, after school ended, but she was right. Learning never ends."

After he took it from her, she looked all around her. "Isn't this a wonderful place? It's like a primeval forest! These trees must be hundreds of years old." She looked almost dazzled. "Imagine how much these old trees have seen and heard over the years." She ran her hand along the giant beech, gave a satisfied sigh, and turned back to Ephraim. "So. Rehearsal didn't go too well."

Ephraim shook his head. "I c-can't." He had a gut-wrenching fear of speaking in front of class. In the Deep Woods he had no such fears—the trees and flowers and birds and squirrels that thronged the forest never laughed at him like the other kids would. Like Esther Swartzentruber did on a daily basis.

"Sure you can, Ephraim," Jorie said. She nudged him with her elbow. "You're a Zook."

"I'm n-not. I'll n-never b-be like them."

Jorie's sky blue eyes looked intently at him. As if he was worth something. "Why wouldn't you want to be like your brothers? I don't know another family who is as well respected as the Zooks. It's been that way as long as I can remember."

Ephraim glanced away. She didn't understand. His brothers—each one so different from the other—were smart as a whip. He couldn't even talk fast. When he tried, the words piled up in his throat like sticks in a beaver's dam.

"And the Zook stubbornness is legendary. I can see right now that you've got that trait."

Ephraim tried not to smile.

Softly, she added, "Ephraim, don't you know you're more like Cal than Ben or Matthew?"

He felt tears prickle his eyes and looked away. "I c-can't m-memorize the whole thing. I t-tried."

"Memory is such a mystery. You don't have to have the whole thing in your head, like reading from a book. Your mind will lead you from one thing to the next, the same way a flashlight can light a step ahead of you. In time, you'll learn to trust your memory."

They sat there quietly, listening to the songbirds, while he took in what she said. Then she rose to her feet. "If you want some help memorizing your lines, I'd be happy to help you after school."

A stain of flush brushed his cheeks. "Since M-Matthew's away and M-Mary Ann is ailing, C-Cal n-needs me at h-home right after school t-to help chore."

"Saturdays, then. You can usually find me at the schoolhouse on Saturday mornings." She pointed to the sketch pad she had brought him. "I've noticed you have a knack for sketching. I thought it might be helpful if you had a real pad to draw your observations. About birds and trees and all kinds of wild creatures." She looked up at the sun beaming through the treetops. "Nature like this, it's a sanctuary, isn't it? A solace. To me, the God who created all this beauty must be a wonderful and loving Being. A realm of limitless love." She sighed happily. "I'd better get back.

Don't stay too late. You know how Mary Ann gets to fretting."
She turned to leave, then spun around to add, "Everything's going
to be fine, Ephraim." She headed out the way she came.

Ephraim watched her for a while, then opened the sketch pad
and scribbled his name on the inside corner.

As often as she could, Jorie stopped by to visit Mary Ann at
Beacon Hollow, but this time the sight of her dear friend had
her close to tears.

"I brought some books for Ephraim," she said, putting the
books on the side table where Mary Ann sat in a porch rocker.
She tried to keep her voice sounding lighthearted and carefree,
but the truth was, she was shocked by how quickly Mary Ann's
appearance was deteriorating. When she arrived, Mary Ann had
been folding laundry, but she had to stop and rest after each gar-
ment, as if it was too heavy to lift. Her skin was milk pale, nearly
translucent, and there was a bruise on the hollow of her throat.

Mary Ann's eyes swept over the titles on the books' spines.
"Did Cal ever tell you why he was so determined to have you be
the schoolteacher?"

"No. He just kept telling me I needed to do this, for the good
of the community."

"That sounds just like Cal, doesn't it?" she said with a fragile
smile. "It has been good for the community, but the real reason
was because he knew you would be good for our Ephraim." She
looked out to the pasture where Ephraim and Maggie were tossing hay to the horses, carted from pasture to pasture in a little red
wagon. The horses nickered and rumbled and stretched out their
necks, snatching mouthfuls of hay before it even hit the ground.
"Ever since Ben left, he's grown quieter. And his stuttering seems

to be getting worse. We've all tried to encourage him to talk. But still, he's just getting quieter. The sight of him fighting to form words never fails to pierce my heart."

"He's a fine boy, Mary Ann. He's just at that age where he's very bashful."

"Think he'll ever outgrow his stuttering?"

"Absolutely. As his confidence grows."

"He reads all of the books you loan to him. Sometimes in the same day." Mary Ann sighed. "I always wished I was more of a scholar. Like Cal. So that I had more things to talk about with him. I just never liked to read much."

Jorie patted her on the knee. "I don't think your marriage to Cal is lacking in any way."

"Jorie, why didn't you marry Ben before he left?"

Jorie grew still. As close as they were, she hadn't expected such a personal question from Mary Ann.

"I don't mean to pry," she hurried to add. "I just have always wondered, that's all, and this sickness has given me boldness. Why would you wait for him but not marry him? You might have had a child by now. Maybe two."

Jorie took a towel from the laundry basket and folded it. "Ben never asked me."

Mary Ann's eyes went wide. "What?! Then . . . what have you been waiting for?"

Jorie shrugged and picked up another towel to fold. "I guess I've been waiting for Ben to grow up." She put the towel on top of the stack and picked up a sheet.

"There are other men to consider. They've certainly given *you* a lot of consideration."

Jorie anchored the corner of a sheet under her chin to fold and rolled her eyes to the heavens.

"Jacob Schwartz? Daniel Riehl?" Mary Ann spread out her fingers and started counting. "Levi Lapp. Zach Glick. His cousin Sam Glick. Then there's—"

Jorie put up a hand to stop her. "It's always been Ben for me. You know that." She put the folded sheet in the basket, on top of the towels.

Mary Ann leaned back in her chair and closed her eyes, as if spent. "Oh Jorie. What if you're waiting and waiting for Ben to be something he's not?"

Jorie had nothing she could say to that. It was not a new thought to her. She stood. "Well, there just aren't enough Caleb Zooks to go around. The rest of us have to make do." She reached down to lift the basket. "I'll take this laundry in. Shall I bring you a lemonade?"

Mary Ann's eyes flew open, as if something just occurred to her.

"Are you all right?"

"Yes. Yes. Lemonade would be fine."

Jorie hoisted the basket on her hip and took a few steps, then turned back for a moment. "Sure you're all right?"

Mary Ann nodded, a serious look on her face. "I'm just fine."

By the time Jorie was leaving to go home, the sky was lit with color as the sun started its descent into the horizon. Cal was outside harnessing a buggy horse as she passed by him on her way down the driveway.

"Cal, stop for a moment and look up! It's a spectacular sunset," Jorie said. "I've always thought of a sunset as God's last painting of the day. It's the last gift he gives to us before he gives us the gift of a sunrise."

Cal looked in the direction she was pointing. "'His name shall endure for ever: his name shall be continued as long as the sun: and men shall be blessed in him: all nations shall call him blessed.'" He glanced over at her and read the question on her face. "Psalm 72:17." He turned back to the setting sun. "Thank you, Jorie. I needed a spectacular sunset today."

The horse nudged Cal with his long nose, as if to remind him that he was waiting. Absentmindedly, Cal reached out a hand and stroked his forelocks. "I appreciate you stopping by when you can. The two of you had your heads bent together, whispering like schoolgirls."

"I was telling her stories about our scholars. How are you holding up, Cal?"

"God will not lead us where his grace cannot take us." He spoke the words and he knew them to be true, and the thought behind them was true, but still, they didn't quench the fear in his heart of what was coming.

"That doesn't mean this isn't a hard thing to endure." Her gaze met his over the horse's head. "So how are you holding up, really? You look . . . positively wrung out."

He fit the bit into the horse's mouth, slipped the bridle over its head, and buckled its chinstrap. "Truth be told, I'm a little stunned. Like I'm going to wake up any day now and realize it's all just been a bad dream." He hooked his hands on his hips. "It's all happening so fast. It's like time has turned into a fast-running river. And all I want is for the river to run backward."

Jorie's eyes filled with tears. "She's like a sister to me."

He gave her a gentle smile. "She feels the same way about you." His attention turned toward the clip-clopping of horses' hooves on the driveway. "Speaking of sisters. Here comes Sylvia."

"I'd better be getting home," Jorie said quickly. She slipped away, taking the trail behind the barn, so that she would be out of sight before the buggy reached the rise.

"What's your hurry?" Cal called out, grinning, watching her go.

It didn't seem right to smile, under such circumstances, but he couldn't help himself as he watched her scoot off. Sylvia had always been hard on Jorie. Mary Ann thought it was because, long ago, Atlee King insulted Sylvia's father by not selling a Percheron to him. Atlee was particular about his horses and wouldn't sell to just anybody. Sylvia's father had a reputation for being too harsh with animals. It would be Sylvia's nature to bear a grudge even if it wasn't her grudge to bear. But Cal thought Sylvia's rancor had more to do with the close friendship between Jorie and Mary Ann.

Sylvia's horse came to a halt and he knew he should go greet her. He usually tried to make himself scarce when Sylvia paid a visit. Mary Ann often teased him that it was strangely coincidental how many chores in the barn demanded his immediate attention when her sister came calling. Today, with Mary Ann feeling so poorly, it wouldn't be right to leave his wife alone, unfortified.

The rain came down in waves, making up for weeks of bone-dry weather. Cal was trying to spend every spare minute he could with Mary Ann, so he was doubly grateful for the rain. It gave him an excuse to go inside the house and not have Mary Ann accuse him of hovering. She was curled up on the living room sofa, looking out the window at the rain as it fell sideways in the fierce wind. Cal was at his desk, paying bills. They hadn't spoken in a long time, but it didn't bother him. He just wanted to be near her.

Interrupting the tranquility, Ephraim burst into the kitchen.

"Cal!" he shouted when he spotted his brother in the living room. "There's an important l-looking l-letter for you." He thrust the letter at Cal. "From the g-government." He pulled off his raincoat and hat and hung them to dry on the wall peg.

"Is it about Ben?" Mary Ann asked.

Cal nodded. Shock coursed through him and it took all of his willpower to appear calm as he finished reading the letter. "They want his dental records."

"Now why would they ask for those?" she asked. "I don't know if he has any."

"He doesn't." Cal folded up the paper and tucked it back in the envelope. He walked over to the sofa and sat down with the letter in his hand. "Ephraim, please go feed the sow."

"Aw, Cal! I just c-came in! It's p-pouring b-buckets."

"Go!" Cal said firmly, pointing to the door.

Choking over words of protest, Ephraim snatched off his hat and slammed it on his head, jerking open the door.

Mary Ann put a soft hand on Cal's forearm.

"They want dental records to identify his body," Cal said quietly, covering her hand with his. "It's probably a mistake. The Army is famous for making all kinds of mistakes. Until we hear more, we'll keep this news to ourselves. No point in worrying anybody about something that is most likely wrong."

As soon as the rain let up, Cal walked over to Bud's and made a call to the government phone number listed on the letter.

The wait was over three days later. Two Army officers arrived at the house in a dark green car with news about Ben. "We're confident that we have a positive identification on Benjamin S. Zook," they told Cal after he greeted them on the front porch where Mary Ann was taking some sun. "He was killed by an enemy sniper while he was evacuating a wounded soldier. He died a hero's death and is eligible to be buried in a military graveyard." One officer held out Ben's dog tags in his hand.

Cal picked up the dog tags as if they were made of spun sugar. After a long moment, he lifted his head and said in a voice roughened with pain, "No. He belongs here, with us." He ran his finger over the indentation that read BENJAMIN S. ZOOK. "We didn't have dental records, but if I saw his body, I could confirm his identity. Maybe there's been a mistake."

The officers exchanged a glance. One cleared his throat and said, "The body is . . . well, there was a misunderstanding when the body, I mean, your brother's body . . . well, you see . . ." He looked to the other officer for help.

"Sir, Benjamin S. Zook was cremated," the other officer said. He started out boldly, then he too, watching Cal's and Mary Ann's horrified faces, lost his composure. "Apparently, the jungle heat . . . bodies decompose so quickly . . . and the commanding officer made a decision . . . well, we're terribly sorry. I realize— now—that cremation isn't your religion's customary way of . . ." His words drizzled to a stop.

"Lieber Gott . . ." Mary Ann put her head in her hands. *Dear God.* Cal put his hand on her shoulder.

"I have his remains in the trunk. I'll go get them . . . uh, it." When he returned, he held out a small metal box for Cal and a flag. "Here's the flag for you, for the funeral."

Cal shook his head. "Thank you, no. We don't fly flags."

The officers exchanged another look of confusion, then quickly said goodbye and drove off.

Together, Cal and Mary Ann sat for a while, staring at the small metal box that held all that was left of Benjamin Zook.

"I'd better tell Jorie," she said, breaking the quiet.

"I'll go," Cal said as he stood up, raking a hand through his hair. "You need to rest. We have a funeral to plan. I'll stop by a few other neighbors and let them know too. And I'll stop at Bud's to call Matthew at work."

Mary Ann rose to put her arms around his waist. "I'm so sorry."

Cal wrapped his arms around her. Over her shoulder, he looked down at the dog tags, clenched in his fist. "I just thought I would've known, deep in my bones, if something had happened to one of my own."

Cal was told by Atlee that he could find Jorie at the schoolhouse. He came over the hill and saw the yellow light of a lantern glowing. He knocked on the door, waited, then knocked again before she came to the door.

"Oh, Cal!"

"You working?" he asked.

"Yes." She opened the door and stepped back so he could enter.

Cal took a deep breath. "I have some news. About Ben."

Her face lifted to his, filled with hope. It broke his heart, having to tell her this terrible news. He dropped his eyes to the ground, unable to look at her any longer.

"He's been killed, Jorie." He glanced up as the shock registered through her. She sank down on the bench behind her. "Two Army men came to the house this afternoon to give us the news."

She didn't say a word. She just sat there, looking stunned. It wasn't proper for him to touch her in any way and so he didn't, but he wanted to do or say something that would help to ease her hurt. He shared the pain she was feeling.

"Jorie," he whispered as he sat down on the bench beside her. "Say something."

She looked at him, startled, as if she had forgotten he was there. "Things were left so badly between us."

"What do you mean?"

"Ben. He did it on purpose."

"Did what?"

"At the Recruiting Office. He knew to sign up for being willing to serve. He knew the difference."

"That's not true. He didn't know. He was fooled."

She shook her head. "He knew. This was his chance to see the world, he said."

Cal leaned back. "Why would he tell me he had been tricked?" He found he wasn't entirely surprised, as if he himself had a doubt in his mind but kept it stifled.

She sighed. "Cal, you always believe the best in others. Ben didn't want you thinking he was less than he was." She put her hands against her face. "When he told me what he had done, we argued. I told him I wouldn't wait for him." Then her eyes started to fill with tears. "But I *was* waiting. I've been waiting and waiting for him to come home."

Cal felt hot tears burn the back of his eyes. "He cared for you, Jorie."

"I know. I know he did. But not enough to keep him home." A tear leaked down her cheek. "And I didn't love him enough to leave."

And what could he say to that? It was the truth. He had known Ben had tried talking her into leaving the church with him, before he was even drafted, but she refused. He had always

66

admired Jorie for standing her ground with Ben. "I'll walk you home."

"No. Thank you. I'd rather be alone for a while."

He stood and walked to the door. "As soon as I speak to Isaac, I'll let you know when the funeral will be held."

She nodded and followed him to the door. "Tell Mary Ann that I'll come help dress him for the viewing."

"There will be no viewing, Jorie." He looked away. "They cremated him."

She had to grab the doorjamb to steady herself. "Oh Cal, have we seen our Ben for the last time?"

He did touch her then. Ever so gently, he squeezed her shoulders with his hands. "No, Jorie. Not for the last time. We have hope for a life together in the presence of Almighty God."

Ben's funeral was planned for Saturday. The night before, in the predawn hours, Mary Ann woke up, realized Cal was not there, and tiptoed downstairs. She saw a lantern light in the barn and grabbed her shawl to pull around her. Before she even reached the barn, she heard the sounds. Sounds of Cal weeping. She had only known him to cry once, four years ago, when they buried their stillborn son. She stopped, knowing he would feel shamed if she found him grieving so deeply. It wasn't their way to express deep emotion. Doing so would seem like a complaint against the Lord.

She knew it would be best to let Cal grieve for his brother in private. Besides, Ben was a sore spot between them. Mary Ann couldn't pinpoint why, but she never quite trusted Ben. Cal would hear none of that; to him, Ben was a Zook. She dropped her head and returned to the house, finding her pathway in the dark with a flashlight.

When she passed by Cal's desk, she stopped and took out four sheets of stationery. She wrote and wrote, words from her heart, then sealed each letter in its envelope and addressed one to Matthew, one to Ephraim, one to Maggie. And one to Cal.

When Matthew asked Lottie for time off to attend his brother's funeral, she threw her plump arms around him and hugged him so tightly that he nearly felt the wind was getting squeezed out of him.

"Oh baby, you take all the time you need," she told Matthew, rocking him back and forth, her eyes brimming with tears. Lottie's son was a soldier in Vietnam and she talked about him every single day.

Ben's death seemed more real to Lottie than it did to Matthew. He just couldn't believe he would never see his brother walk up the steep incline of Beacon Hollow with that long stride of his, or pitch a softball to Ephraim on their front lawn, or toss Maggie in the air, or watch Ben drive off in his courting buggy with Jorie by his side. Or . . . skipping out the side door of the barn to head to town—letting Matthew finish up choring for him. Ben was famous for that. Matthew could never stay mad at him for long, and he never let Cal know how often it happened, either.

After work on Friday, Matthew caught the bus to Stoney Ridge and was surprised to see Cal waiting for him at the station. Matthew knew something was on his mind when Cal didn't even comment on his hair, hidden under his black felt hat. He left the baseball cap back at Mrs. Flanagan's, along with his new English clothes. He had expected to get a raised eyebrow and a gentle lecture about staying on the Plain and narrow way. Instead, on the drive to Beacon Hollow, Cal explained that Mary Ann had a type of blood cancer.

"You might be surprised when you see her," Cal said. "She's as frail as a bird."

"But I just saw her a few weeks ago. How could she get so sick so fast?"

"That's the acute part, I suppose, of acute myeloid leukemia."

"But she'll be okay, won't she? I mean, those doctors can work miracles. At least, that's what they tell us at the Veterans Hospital."

Cal swallowed hard. "I don't think so, Matthew. It's like she's fading away, right before our eyes."

Matthew was quiet for a long while. First Ben, then Mary Ann. Here he had been enjoying his new life, even if it was in tired old Lebanon, while Cal was coping with tragedy after tragedy. Without thinking, he took off his hat and turned it around and around by the brim. "Life can sure change fast, can't it?"

Cal nodded. "That it can."

Matthew glanced at Cal, at the strong set of his jaw. His brother reminded him of a plowed field, with furrows straight and deep. "Cal, we all count on you. Who do you count on?"

Cal's eyes turned to the ridgeline that defined Stoney Ridge. "'I will lift up mine eyes unto the hills, from whence cometh my help. My help cometh from the Lord, which made heaven and earth.' If the Lord God is wise enough to manage this world, he knows enough to help me through these troubles." A brief smile passed over his face as he gave a sideways glance at Matthew. "So, little brother, I see you got your money's worth at the barbershop."

Later that afternoon, after Ben's funeral service, the last of the women washed and dried dishes in Beacon Hollow's kitchen while husbands gathered outside by the buggies. Jorie stayed as long as she could, but the moment came when she had to get off by herself. She slipped out the back door and walked down to the willow tree by the creek. It was a glorious September afternoon, almost cruel in its beauty. She saw Ephraim walking around in the creek, barefoot with his pants rolled up, watching the water swirl around his ankles.

"Hello there, Ephraim."

He whirled around, looking as if he expected to be called back to the house. Instead, Jorie sat down on the creek bank.

"Nice to have a few moments to yourself, isn't it?"

He nodded.

"The creek is so clean that you can see to the bottom. Did you know that water is actually made up of different colors? All clear, but colors all the same."

He dug a toe into the creek bottom, kicking up a swirl of dirt.

"I'm sorry about Ben. I know you and he were especially close."

Ephraim gave a big nod. "I'm s-sorry too. F-for you."

She nodded, then swallowed hard to fight back the tears that started to prickle her eyes. They came so suddenly, those tears. "It's hard to understand God's will sometimes. It's hard to understand why he took our Ben."

"A-about Mary Ann t-too."

Jorie studied Ephraim's profile as he watched the ripples on the top of the water. He was so dear to her, her Ephraim. He reminded her of one of her colts: gangly, long limbed, awkward, skinny as a broom handle, but filled with so much promise. She

70

shouldn't have been surprised that he had figured out Mary Ann wasn't going to get better. Ephraim was perceptive like that. They sat there quietly for a long time, watching bugs land on the top of the water. "The bishop's words at the very end of Ben's funeral today helped me feel better. Do you remember what he said? He repeated it twice."

"God a-always h-has a p-plan."

"Promise me you'll say that to yourself whenever you start thinking about Ben and feeling sad. And whenever you feel worried about Mary Ann. I promise to do the same."

She rose to her feet. "I'd better get back up there. My grandmother had her eye on Sylvia's sour cream coffee cake. I don't think Sylvia would understand if that entire cake went missing."

She smiled a little, and that made Ephraim smile. It felt good to smile, she thought, even on a day like today.

On the bus ride back to Lebanon late Sunday afternoon, Matthew's heart felt heavy. He didn't know what troubled him more: the reality of Ben's death or the sight of Mary Ann. Both, most likely.

When he had walked into the kitchen, the sight of her tore a choking gasp from his throat. She was thin and pale, with dark circles under her eyes. He could hardly say hello, trying to get it past the knot in his throat. He noticed bruises on her arms and suspected they were on her legs too, though she covered them in stockings. For the first time since he had left home, he found himself wishing he was still at Beacon Hollow, to help his family. He had planned to spend his days off exploring the area, maybe even take the bus to Philadelphia. He wanted to visit museums and well-stocked libraries, to attend different churches, and even to sit downtown on park benches and watch people. Mostly girls. So far, he had hardly seen any girl under fifty in Lebanon, and the one he did meet—a candy striper at the hospital—had a very impressive overbite.

Instead, he decided he would head back to Stoney Ridge as often as he could. Cal needed him.

The last few nights when Mary Ann woke in the night, she found Cal in the chair next to the bed, watching her, like a mother looking after a sleeping child. She wished his last memories of her wouldn't be these but of other times, when she had been young and full of life. She smiled and patted the bed so he would lie down beside her. He slid into bed, stretched out, and put his arm around her, so that her head was on his chest. She could hear his heart beating. What a beautiful sound, she thought. The sound of your husband's heartbeat.

"Cal, I told Dr. Lachman today that I am going to stop the treatments." She listened for him to respond, but he didn't say a word. "The treatments aren't working. The cancer is going too fast. I need to die well."

She glanced up at him. He was staring at the ceiling.

"Dr. Lachman agreed with me."

A tear slipped from the corner of Cal's eye and rolled down his cheek.

She propped herself up on her elbow to face him. "I need to show Ephraim and Maggie, even Matthew, that our faith matters, even facing death. Maybe especially then. I can't do it while I'm sick from the chemotherapy, lying in bed, looking and feeling like a plucked chicken. This is my time. I'm at peace with it." She reached over him to pull the nightstand drawer open and take out the letters. "There's one for Matthew and Ephraim and Maggie. To be given to them on their wedding day." It could have been hours later or only moments when she lifted the fourth letter and placed it gently on top of his chest. "This one is for you, Cal. For your wedding day."

"Don't," he said, his voice breaking.

She brushed the tears off of his cheeks. "I've never asked anything of you, Cal, but I am asking you to consider this. After I am gone, it's normal to grieve. I hope you'll miss me sorely." She paused and took a deep breath. "But after a time I want you to ask our Jorie to be your wife."

Mary Ann could read the shock of her words on Cal's face by the moon that was casting its long pale light through the window.

He turned away. "You can't pick out another woman and tell me to love her," he said after a long moment. "You can't be thinking I'll marry her after you're gone. You can't will someone into taking your place."

She touched his cheek, turning his face back to hers. "I've given this thought and prayer, Cal. Jorie would be just the kind of mother our Maggie and Ephraim need. And the right wife for you too."

"Jorie King is my brother's girl."

"Not anymore." She felt him take in a hard breath. "It might take awhile to think of her in a different way, but I hope you won't let that stop you, Cal. Not Ben's memory, not meddling relatives." She sighed. "Things have changed, for all of us. I'm blessed, in a way, having this time. Knowing I'm dying. Your folks never had that chance." She laid her head back down against his chest, her cheek nestling into the hollow above his heart.

In a voice roughed by pain, Cal said, "I just don't know how I'm going to live through your dying."

A cold spell hit the next week, complete with gusting wind and frost on the roofs of the farmhouse and outbuildings. It took them all by surprise after such a long hot summer.

"M-Mary Ann, are you . . . g-going to g-get b-better?" Ephraim asked her one morning when he brought a pail of steaming milk into the kitchen from the barn.

Mary Ann turned slowly, careful to keep her face calm, for even with the gusting wind she'd caught the note of fear in Ephraim's voice and it touched her heart. He was standing in front of the wall pegs that held Cal's hat and large coat and looked so small by comparison. His bony wrists, chapped red from the cold, stuck out from the ends of his coat sleeves. She came up to him, her gaze moving gently over his face, a face that was so dear to her.

"I don't think I am, Ephraim," she said.

The words flew from Ephraim's mouth, fierce and whole. "Please don't die."

Mary Ann dug her fingers into his shoulders as she pulled him against her.

It was hard, so hard sometimes to accept God's will.

The weather warmed up by week's end. One evening, Mary Ann had just enough strength to ask Cal to carry her outside to watch the day end. He bundled her up in quilts and sat her in the porch swing so she could watch Maggie and Ephraim play softball. Cal sat next to her, holding her hand. Her heart was suddenly too full for words as she let her gaze roam lovingly over Beacon Hollow: the corn shocks built like tepees, her vegetable garden that had been started and tended by Cal's mother, the neat shed that held their winter wood supply, the lofty white barn. Flat, carefully plowed fields with rich, loamy soil. And a creek that ran almost the year round to give water to their cows and sheep and horses that liked to graze under the willow tree's shade. Cal kept the farm in immaculate condition, just like his father had. Beacon Hollow, it was part of them; this place was their history. This farm—it was a good home to raise a family.

They watched the sun slip under the horizon, slowly and silently. She wondered if this was what dying would feel like. Slipping away slowly and silently. She didn't fear death, for she would be in the loving arms of her Father in heaven. But it was the thought of the loving arms of those she was leaving behind that broke her heart, the thought of all those joyful moments they shared that would be lost.

She knew she didn't have much longer. She had grown so weak, so tired. Her body was covered with deep, eggplant purple bruises. Dr. Lachman had told her such bruising would be a sign that her time was near. He said that most likely, hemorrhaging would occur in her brain. He wanted her to come to the hospital, but she and Cal refused to consider it.

"It's not our way," Cal explained. "Our people pass at home, surrounded by loved ones."

Cal and Maggie made hot chocolate and brought it out on the porch to watch the full and creamy moon rise in the evening sky.

"What will it be like in heaven?" Maggie asked Mary Ann as she handed her a warm mug.

Mary Ann wrapped her arms around her daughter. Maggie had hardly left her side in the last few days, only leaving to go to school, and then she rushed home as if she feared the worst. Mary Ann knew she had to answer this question well to help her daughter find peace. She didn't want to leave Maggie with bitter feelings about God, as if he had played a mean trick on them by taking her too soon. The way Mary Ann felt growing up without a mother. It was through knowing Cal that she came to understand God didn't play tricks; his ways were good and wise.

"Maggie, how do your hands feel right now, holding on to that warm mug after playing in the cold?"

"Good."

"Really good?"

She nodded.

"But after a while, that good feeling fades away."

She nodded again.

"In heaven, that good feeling won't go away. That warm, good feeling is like the presence of God, and it will last for all eternity."

Cal's gaze settled gently, lovingly, on his wife.

That night, Mary Ann died in her sleep.

4

On the kitchen counter at Beacon Hollow were pies and casseroles, sliced cheese and ham, bowls of black and green olives and sweet pickles, slices of bread slathered in peanut butter. Sylvia examined the bounty with a critical eye and moved the mayonnaise and mustard closer to the sliced ham. Marge King tried to shoo her out of the kitchen to take her place with the family near Mary Ann's coffin, but Sylvia wouldn't budge. She was determined to oversee the food. The last time Marge King helped in the kitchen for a funeral, she absentmindedly added marshmallows to the chicken salad. Sylvia was going to make sure things were set out right. It was the least she could do for her only sister.

Besides, Sylvia knew she had to keep moving. She had to stay busy. If there was one thing she knew, keeping busy helped ease a heartache.

Jorie could not eat much of anything today, but Sylvia kept thrusting plates at people and encouraging them to "Eat, eat!"

77

Finally, Jorie accepted one just to appease her. Watching Sylvia, knowing how her heart must be suffering with her sister's body laid out in the other room, Jorie was filled with compassion for her. Sylvia was a devout woman, trying to do the right thing, whose greatest need was to be needed.

Jorie had driven her grandparents over for Mary Ann's viewing and stayed close by Marge's side. Sometimes, her grandmother could be a little . . . unpredictable. Downright inappropriate, Atlee would say, though with amused respect for his wife. Jorie felt almost relieved to focus on Marge; it helped her set aside the heartache of loss that shadowed her lately.

When their turn came to view Mary Ann's body, Marge reached out and stroked Mary Ann's cold cheek, as tenderly as if she were a sleeping child. "If only she could have just hung on a little longer. I was working on a remedy that could've healed her for sure."

Jorie bent over and kissed Mary Ann on the forehead. "Goodbye, dear friend," she said, before turning quickly away to stop from tearing up.

Her eyes caught Cal's across the room, and he gave her a brief nod. She didn't know how he was able to cope lately. Two funerals in scarcely two weeks' time. Such grief, such grief. She knew she felt speechless under its weight.

As the line continued, she followed her grandparents to shake the family's hands. Cal spoke soft words of gratitude, but his eyes were two flat, smooth stones. Even Matthew, who usually couldn't wipe the laughter from his eyes, answered everyone who spoke to him in a polite, subdued voice. Maggie was silent, not even humming. Ephraim was nowhere to be seen.

When the twentieth buggy turned onto Beacon Hollow's lane,

Ephraim felt as if he couldn't breathe. He had to get out of the house, away from the neighbors who kept patting his head and telling him Mary Ann was in a better place. He knew that couldn't be true because, for Mary Ann, there was no better place than Beacon Hollow.

He decided to go across the road to Stoney Creek and see how big the yearling Percherons had grown. He was crossing the road when he noticed a car stopped at Marge King's roadside fruit stand. He recognized the driver: that dark-skinned man who had run out of gasoline back in August.

"Hello there! Remember me?" the man called out to Ephraim.

Ephraim walked up to his car and leaned down to peer inside. A woman was next to the man, about the same age. She was just as dark as the man but her hair wasn't kinky—it was long and straight—and her stomach was as round as a volleyball.

The man smiled at Ephraim. "I don't think I caught your name, last time we met."

"Ephraim Z-Zook."

"I'm Dr. Robinson, Ephraim. I'm the new veterinarian in town. This is my wife, Mrs. Robinson." He turned to his wife. "He's the boy who helped me when I ran out of gas a month or so ago."

So *this* was the man, Ephraim realized, who Ron Harding was talking about at the hardware store. For the life of him, he couldn't understand why people would listen to Ron Harding and Jerry Gingerich. He'd rather have a man like Dr. Robinson live in Stoney Ridge than the likes of those two. He had asked Cal why folks wouldn't let a colored man live here, especially a vet when they needed one so desperately. "Folks can be mighty ignorant," was Cal's explanation.

Ephraim had told Cal *that* sounded like another thing to add to his list of questions without answers. Lately, Ephraim's mind, his whole being, was questions.

Seeing the frustrated look on Ephraim's face, Cal spoke up again. "Give people a chance to get to know him. Then he'll change their minds. You just watch and see."

Dr. Robinson broke in on Ephraim's musings. "We just came from a house down the road that was up for sale, but when we got there, the lady said she had changed her mind. Wasn't for sale, after all."

Ephraim felt a twisting in his stomach.

"I noticed that roadside stand and thought we'd stop to get some tomatoes. I don't see anyone working, though."

"That's M-Marge's s-stand. She's over at B-Beacon Hollow. At the f-funeral."

"Who died?" Dr. Robinson asked.

Ephraim looked down at the ground. "My s-sister-in-law."

"Oh. I'm sorry, Ephraim."

He didn't want to have to answer any questions about Mary Ann. He pointed to the stand. "M-Marge usually l-leaves an h-honor j-jar."

"No kidding?" Mrs. Robinson asked, leaning forward in her seat to look at Ephraim. "An honor jar? What happens if people forget their honor and walk off with the money?"

Ephraim shrugged. "I g-guess they n-need it m-more than we d-do."

Dr. Robinson looked at Ephraim for a long while. "Have you been able to get to that circus yet?"

Ephraim shook his head.

"I think it's only in town another month before moving on to Harrisburg."

Ephraim nodded. "I'll try to g-go soon."

Dr. Robinson stuck out his hand to shake Ephraim's. "Glad to have seen you again, Ephraim."

"H-hope you find a place s-soon."

"I hope so too," Mrs. Robinson said. "We're staying in a dumpy little motel in Stoney Ridge and eating our meals at the diner. We'd better find a place before this baby comes or I will go stir-crazy." She twisted her fingers around her head like she was winding a clock.

Ephraim didn't expect that; he felt a smile tug at his lips.

"Lisa, that's the farm I was telling you about." Dr. Robinson pointed to Beacon Hollow. "That's your home, Ephraim. Isn't that right?"

Ephraim turned and looked up at the farmhouse. A buttery glow from kerosene lanterns lit the windows. Buggies were lined up, shoulder to shoulder. The sun was setting low in the west, casting a long reddened light onto the carefully tended fields.

He turned back to Dr. Robinson. "Me and my f-family, that's where we l-live."

The weather turned unseasonably warm again after Mary Ann's passing. Sylvia dropped by Beacon Hollow every day to help. She organized meals to be delivered for the next month and hired two teenaged girls to clean the farmhouse, do laundry, and cook.

"Caleb, I realize now is not the time, but—" Sylvia started before leaving to return home one afternoon.

"Then perhaps it's a conversation that could wait until some other day," Cal interrupted wearily.

"There has been quite a bit of talk about what's going on in that schoolhouse," Sylvia continued, as if Cal had asked her to elaborate. "Actually, about what's *not* going on in that schoolhouse. Do you realize that they spend more time outdoors than in?"

"It's been beastly hot this fall, Sylvia. Soon enough, they'll be stuck indoors. Until then, Jorie feels spending time out in nature actually helps promote learning."

"Promote fiddlesticks!"

Cal put a hand up to stop her. "Let Jorie do the teaching, Sylvia. You have enough to do, taking care of your own farm." What he wanted to say was that Sylvia didn't need to stop by every day.

"Speaking of my farm, Caleb," she said, "I've been thinking that Maggie should come and stay with us for a while."

Cal was just about to take a sip of coffee when he froze. "*Take* my Maggie?"

Sylvia sat down next to him. "It would give you time to get used to things, get a new routine established. You know how close she and Esther are. It would be good for her to be around females."

Cal kept his eyes lowered. "She's my daughter, Sylvia. My only child. It would be like taking the light from the sun. I just couldn't bear it."

"Think about what *she* needs, Caleb. And what Mary Ann would want for her."

After Sylvia finally went on her way, a sadness welled up inside of Cal. He wanted Mary Ann alive, to take care of their daughter and to deal with Sylvia's meddling. He wanted his brother Ben alive to help run Beacon Hollow. He pressed his lips together against his weakness. His wife and his brother knew a better life now. The eternal life, warm and safe with God and the glory of heaven. It was selfish of him to miss them. If only for the sake of Ephraim and Maggie, he had to find the courage to surrender

to God's will. Mary Ann and Ben were no longer with them—
they'd gone to God.

The Lord giveth and the Lord taketh, but it was wrong of him
to dwell so much on the taking. God had given him so much too.
Happy years with Mary Ann and a beloved daughter in Maggie.
Two other brothers to share the work of Beacon Hollow.

Death was certainly a hurtful thing, he couldn't deny that, but
only to those left behind.

As Jorie watched Maggie working at her desk, she wondered
what was going through her head lately. How did a little girl
make sense of death? Maggie often had a knowing look on her
face, the hint of a smile that made Jorie think she knew more
than she was letting on. Jorie had always gotten the impression
that Maggie was smart beyond her years. Her gaze turned to
Ephraim, sitting in the far back row. She worried about him,
sweet Ephraim. His stutter had grown worse since Mary Ann's
passing, and that was when he did talk, which was seldom. It
seemed as if he was trying to be invisible, but Jorie refused to
let him. She hoped that by having him do well in the role of the
angel Gabriel in the Christmas play, it might give him some
confidence he lacked.

She glanced up on the wall to see the growing list devoted to
an inventory of first sightings. It was an idea she came up with
to try and encourage the scholars to become more observant of
nature. As her eyes scanned the list, she realized that most of the
first sightings were Ephraim's. Red fox. Cooper's hawk. Northern
bobwhite. Great egret. Ray added a cottontail, which made the
scholars laugh at its ordinariness, but then he looked so offended
that Jorie added it to the list.

On the opposite side of the blackboard was another growing list, titled "Very Important Questions." Whenever the scholars had a question they couldn't answer, they wrote it up on the board for the class to discuss. "How does the moon stay up in the sky?" "When bees head to the hive, how long until it rains?" "What do you get if you cross an elephant with a rhinoceros?" She was pleased with the questions and the discussions they prompted; she wanted to ignite the children's curiosity about this big, beautiful world God gave them. If there was one thing she wanted to leave them with, it was . . . wonder.

Ephraim thought briefly of telling Cal about the circus tickets, but quickly dismissed the notion because he was pretty sure Cal wouldn't let him go. He just wanted to see the wild animals, up close, but Cal would be worried he'd be tempted to see the entertainment. His brother Ben had gone once and came home with jaw-dropping tales of circus ladies who wore practically nothing. No, he thought it would be best not to bother Cal with this right now. Cal had enough on his mind. He thought of what Ben often advised when faced with such a knotty problem: "Better just go now and apologize later."

Ephraim would need to skip school to go to the circus. He had given this plan a lot of thought and settled on Friday. Jorie took the class out on all-day expeditions on Friday, and Ephraim figured that, if absolutely necessary, he could use the excuse that he was late to school. Once, Levi Yoder was so late that the class left without him. There wasn't church this Sunday, either, which reduced the chance of Cal crossing paths with Jorie, and hopefully, she might even forget that he was absent. Jorie could be forgetful like that, especially if she got excited about something the scholars found on a Friday expedition. He might just get away with it.

On Friday, he and Maggie left for school like always, but he stopped at the road. "You g-go ahead, I'm g-gonna head through the D-Deep Woods."

"I'll come too."

"No!"

Hurt, Maggie spun around and marched up the street toward the schoolhouse. Ephraim bent down to tie his shoe. As soon as she disappeared around the bend, he ran down the street in the opposite direction to catch the bus.

At the part of the road where the bus usually stopped, Ephraim waited anxiously, hidden behind a tree. He was worried a buggy would pass by and spot him playing hookey. Suddenly, behind him came a familiar tuneless humming.

He whirled around to face Maggie. "Aw, Maggie. C-can't I d-do anything alone?"

She pushed her glasses up on her nose. "If you don't let me come with you, I . . . will . . . tell."

He scowled at her but explained the plan for the day and told her that if she went along with it, she might have to lie. She cocked her head and thought about it for a split second. "Dad says that repentance is a daily thing. So I'll just plan on doing some extra repentance-ing today."

As soon as she finished the sentence, they heard the bus chugging up the hill and waved their arms so the driver would stop. Less than an hour later, they stood at the Lancaster bus station, wondering which way to go. It wasn't hard to determine that West Lampeter Fairgrounds was the answer to that question—circus posters covered every surface. Before even reaching the fairgrounds they caught sight of the unmistakable peaked top of a canvas circus tent, thickly striped in white and red.

"There it is," Maggie said, eyes wide.

They found the ticket booth at the circus entrance. Ephraim handed the ticket taker his two prized tickets. "W-which w-way t-to the menagerie?" he asked, trying not to stare at how small the man was. This man was smaller than anyone in Stoney Ridge.

The dwarf pointed a finger down the path along the large tent. "Animal dens are that way. It's feeding time now, if you hurry."

Ephraim and Maggie wandered around the tents, led by the smell of animals—a smell that wasn't much different from a barnyard.

"Oh, Ephraim, look!" Maggie called out. "See the horses? They're Percherons, aren't they? Just like the Kings'!" A make-shift corral held a half-dozen draft horses, their heads buried in mounds of hay.

"K-Kings' horses are b-better," Ephraim said loyally.

Spotting the animal dens, he grabbed Maggie's hand and pulled. In a long row, shaded by the tent, were cages on wheels, brilliantly painted scarlet with gold trim. Their sides were propped open to reveal an assortment of unusual animals. Three chimps, with large patches of missing hair, were huddled in a corner of a dirty den. Next den over, an old black bear with paws as big as dinner plates squatted in front of his food dish. Then there was an angry-looking eagle, tied to a post. A tired and toothless lion lay on his back in another den. At the very end was the cougar den. *This* was the reason Ephraim had come. He walked up to the cougar cage, as close as he dared, and quietly watched. The cougar licked its paws, tail swinging, before noticing Ephraim. Its lithe, tawny-colored body jumped off of a ledge and went up to the bars, as if sizing Ephraim up. The cougar sniffed the air, then settled back on its haunches. Ephraim had never seen anything so beautiful. The cougar and Ephraim exchanged a long look. He took a step closer.

"Not so close, Ephraim," Maggie whispered.

"It's ok-kay. She knows," Ephraim said, eyes still glued to the cougar's.

"Knows what?" Maggie asked, hiding behind him.

"She knows I th-think she should b-be free."

A sudden clanking of metal surprised the cougar and she turned toward the sound, curling back her lips to bare her teeth. It was a circus worker, not much older than Matthew, throwing lunch to the cougar. He had an electric prod that he kept in front of him and used it to poke the big cat in the flank as she ate. The cougar lunged toward him, but he shocked her with the stick, then laughed when she fell back in pain.

"S-stop!" Ephraim shouted with such force that his spit sprayed through the air.

"Beat it, kid," the worker yelled. "Or I'll try it out on you." He pretended to jab the prod toward Ephraim.

"Come on," Maggie said, pulling Ephraim away. "Let's go find the human cannonball." They had seen large banners for the human cannonball, plastered on sides of the big tents. "And I want to see the world's fattest lady. And I want cotton candy too."

Ephraim scowled at the worker but went off with Maggie. They walked into the main tent and saw trapeze artists and a tightrope walker, but the human cannonball, they were told, was at the dentist with a toothache. When they found the fattest lady in the world, they decided that Fannie Byler, a woman in their church, was even fatter. Ephraim bought Maggie cotton candy on a paper cone. Too soon, he knew they needed to catch the bus to get home by the time school let out.

Before they left the circus, Ephraim wanted to walk past the cougar den one more time. The cougar was waiting as if she had been expecting him. She stuck her nose through the bars, drawing in a scent of him. Her golden eyes were bright and she stared right at him, and he had the strangest notion that she was begging him to set her free. Ephraim put a hand up as if he was going to touch her, but the trainer shooed him off.

On the bus ride back, Maggie fell asleep. A bump in the road woke her up and she looked at Ephraim. "This was the best day of my life." Then her eyes drifted shut again and she leaned her head against his shoulder.

Today had been worth it.

It was purely accidental that Jorie was walking on the road when the city bus pulled up and Maggie and Ephraim hopped off. She was heading home and thought she might stop by Beacon Hollow to see if they were sick, but the timing of the bus was just a coincidence. They didn't notice her following behind them. She knew they were up to something, and she was pretty sure Cal wouldn't be happy about it. But they were safe and they were home. She thought she even heard Maggie humming. The sound of it tugged at her heartstrings like a well-loved hymn. Whatever they had been doing, she knew they needed time for things like that, where they could just be two happy children.

She crossed the road and turned left at Stoney Creek's drive.

On a rainy morning in late October, Matthew surprised Cal by showing up for breakfast. The windows were open and an acrid smell of burnt oatmeal filled the room.

"Did you burn the coffee too?" he asked, when Cal opened the door for him.

"No, but I can't guarantee that it's drinkable," Cal said. "How'd you get here?"

"Bus. I have a couple of days off and thought you might need some help getting that third cutting of hay in."

Cal looked a little confused. "I hadn't given much thought to that third cutting yet."

"Hadn't thought about it? This time last year, you had that third cutting stacked and in the hayloft."

Matthew was worried about his brother. Cal was always the strong one. He kept the family together after their folks died, stepping into their father's footsteps as if he was born for it. But Cal seemed as if he were walking around in a fog, preoccupied and distant. As Matthew looked around, he could see only the bare minimum was getting accomplished at Beacon Hollow. The cows were getting milked, of that he had no doubt. And the milk was getting picked up regularly by the milk truck every other day, just like always. But not much else of the normal farm routine seemed to be happening. Even the fields—usually plowed under with manure as soon as the harvest was in so that they would spend the winter gaining nourishment—looked about as well-plowed as if a cat had scratched around on them. He looked outside at the steady rain. Well, the hay wasn't going to get cut today.

Cal went to the stairs. "Ephraim! Maggie! Time to wake up!"

"They're not here. I met them on the road. They were on their way to Jorie's."

"What?" Cal said, dropping a spoonful of paste colored oatmeal into a bowl. "Why would they be going there at such an early hour?"

"Something about hunting for a beaver's den. Ephraim said he had just read that beavers have extra-large lungs and that's why they can go underwater for seventeen minutes. Said he wants to time them." Matthew stirred the oatmeal, took a bite and frowned, then pushed it away. "They went early to get breakfast at Jorie's." Quietly he added, "I shoulda gone too."

"There's fresh eggs," Cal said, pointing to the basket, still on the counter. "You can help yourself."

Matthew looked for a clean bowl in the cupboard, couldn't find one, so he rinsed one that sat piled up in the sink. He cracked three eggs, tossed the shells in the sink, and started whipping up the yolks. He cooked the scrambled eggs in the only fry pan he could find that wasn't dirty, then looked for a clean plate, and finally just gave up. He sat down at the table and ate the eggs directly out of the fry pan. "I saw Sylvia in town. She said to tell you she'll be stopping by around noon. Said she's bringing Esther to play with Maggie."

"Oh no," Cal said. "Oh no, no, no." He glanced at the clock on the wall. "Matthew, you need to run over to Jorie's and fetch Maggie. Ask Jorie to come too. Tell her ... it's an emergency." He grabbed Matthew's fry pan and started filling the sink with hot water.

Matthew pushed himself back from the table. "What's the emergency?"

"Sylvia wants Maggie to live with her."

Matthew's eyes went wide. "You gonna let her?"

"No, I am not. But we have to show her that we're doing just fine and that Maggie isn't running all over the county like a wild Indian." He grabbed the liquid soap bottle and squirted its entire contents into the sink, then started scrubbing dishes like a madman.

Fifteen minutes later, Jorie and Maggie and Ephraim arrived, trailing behind Matthew. When Cal caught sight of Maggie, he could practically hear the squawking Sylvia would do if she caught sight of her. Barefoot, Maggie was wearing Ephraim's shirt and a pair of old pants, held up by twine. Her hair was tucked loose in a bandanna, flowing down her back in tangles and snarls.

Cal ran outside. "Jorie! Maggie needs to be—"

"To be turned back into a girl," Jorie said, laughing. "Don't worry, Cal. Matthew explained the situation."

"No, I do not!" Maggie said, scowling, an indignant look on her face.

"Yes, you do," Cal answered, in a tone of voice which meant she had to obey.

"This is all because of Sylvia . . . and Ephraim says she's not really even his aunt!" Maggie shouted.

"Maggie, calm down." Cal gave Ephraim "the look." "That's true, she's not Ephraim's aunt."

"Mine either," Matthew chimed in.

Cal rolled his eyes.

"You can't deny," Matthew said, "that somehow Sylvia Swartzentruber manages to exude disapproval at fifty yards."

At first, Cal wanted to put a stopper in Matthew, but as the meaning of his words sunk in, he let out a laugh. It surprised him, that laugh. A small laugh. In that messy kitchen, with dishes piled up in the sink and a floor so dirty that shoes could stick to it, with Matthew and Ephraim and Maggie looking at him as if he was coming unhinged.

A small, tiny laugh, but it was there. His first laugh since Mary Ann had passed.

Jorie seemed to understand; her eyes were smiling as Cal tried again to persuade Maggie to change into girl clothes.

"But I *am* a girl!" Maggie said, stamping her feet.

"Of course you're a girl," Jorie said. "We just need to have you looking like one." She put a hand on Maggie's head and gently guided her upstairs to get a bath.

Downstairs, Cal, Matthew, and Ephraim swept and cleaned and hid the dirty laundry down in the basement. Jorie came back down and tried unsuccessfully to swallow a grin at the sight of Cal with an apron around his waist. "Maggie says she doesn't have any dresses."

"That's not entirely true," Cal said, feeling his cheeks grow warm. "She just doesn't have any *clean* dresses. That's why she's helped herself to Ephraim's hand-me-downs."

"What happened to the girls who were cleaning for you?" she asked.

"They're working as waitresses for that new restaurant in town." He swept an overlooked pile of dirt into a dustpan. "I haven't had time to find someone else." Truth be told, he was overjoyed when the girls told him about their job offer. They made him nervous in his own house, and he knew Sylvia grilled them for details—which only added to Sylvia's ability to leak a constant stream of complaints about him, like a rowboat with a hole in it.

Jorie glanced at the kitchen wall clock. Ten thirty. "Where do you think I could find some of Maggie's dresses?"

Cal pointed to the basement stairs. "Down there, in the basement. In a pile. The machine broke down and I haven't had a chance to fix it."

At eleven, Jorie brought Maggie to see Cal. She was wearing a lavender dress with a starched white apron over it, black stockings, and polished shoes. Her shiny clean hair was tightly pinned down under a stiff prayer cap.

"Maggie," Cal said, a smile lighting his face, "you look like—"

"A dumb girl." She wiggled. "These dadburn pins keep poking at me. I wish I was a boy like Ephraim."

Cal crouched down. "I'm sure glad you're my little girl."

"If I were a boy, then I wouldn't have to play with Esther," Maggie said. "She likes to play house and make me the baby just so she can boss me around."

"S-she tries to b-boss me t-too, Maggie," Ephraim said. "She'd b-boss you whether you're a b-boy or a g-girl. She's just p-plain b-bossy."

Jorie looked around the kitchen. "You men worked a wonder!"

Matthew leaned over to whisper loudly in her ear, "Just don't look in the oven. You'll see a week's worth of dirty pans."

"Maggie, stop wiggling," Cal said.

"I can't help it!" she said with a scowl. "These clothes are still wet."

"They'll dry soon." Jorie squeezed Maggie's shoulders. "We'll go find that beaver's dam another day." Something at the window caught her eye. "Sylvia's here. I think I'll just slip out the back." She went out the side door as Ephraim darted upstairs.

Mary Ann's garden! Cal hurried out behind Jorie. He saw the shock register on her face when she saw the garden, overgrown with weeds as scraggly as the pumpkin vines. Mary Ann had loved this little plot of soil. She had treated it like a sanctuary. When the house got crowded, he could always find her in the garden, fussing over her plants.

"It's been a little hard to find time to weed," he said. That wasn't entirely true. Everything just seemed to take him longer these days, as if his head was stuffed with cotton and he wasn't thinking clearly.

Jorie spun around on her heels. "Lizzie Glick! She'd be just the right girl to keep house for you. I've never seen anyone work as hard as Lizzie."

"What makes you think she'd quit a good job at the hardware store to keep house for me?"

She looked at him as if it was the most obvious thing in the world. She pointed toward the window. "Because of Matthew."

Cal turned toward the house. Through the window, they could see Matthew attempting to juggle three eggs. Maggie was clapping her hands in delight until Matthew dropped an egg on the floor. Cal turned back to face Jorie, puzzled. "What about Matthew?"

She gave him a patronizing smile. "Why are men so smart in some things and—"

He held up a hand, grinning. "No need to finish that thought."

"Talk to Lizzie."

"Jorie, thank you." His eyes held hers just a beat too long, and then he looked away, feeling guilty, as if he had done something wrong.

Jorie didn't seem to notice his discomfit. She pointed to his waist. "Don't forget to take off that apron."

The kitchen door banged shut and he knew he needed to go back inside to face Sylvia. He yanked off the apron and tossed it behind a bush, then returned to the kitchen with a sigh.

Sylvia wasn't fooled by Maggie's freshly scrubbed look. "I saw

Maggie running along the road this morning in Ephraim's old trousers. And her hair was tied back, looking like a tail on a runaway horse."

Cal scratched his head. "Well, you see, she likes to help outside and those dresses and pins just . . ." He stopped himself. There was no point defending it. The truth was that he let her dress the way she wanted.

Within five minutes, Sylvia found the dishes in the oven and the mountains of laundry in the basement. "What happened to those girls I hired?"

"They were offered jobs in town at the new restaurant. They offered to stay, but I told them to go on, take the jobs. They'd make more money than I could pay them and they'd get to be around young folks."

"You're too soft on people, Caleb. Always have been." Sylvia sighed, then waved her hand. "I'll find you new helpers."

"Well . . ."

Esther smiled a Cheshire cat smile as her mother added, "And Maggie will be coming home with me today."

Maggie's eyes went wide.

"Maggie is a strong-willed child, Caleb. It's not your fault you can't manage her. She needs a firm hand."

"Sylvia, I know you mean well—" Caleb started. He knew from the set of Sylvia's chin, lifted high and aimed dead straight at him, that he was in for a fight. He had enough experience with Sylvia to know it was wise to tread carefully when she was in this frame of mind.

"I'm only doing what's best for my niece. It's what my sister would have wanted. No little girl is going to grow up properly in an all-male household. She's already wearing pants. Next thing you know she's going to cut her hair short and carry a slingshot to shoot down a duck for dinner." Sylvia looked Ephraim over, head to toe. "Perhaps Ephraim should come with me too." Her crisp words knifed through the air.

Now Cal set his jaw. As calmly as a frustrated man could, he asked, "You're saying that these children are better off without me?"

"No, of course not. But you're a minister now. That was God's doing." She rolled her eyes as if God should have consulted her first. "He knew Mary Ann would be taken from us. You don't have time to be doing laundry and ironing clothes and cooking meals and milking cows and taking care of two children. I can't imagine how you're doing your minister duties too."

What she meant, Cal knew, was that he probably wasn't doing his minister duties. It wasn't far from the truth, either. He felt like he was treading water and barely able to keep his head up.

Sylvia started up the stairs. "I'm going to pack a few things for Maggie."

Matthew scooted his chair next to Cal's. "Are you going to let that happen?" he whispered forcefully. "I know you're grieving, but get hold of yourself."

Cal planted his elbows as if anchoring himself into the tabletop. "Sylvia!" She stopped, midway up the stairs, and came back down to the kitchen with a curious look on her face. "I am the head of this family. And I will not let you take my family from me." He stood, his palms facedown on the table, drawing strength from all that a family table symbolized. "That's the last I want to hear on this subject."

Sylvia's face grew hard and her mouth set in a stern line. She grabbed Esther's hand and marched out the door.

Matthew stood by the window, watching them climb into their buggy. "Why do I feel you just poked a sleeping bear?"

On the buggy ride home, Sylvia silently fumed while Esther, bored, dozed off. Sylvia reviewed the many red flags of trouble she observed at Beacon Hollow. First and foremost, *what* was Jorie King doing there? She saw her talking to Cal by Mary Ann's garden, saw them look into each other's eyes. Sylvia knew she wasn't supposed to hate, that it was a sin. But it was a sin to think you were something special too, and that was Jorie King, in a nutshell. She remembered Jorie as a little girl, with an impish face and unruly hair. She had been headstrong and daring. No doubt spoiled, as the daughter of a far-too-lenient minister. And as a young woman, Jorie was famous for the number of suitors she had turned down. It dawned on Sylvia that Jorie might be trying to set her cap on a prize like Cal, now that Ben and Mary Ann were gone.

Poor Cal. He was distraught without Mary Ann, that was plain to see. He looked as haggard and worn out as his clothes, all wrinkled and rumpled. And that house! Why, she had never seen such an unkempt house. Her sister would be shamed.

Somehow, she needed to help Cal. *If only he weren't so stubborn! Why couldn't he accept help?* As Sylvia turned onto her drive, she came to a decision: she would not let poor Mary Ann down. Maggie needed her, Ephraim needed her, and, clearly, Cal needed her.

After Sylvia left, Cal sent Maggie and Ephraim to the garden to weed. Matthew offered to help fix the wringer washer, so Cal went to the workshop in the barn to look for the tools he would need. Bud Schultz walked over from his farm and joined him.

"I saw Hurricane Sylvia leave." Bud whistled. "Roar in, roar out." A beefy man in his late sixties, Bud's eyes grazed over the tools hanging on Cal's neatly organized pegboard.

Cal found his toolbox and looked through it for his wrench. "She wasn't too happy."

Bud unhooked a hammer from the wall and held it up, lifting his bushy upswept eyebrows in a question to borrow it. Cal gave a nod and Bud tucked the hammer claw on the hook of his overalls. "Any reason in particular this time?"

"She doesn't think I'm much of a mother, I suppose. Or a father. Or a minister, for that matter."

Bud leaned against Cal's workbench. "You know, Cal, people have been known to marry again."

Cal jerked his head up. "She hasn't been gone very long."

Bud breathed loudly through his nose. "Have you even thought about it?"

"No."

"Maybe you should. That's all I'm saying."

"Marrying a woman I do not love is apt to be a cure worse than its affliction." Cal found the wrench he was looking for and closed up his toolbox.

"Who said anything about marrying a woman you don't love?" Bud said, lifting his shoulders in a shrug.

"Aw, Bud, I just never expected to grow old with anyone else." Cal looked at his neighbor, a man who was dear to him.

Over the years, Bud had become a part of the Zooks' family. He joined them for supper nearly every Sunday. They felt comfortable borrowing Bud's telephone and asking for rides. Bud had a son who left farming behind to become a stockbroker in Philadelphia and visited once a year, only to badger his father into selling the farm and moving to the city. Every year, Bud refused and his son left in a huff.

"You're going to have an awfully long and boring life if you don't give yourself the freedom to love again," Bud said, thumbs hooked under his overall straps. "Why, you're a young fellow—scarcely thirty years old! Unless of course, you don't feel the need . . ." His voice trailed off as a mischievous glint came into his eyes.

Cal stiffened. "I am a man yet."

Bud grinned. "Hoo-boy, that's a relief." He leaned against the wall and crossed his arms. "You know, you Amish folk do a better job than most of us by facing the future as it is."

"You've been alone an awful long time, Bud. You seem to be doing just fine."

Bud walked over to the open door of the barn and scanned his fields. "Maybe I'm a little sorry I didn't take my own advice."

When Jorie returned home from Beacon Hollow, she spotted Doc Williams's car in the driveway. She went first to the barn, assuming she would find him there. The Kings' barn was a huge structure, made of stone at the bottom and whitewashed wood at the top. Beyond the barn were forested hills that followed the entire perimeter of the property. Jorie stopped for a brief moment to take in the sight. In autumn, the hills were spectacular—aflame with trees of red, orange, and yellow foliage.

As Jorie slid open the door, a slice of fading sunlight fell across the freshly swept barn floor. She breathed in the familiar smell of animals and hay. The main part of the building consisted of two aisles of box stalls, separated by a dark, narrow corridor. Most of the stalls were empty at this time of the day. Atlee managed the barn with a precise regimentation: the horses were turned out to graze by rotating pastures. A barn swallow swooped over her and landed on a mud-plastered nest; she could see the hay sticking out of the layers of mud in the nest. She walked through the center of the barn and out the other side, and there she found her grandfather talking to Doc Williams. Standing beside them was that tall, dark-skinned man whom Jorie had met awhile back, when his car ran out of gas in front of Stoney Creek. So *he* was the new veterinarian.

"Jorie, I was hoping to see you." Doc Williams waved her over. "This is Jim Robinson, a vet from Virginia who's going to be taking over for me. I've been showing him around, introducing him to my patients."

Jorie knew Doc Williams better than she'd ever known an English person. She always thought he had the makings of a Plain man—when he didn't know the answer to something, he said so.

"We've met once before." Jorie shook hands with Dr. Robinson. "Do you know much about horses?" She hoped the answer was yes. Doc Williams knew cats and dogs, but when it came to sheep, cows, and horses, he had to consult his books. He had retired from a city practice and moved to the country, then ended up practicing because there was no nearby vet in the area to handle the Amish farms. Last year a series of misfortunes—a mastitis outbreak at Jonas Lapp's dairy, bloated sheep from sweet clover at Samuel Riehl's, and the loss of Stoney Creek's prize broodmare—and Doc Williams knew it was time he found someone else.

"My specialty is large animals," Dr. Robinson told her. "I grew up around horses." He walked over to the fence where a stallion, Big John, looked at him curiously with glossy black eyes. Big John stuck his nose over the fence to see if Dr. Robinson might be hiding a carrot or two in his pocket. The doctor chuckled as Big John sniffed his face and hands. "He is absolutely huge! Must be at least seventeen hands."

"Eighteen," Atlee corrected. He wasn't being proud, he was just stating a fact.

"These Percherons are such gentle giants." He stroked Big John's long forelock.

"Are you familiar with the breed?" Jorie asked.

"A little," Dr. Robinson answered, rubbing his hands along Big John's large-boned face. "Let's see, Percherons are from the northwest part of France. Their Arabian ancestry is evident in their large, dark eyes, and gives them an elegance despite their massive size—"

Jorie's eyebrows lifted in surprise. It almost seemed as if he was reading from a textbook.

"—a versatile breed known for their intelligence and gentle temperaments. Easy to train, gentle and patient around children."

Jorie and her grandfather exchanged a look, impressed.

Dr. Robinson turned to Jorie. "I knew of a man who lost his voice to throat cancer. He was able to guide his horses with the slightest touch of his hand." He looked around the pastures. "Your horses are magnificent. Beautiful conformation. They're compact and muscular, the neck is crested, with a little feathering on their legs. Are they all dapple gray in your line?"

"Most," Atlee said. "We've got a new broodmare, though, who looks like she's been dipped in ink. Name is Fancy."

"Because she thinks she's something special," Jorie added.

Dr. Robinson noticed the chalkboard on the barn wall with statistics written about expected foaling dates. "Any chance you keep breeding records?"

Jorie smiled. "My grandfather keeps very precise records. He's been breeding these horses for thirty years. Why do you ask?"

"Not sure if you're in need of customers, but I have a friend from vet school who's asked me to keep a lookout for a good Percheron stud."

Jorie exchanged another glance with her grandfather. Atlee took a few steps toward Dr. Robinson. "Welcome to Stoney Ridge. We're delighted to have you here."

Two months had passed since Mary Ann's funeral. The initial shock had worn off and some of the Zook family routines were established again. Ephraim and Cal spent a morning in the fields, pitching ears of dried corn into the stake-side wagon. It was a finger-cold day, when a farmer was forced to accept that winter was right around the corner. Cal had been trying to pasture the livestock each day to save on winter feed, but it was time to keep the animals in the barn, protected from the rain and cold.

"M-most of the b-birds are gone," Ephraim said, as they walked between rows.

"Sometime during this month, we can expect a few northern visitors," Cal said. He pointed out some northern juncos, feeding on weed seeds along fencerows. "We're going to have to keep those feeders stocked. Those birds depend on us for handouts."

"We'll be ice-skating on Blue Lake Pond soon," Maggie said.

"Not too soon, I hope," Cal said. "I have a lot to do before nature ends the year."

Ephraim gave a little whistle and the two horses stirred. They leaned patiently into their load and pulled ahead fifteen or twenty feet, then stopped. They were so well trained that they could be started and stopped and held in place with nothing more than a whistle or cluck. Matthew was the horse trainer at Beacon Hollow.

He had picked out these two horses—then foals—from the Kings' three years ago and spent time every day working with them.

Maggie ran back and forth to the house, returning with a fresh water jug. By midmorning, they were ready to let the horses rest and take a break. Cal sat, leaning against a fence post, when Ephraim saw a look of crushing weariness come over him.

Cal took his hat off and raked his fingers through his hair. "We've barely made a dent," he said, more to himself than to Ephraim. "So far behind and there are still acres and acres to go."

"We'll g-get it d-done, Cal," Ephraim said, trying to be encouraging. He looked up at the gray flannelled sky and wondered himself how they were going to get all of the corn into that silo. The day had begun with clear skies, but now a layer of threatening clouds had come in and the temperature was dropping, which meant snow was on its way. Rain and snow could ruin the silage, causing it to mold. "I could s-stay home from s-school."

"Me too," Maggie volunteered.

"No," Cal said. "You need your schooling. Somehow, it will get done." He smiled. "Might take a small miracle, but it will get done."

Sometime later, they heard the clip-clopping of horses' hooves turn into Beacon Hollow's drive. When the buggy driven by a chestnut gelding reached the yard, five bearded men hopped out. They looked around and waved when they saw Cal and Ephraim and Maggie in the field. Cal stood, brushed off his pants, and left the cornfield to cross the pasture and reach the men. Ephraim and Maggie followed behind him.

"Thought you could use a hand getting the corn in before the snow starts," said Samuel Riehl, the other minister. Without waiting for an answer, he led the other four neighbors out to the place where Cal and Ephraim had stopped working to rest.

Ephraim looked up at Cal and saw him blink back tears. Seeing the relief flood his brother's face made his chest ache.

The men fanned out, working row by row, clucking the horses to move forward as if they were their own. Cal put his hat back on and adjusted its brim while looking at the men as they worked.

"You're right, C-Cal," Ephraim said, grinning. "Somehow, it'll g-get done."

Cal rested a hand on Ephraim's back. "The Lord answered our prayers, Ephraim. He gave us neighbors." He grabbed Maggie's hand and the three walked over the hay stubble to join the men.

That evening, as they sat down to evening prayers in the living room, Ephraim noticed that the weariness on Cal's face was gone, replaced by a look of satisfaction. The fire was crackling in the hearth as Cal read aloud from his Bible. Maggie snuggled close to him on the couch.

When Cal finished reading, he closed it, and his hands lovingly grazed the top of the old leather Bible. "It was a good day."

It was, Ephraim agreed. *A very good day.*

5

Thanksgiving came and passed. It brought the first real snow-fall that harkened winter's arrival. Ephraim woke in the night to the sound of a woman's scream. He threw off his blankets and ran to the window, lifting it open. He heard Cal's footsteps heading down the stairs and hurried down to catch up with him before he left the house.

"D-did you hear it?"

Cal pulled the rifle off of the wall. "I did. Now go back to bed." He opened the kitchen drawer for cartridges.

"W-what w-was it?"

"I don't know. Some kind of wild creature. It's not a sound I've heard, at least not since I was a boy."

"I'll c-come. I c-can t-track for you."

"I need you to stay here with Maggie."

"But Cal—"

"Stay." Cal spun around to give him a look that said he meant it. Then he grabbed his hat and coat from the wall pegs and left.

Ephraim watched him head out past the barn, down to where the sheep were in the meadow. He wanted to go with Cal so badly he could taste it. He thought for a moment of sneaking off anyway, but knowing Maggie, she would get up and wander outside looking for him. He sighed, deeply annoyed, and went back to bed.

He tried to stay awake to listen for a shot—to know Cal had found the animal—but next thing he knew, someone was shaking him on the shoulder to wake him up.

"Milking time." It was Cal's voice. Sometimes his brother was like a human alarm clock.

Ephraim opened one eye and saw that the sun was starting to rise. He bolted up. "D-did you get it?"

"No. But it got our Delilah."

Delilah was their best ewe. Matthew had named her Delilah because she welcomed the attention of the rams—any ram—never failing to get pregnant each year. She usually gave them twins too. As Ephraim leaned over to put on his pants, a tear dropped on the floor. He wiped his eyes with his hands, mad at himself for going so soft on a dumb sheep. But he hated animals getting killed. When he trapped the bobcat that kept getting into Amos Esh's sheep pasture last September, he didn't mean for it to be killed. He wanted to catch it and take it far away, but Amos Esh got to the trap first and shot it dead.

Each December, when the air grew cold enough for hog-killing, Ephraim had always found a way to absent himself. He would be in the house or in the barn, far enough away so that he wouldn't hear the squeals of the hog as it was tied up before being shot in the head, mercifully quick. The hog was dipped in boiling water and hung from a tree next to the toolshed, then gutted and butchered into a thousand pieces. From it they got bacon, ham, loin, sausage, and ribs. Everything was used—"Everything but the squeal" was a line he'd heard all his life. Cal tried to explain that if you wanted ham and bacon, you had to kill a hog. It wasn't for sport, he said, but for eating. Still, the first time Ephraim witnessed a hog-killing, he ran behind the barn and threw up.

Ephraim had never even killed a chicken. If Mary Ann asked him to go get a hen for dinner, even an old hen that had stopped laying eggs, he would find Maggie to do the killing for him. She had watched Mary Ann do it so often she was already good at it. A quick twist of the neck and the hen never knew what had happened. Maggie offered to show him how, thinking Ephraim just couldn't get the hang of it. He would decline, saying it was girl's work, but that wasn't true. He just couldn't stomach it.

On this morning, out in the barn, Cal let out a big yawn as he wiped down the cows' teats with antiseptic before attaching the milking pump. The diesel generator that ran the pump hummed in the background. "Ephraim, I'm sorry about last night. I know you could've probably found it."

Ephraim shrugged.

"If you get time after choring, go out looking for tracks to see which way it was heading. I need to know if I should sleep in the barn tonight in case it comes back."

"Did it t-take Delilah?"

Cal looked away. "Most of her. So we know it wasn't a coyote."

Ephraim knew that coyotes go for the neck of their prey and usually come back later for the kill. A coyote wouldn't drag it away, like this one did. "C-Cal, have you ever heard a s-sound like that?"

"Once," Cal said. "When I was a boy. It was the scream of a mountain lion. There are still a few of them around."

From the barn, Cal could hear a horse and buggy turn into the lane of Beacon Hollow. He hurried outside and was surprised to see Jorie King in the driver's seat, out of breath.

"What's making you look as pleased with yourself as a pig in pokeweed?" He couldn't help but smile when he saw the shining intensity in her eyes.

She was so pleased she beamed a smile back at him. "I have an idea! I was driving to town and saw it and I just knew! I knew it could be fixed up and it could be just the place. I turned the horse right around to tell you!"

"Slow down and catch your breath. I have no idea what you're talking about."

"For the new vet! A place to live! It's that old cottage that my grandparents lived in when they first bought Stoney Creek, before they built the farmhouse. It's not in good shape, but we could fix it up. And maybe he could even use that room off the back for his patients. It's got a separate entrance."

Cal turned around to look at Stoney Creek's large barn, the rooftop visible from Beacon Hollow. "That's on your land," he said in a flat tone.

"Practically on the main road, though. That's why my grandparents wanted to live on this side of the farm. But for a vet, he'll be close to the major roads during winter. And it's wired for electricity. We just need to get someone from the electric company to come out and turn everything back on."

He gave her a wary look. "I don't think you should be getting involved in this."

She cocked her head. "I already am involved. Stoney Creek needs that vet as much as anybody else."

"What does Atlee say?"

"I haven't told him yet, but I'm sure he'll agree with me."

"Jorie," Cal said in a warning tone.

"He's a *good* vet, Cal. You know that. We need to help him." She picked up the horse's reins, preparing to leave. "If you have time soon, would you mind going through the cottage and making a list of repairs? I'll talk to some of the neighbors and see about getting some curtains made and furniture donated. Maybe we could have a work frolic. Then Dr. Robinson and his wife could move out of that motel well before the baby arrives."

He nodded, trying to follow everything she said, as a small needle of worry began to plague him.

All morning, Cal and Ephraim worked in the barn, side by side. After Ephraim finished his chores, he went out to see if he could find any animal tracks. As he passed by the sheep grazing under the willow tree, he was glad to see that Cal had already taken care of what was left of Delilah. All that remained were some tufts of wool. Ephraim knew Cal had probably put her in the manure pile to return to the earth. It was hard, loving animals like he did. They were always getting themselves into some kind of trouble.

Along the fence was a low spot where puddles had formed from melting snow. He looked carefully and spotted tracks in the mud where an animal had jumped over the fence. The paws were large, nearly four inches. He wished Matthew were here this weekend. He would have liked to show Matthew those paw prints before they were washed out with rain or snow. With paws that big, it could be a bear. But then he dismissed that notion. The sound of that scream, that was no bear. He hopped over the fence and picked up the trail again as it led into the Deep Woods. He knew that wild animals were most active at dawn and at dusk, so he wasn't too worried about meeting it face-to-face in the broad daylight. He hoped he would, though, but as he went farther along the creek, the paw prints vanished.

The persistent rumble in his belly reminded him it was past lunchtime, so Ephraim gave up the hunt and returned home.

Cal was in town later that week and saw Marge, Jorie's grand-mother, in the hardware store. He had been planning on stopping by the Kings' on the way home, so this was a pleasant coincidence. He wanted to talk to Marge about Maggie.

Marge King might fancy herself as a healer, but Cal had al-ways thought of her as being more of a fixer. She liked to fix people, mostly. She had a keen insight that he respected and rarely gave him poor advice, with the exception of her medicinal know-how.

Some people thought Marge was far too outspoken and a little quirky. Maybe so, but he had always liked quirky. In fact, now that he thought about it, Jorie was quirky. He'd assumed she was more like Atlee with her devotion to those horses, but there was a side of Jorie that lived up in the clouds. Maybe she got some of that cloud living from Marge.

"Just the person I've been wanting to see," he told her and she looked so pleased. "Marge, you've raised five daughters of your own."

"Indeed I did. Twenty-seven grandchildren at last count! But they're scattered all over the countryside now—Ohio, Indiana, Illinois, even Canada." She clucked, deeply distressed. "My own parents could never have imagined the changes we're facing."

"Every generation faces a set of unique challenges," Cal said. "But we can handle those challenges with the Lord's help." The clerk rang up his batteries on the cash register. Cal paid for his purchase and walked outside with Marge. "I've been wanting to talk to you about Maggie."

Marge looked at him, interested. "Something ailing her? The flu is going around."

"No, no, nothing like that." He wanted to veer away from talk about home remedies. "She doesn't like anything to do with being inside, kitchen work, or any woman's work, for that matter. Just the other day, Sylvia offered to take her to a quilting bee and we couldn't find Maggie anywhere. She hid herself in the hayloft to avoid going." He winced. "Sylvia wasn't too understanding."

Marge covered her mouth with her hand, her eyes widening with near laughter. Jorie had the same habit, he realized, when she was amused by something but knew she shouldn't show it. Maybe Marge and Jorie were more alike than he had realized. Mercifully, Jorie had no interest in doctoring.

"Maggie just wants to be outside, choring with Ephraim and me," he continued. "I'm worried she won't learn the . . . feminine skills . . . she'll be needing."

Marge nodded.

"What would you advise, Marge?"

"Well, since you've asked my advice," Marge said amiably—she dearly loved to be asked for advice—"I would just let her be."

Cal just looked at her, nonplussed. "Really?"

"Maggie's grieving for her mother, Caleb. Doing women's work probably just reminds her of Mary Ann. It's easier to be outside. She just wants to be near you."

Cal took that thought in for a long moment.

Marge patted his arm, as she would a small child. "If you're worried that Maggie won't learn the things she needs to know about being an Amish woman, you can quit your worrying. When she's ready, she'll learn. Just give her time." She tilted her head. "But you sure look a little careworn. How about if I bring you a new tonic I whipped up? I call it 'Phoenix Wings.' It'll boost your energy. You'll rise like the phoenix!" She lifted her arms as if to take flight.

Cal's dark eyebrows shot up. The last time he tried Marge's remedy—a cough syrup—just to be polite, he couldn't hold anything down in his stomach for the rest of the day. And his stomach hadn't been the problem. "Thank you, Marge. I think I'm fine, though."

Marge shrugged, disappointed. "Suit yourself." She peered out into the street, searching left and right, and for a split second Cal could see how lovely she must have been as a young woman. "Now where did I put that horse and buggy?"

As a habit, Jorie went to the schoolhouse early to start the stove and get the room warmed up. On Monday morning, the door swung open as if it hadn't been latched. She couldn't believe she hadn't shut it tight. She walked in slowly and carefully, sensing something wasn't quite right.

She saw nothing out of the ordinary. Nothing looked out of place, but she couldn't shake the feeling that someone had been inside.

Cal couldn't postpone cleaning out the barn any longer. Under normal circumstances, he kept it in pristine condition, but these times weren't normal. However, Bud—a man unconcerned about pristine conditions of *any* barn—looked around Beacon Hollow's barn with disgust just yesterday and wondered aloud when the milk inspector would be coming through. That was the moment when Cal knew it was time to get the barn back into shape.

At breakfast on Saturday morning, he told Ephraim and Maggie the plans for the day. They responded by folding their arms on the table, clunking their heads, and groaning.

But Matthew saved the day. He walked into the barn, unannounced, as Cal was doling out pitchforks. Matthew told Cal that it was a good thing he had come, because he could smell that barn as he stepped off the bus. By late afternoon, they had milked the cows, mucked out all of the stalls, replaced the straw bedding, swept the aisles, and knocked down cobwebs . . . and the barn was back to the Zooks' previously high standards of tidiness. A small thing it was, really, just an ordinary thing, but for the first time in months, Cal felt as if he wasn't draining the sea with a pail. That tidy barn made some broken part of him begin to feel whole again.

Cal had just come into the kitchen and started to open cupboards, wondering if Ephraim and Matthew would object to scrambled eggs and cold cereal for dinner. He knew Maggie wouldn't care one way or the other; she was fussy about food and turned up her nose at most things. He found it just one of many mysteries attached to raising a girl.

"Uh-oh, the aunties is coming," Maggie said, looking out the window.

"Are coming. The aunties are coming," Cal corrected, trying to hide his disappointment. Ada and Florence were Cal's two elderly maiden great-aunts, his grandfather Zook's sisters. They lived in a small house on the far south end of Beacon Hollow's property. "What do you think they want?" Cal wondered as he peered out the window over Maggie's shoulder. What he really wondered was, how long would they stay? Once they settled in, those aunties could talk the air full. "Matthew! Come downstairs and visit with the aunties."

Cal heard an exaggerated moan float down the stairs. He went to the kitchen door and opened it wide. "Ada! Florence!" he said, in as delighted a voice as he could muster. "Come in and sit down."

The aunties walked in and glanced around the cluttered kitchen, hands on their bellies, frowning. Cal moved books and papers off of the kitchen table. He cringed when he saw drops of raspberry jam from today's lunch on a chair seat. He hoped the aunties might not notice, but of course, they did and exchanged a disapproving glance. Before sitting down, Ada wiped the sticky seat with her handkerchief.

"Caleb," Ada began, after easing into a chair, "you need a wife."

His dark eyebrows lifted in surprise. He hadn't expected this: an ambush from the aunties. "It's only been a few months."

"Yes, we know," Ada said. "But these are special circumstances."

"How so?" Cal asked, distracted by Matthew who had come to the bottom of the stairs and was trying to quietly slip out of the room, unnoticed. Cal shook his head and pointed to an empty kitchen chair. Matthew remained where he was, poised, ready to escape.

"You're a minister," Ada said. "You need to be an example to others, even in your grieving. It's time you think about remarrying. We know this is what Mary Ann would've wanted."

"Absolutely would have wanted you to marry again," Florence echoed. Some folks thought Florence never had an original thought in her head; she only finished whatever Ada was thinking.

Wide-eyed, Cal looked at them as if they had just told him they were flying to the moon. He turned to Matthew for help. To his chagrin, Matthew looked back at him with laughing eyes, enjoying every moment of Cal's discomfort.

"So, Caleb, we have an idea," Ada continued, milky eyes flashing. "We're quite excited."

Cal's heart sank. Once Ada had an idea in her head, nothing on earth could shake it from her. A Zook trait, his mother had dubbed it.

Ada slipped on her reading glasses. "We have made a list of suitable wives for you."

As Ada searched through her apron pockets for the list, Cal's gaze wandered to the window. He hoped to spot a cow straying out of its stall, or a loose horse, or something that could give him an excuse to bolt.

"This won't be at all difficult," Ada said. "You are a rarity. An eligible bachelor among a sea of women whose lonely hearts ache for a husband."

"Oh, that's lovely, Ada," Florence oozed.

Positively dripping with self-satisfaction, Ada unfolded the list with a flourish. "Every other Saturday night, we have invited one of the women on this list to come and make supper for the family." She held up a cautionary hand. "Hold your horses. We know that Saturday-before-meeting is your busiest day, so we've only invited the ladies to come on off-meeting Saturdays."

Now intrigued, Matthew pulled up a chair and sat down, leaning his chin on his elbow. Cal shot him a look to intervene, but Matthew only shrugged his shoulders in a gesture of surrender.

"First Saturday," Ada said with a birdlike smile, "will be tonight. Laura Mae Yoder. She's a lovely girl."

"A charming girl," Florence echoed. "She's a good cook too."

"W-who's a g-good cook?" Ephraim asked, bursting through the kitchen door with a swoop of cold wind following behind him.

Cal got up and closed the door tight.

"Laura Mae Yoder," Matthew said. Cal noted that his tone was entirely too jovial. "So who else is on your list, Ada?"

"In two weeks, Emma Bontrager will come."

"Who else?" Matthew asked. "How long is the list?"

Florence pulled the list out of her sister's hands. "So far we have eight on the list."

"What's she t-talking about?" Ephraim whispered to Cal.

Cal crossed his arms and leaned his back against the doorjamb. "Ada and Florence think I need to be married off, Ephraim. So they've made a list of single women and have invited each of those ladies to come over and cook for us." At any other time he would have laughed, for it was such a preposterous thing. To tell him, a grown man with a child of his own, whom he must marry and when. But he shouldn't laugh. Doing so would hurt the aunties' feelings and he knew their hearts were in the right place. They were just trying to help.

"A g-good dinner once in a w-while?" Ephraim asked, as if that were the most wondrous thought in the world.

Cal doffed the tip of Ephraim's black hat, sending it spinning. "You got a complaint against my cooking?"

Matthew snorted and went back to reading the list. "Where Ephraim is concerned, a good meal is nothing to joke about."

Cal pressed his lips together, trying not to smile. Even Mary Ann, who had far more patience with the aunties than he did, was known to hide once or twice when she saw them coming up the road. The aunties kept up a constant stream of dialogue, finishing each others' sentences, and a person ended up feeling exhausted after listening to their chatter.

"We came up with this idea because the way to a man's heart—" started Ada.

"—is through his stomach," finished Florence.

Interesting logic from two maiden ladies, Cal thought.

Maggie sidled up to Florence's side. "Jorie King isn't on there," she said, running a finger down the list.

Ada and Florence exchanged a look. "No."

"Why n-not?" Ephraim asked.

Ada's lips drew in a tight line as Florence blurted out, "She didn't add her name to it."

"What are you talking about?" Cal asked. "I thought you came up with this list yourself."

Florence looked as if she might start to cry. Ada scowled at her and explained, "We were at a quilting frolic the other day and passed around the sign-up list to the unmarried gals."

Cal groaned.

"Jorie King didn't sign up?" Matthew asked.

"Not only that, she said it was a terrible idea and that you were a grown man who could think for yourself." Ada looked indignant. "But all of the other women thought it was a fine idea."

Cal sat down at the table. "Ada and Florence, I know you mean well, but I'm perfectly capable of deciding if, when—and whom—I will marry."

Ada covered his hand with hers. "We think so too, Caleb, but you don't seem to be doing it."

Cal cringed. Whenever the aunties got a certain look on their faces, they weren't going to budge. He was going to have to be tough, really tough. "No, Ada. Absolutely, positively no."

Out of the corner of his eye, he saw Laura Mae Yoder walking up the drive that led to the farmhouse, carrying a large basket.

A few hours later, after the kitchen had been cleaned up and Laura Mae Yoder went home with her emptied basket, Matthew held his stomach and moaned. "I ate so much I'm nearly wobbling on the chair." He opened one eye at Cal, seated across from him at the kitchen table. "So, what did you think?"

Cal patted his stomach. "Laura Mae is a wonderful cook."

"Sure. She's a fine cook. But what did you think about her as a wife?"

Cal glanced at him. "She's a sweet girl," he answered without much conviction. "A real sweet girl. But she isn't the one for me."

Matthew grinned. "I'll say!"

Cal tried not to laugh but couldn't help it.

Matthew grabbed another cookie Laura Mae had left for them on a big plate. "I'll go make sure the barn is locked up tight." He put on his coat and hat, reached for the door, then stopped and turned around, eyes twinkling. "Don't you worry, big brother. You know our aunties. They are going to keep at it until they find you Mrs. Right."

Cal threw a cookie at his head, but Matthew caught it, stuffed it in his coat pocket, and grinned.

"Why, Cal, how thoughtful! For later."

"Line up, everyone," Jorie told the scholars. "Time for a spelling bee."

The class jumped out of their chairs and raced to their well-rehearsed spots—alternating grades on each side of the room. Jorie liked to pair classes together to build teamwork. She thought it kept the shine off of any scholar who had a tendency to puff himself up by spelling the pants off of everyone else.

The big-eyed first graders were paired with the third graders and went first, pitted against the second and fourth graders. "Bough," Jorie said, enunciating it clearly.

Maggie gasped. "I know!" she told the third graders.

"Wait," Davy Mast said. "It's a twick." Davy had trouble pronouncing his r's. L's, too. He looked to Jorie. "We-peat and give in a sentence, pwease."

Jorie smiled at Davy, impressed. "The tree bough broke in the storm."

The first and third grade spelling bee contestants sobered. They whispered in a frenzied conference, made a unanimous decision, and gave Davy the honor of spelling aloud: "b-o-w."

Esther hollered, "Wrong!" The older grades hooted with laughter until Jorie shushed them. She gave Esther a warning look.

"Second and fourth grade team: bough."

They had an advantage after knowing how it was *not* spelled. "B-o-u-g-h," fourth grader Arlene Blank proudly spelled.

"Correct," Jorie said. She turned to the crestfallen first and third graders. Davy Mast hung his head and went to his seat. There was a risk to being spokesman: whoever spoke, if a word was spelled incorrectly, had to sit down. "Davy, you were absolutely right. Words can be very tricky. It's important to know the context, just like you asked for a sentence. Well done." Davy sat a little straighter in his chair, but he still looked as if he had been duped.

After that, the rounds went faster and faster. Finally, the entire eighth grade, all big boys, was pitted against Esther, who was spelling them down, one by one. With every correct word, the scholars went wild with claps and hoots. When a word was misspelled, groans and boos echoed throughout the room.

"Xenophobia," Jorie announced to the last standing contestants: Ray Smucker, Ephraim, and Esther.

Ray looked as if he had been tossed a hot potato. "Z," he started and got no farther before Jorie raised a hand to stop him. Ray lumbered to his chair like a big bear, woken from his hibernation and not happy about it.

"Xenophobia," Jorie repeated.

Esther gave Ephraim a catlike smile. "You go first."

Ephraim looked panicky.

"Remember the roots, Ephraim," Jorie said. "Always look to the root word."

Ephraim looked up at the ceiling as if trying to pull the root words down from the sky. "Xeno . . . stranger," he muttered to himself, "ph-phobia . . . fear." He looked at Jorie and enunciated the letters slow and spoon-fed, as if he was terrified he would make a mistake.

"Correct." Jorie turned to Esther and delicately pronounced, "Cormorant."

Esther scrunched up her face.

"Look to the roots, Esther," Jorie coached.

"Put it in a sentence," Esther demanded.

"Cormorants devour fish voraciously."

Esther looked completely blank. "C-o-r-e . . ."

Jorie put up a hand. "No. Ephraim, your turn."

Ephraim looked up at the ceiling again. "Cor . . . raven . . . mor . . . sea . . . raven of the sea. A g-greedy person." He dropped his gaze and looked right at Jorie. "C-o-r-m-o-r-a-n-t."

The entire class looked to Jorie for confirmation. She smiled. "Correct." They burst into hoops and hollers for Ephraim, who blushed furiously. Jorie was pleased for him; it was the first time he had won a spelling bee. It was the first time he had won anything at all.

Esther squinted in annoyance at this display of high spirits. As she walked past Ephraim to get to her desk, she whispered loudly so everyone could hear, "G-g-g-good j-j-j-job."

A horse's whinny floated up the hill to the barn on the wind. Cal knew the visitor was Isaac Stoltzfus coming up the lane before he even saw him in the buggy. He recognized Isaac's sorrel mare, a horse that arched her neck and trotted proudly, glad to be working. He wiped his hands on a rag and went out to meet the bishop.

"From the looks of those clouds we are in for more bad weather," Isaac said when he climbed down from the buggy.

"Would you like to come in for coffee?" Cal asked. He had to offer, but he hoped Isaac would decline the coffee. The breakfast dishes were still piled high in the sink, and Maggie and Ephraim had tracked muddy footprints through the kitchen.

"Thank you, no. Nell is expecting me home soon."

Cal waited a moment, certain Isaac had something other than the weather on his mind. He had to wait, though, for Isaac to shape his thoughts. Isaac was a deliberating man. Such deliberateness could be exasperating in a minister's meeting, especially when it was time to get home for the milking, but Isaac made few mistakes and Cal held great respect for him.

"So," Isaac started, looking down the driveway toward the road. "Jorie King has offered the old cottage on Stoney Creek to the new veterinarian."

"Yes, she has. The English won't sell or rent a house to him."

"And why is that?"

"I was told because he is a dark-skinned man." Cal took his hat off and started spinning the brim in his hands. "I was warned by some Englishers in town to not allow our people to sell or rent to him."

Isaac stroked his long beard. "Caleb, do you think it's wise to get involved in English problems?"

"The way I see it, Isaac, we already are involved. We need that vet. Dr. Robinson knows farm animals much better than Doc Williams. And Doc Williams has a lot of confidence in him."

"And did you tell Jorie this?"

"I did," Cal said.

"I'm concerned that she may be creating problems for herself, for Atlee, and Marge."

"She believes she is doing the right thing, Isaac." No. It was more than that. "And truth be told, I think she is too. I'm helping her get the cottage prepared."

Maggie and Ephraim burst out of the house and ran down to the barn, laughing loudly, stopping only long enough to throw snowballs at each other.

"I'm going to get you, you yellow-bellied coward!" Maggie yelled as Ephraim ducked into the barn.

Cal cringed as he saw Isaac do a double take when he recognized Maggie: she was wearing Ephraim's hand-me-downs.

"I can explain," Cal quickly said, knowing Isaac was horrified to see a little girl in boys' clothing. "I'd forgotten how often the washing needs to get done. We ran out of clean clothes yesterday so the laundry is drying on the line." He pointed to the clothesline; the clothes hung frozen solid like popsicles. "They'll be dry in no time."

Isaac looked at the clothesline for a long moment, as if he had never seen such a sight. "Shall we walk?" he asked when he finally spoke. They strode out past a field of freshly cut hay, now stubble, and walked along the fence line. Cows in a pasture stopped grazing and stared at them. "Have you given some thought about marrying again, Caleb?"

"No. Others have, though."

"Some folks are worried about you."

Cal grimaced. "Any chance you spoke to Sylvia?"

"As a matter of fact, I did. She stopped by the farm yesterday. Said you don't have any household help."

"Well, not at the moment. I'm looking around, though."

"Sylvia said she's offered to take Maggie for a spell. What do you think of that?"

"Aw, Isaac, you know Sylvia. Maggie would be miserable staying in that house. I'd be miserable without her. She's all I have left."

"Our Sylvia can be quite . . . determined," Isaac said.

Mule-headed, Cal corrected but kept the sentiment to himself.

"Her heart is in the right place. Beacon Hollow is a household filled with males. Maggie needs to be around women, to know how to do women's things." He stopped for a moment and looked out at some cows grazing in the pasture. "There's something else to consider. You're a minister now. You have added responsibilities."

Cal looked directly at Isaac so that he might know the truth of what he said. "Mary Ann is still in my heart."

"There's no greater way to honor her memory than by marrying again."

Cal crossed his arms and looked out over his fields, a mixture of snow with yellow stubble. Empty fields. Frozen earth. Like his heart. "Isaac, I would need to feel something for a woman. And right now, I'm not feeling much of anything. Except for wishing the good Lord might have spared Mary Ann." As soon as he said the words aloud, he regretted them and braced himself for a chiding look from Isaac, to remind him that God does not make mistakes.

Instead, Isaac nodded, seeming to understand. "You might be too young to remember my Annie."

Cal looked at him sharply. "I'd forgotten, Isaac. Nell's been your wife for so long, I just plain forgot you had been married before."

"Nell and I have been married for twenty-five years. But Annie Riehl was my first wife. We'd only been married a year and she died giving birth to our first child. A little girl who died a day later."

Caleb felt a jolt. Isaac didn't have any daughters, only sons. *At least I still have my Maggie, a part of Mary Ann.*

"I felt just like you did, numb inside. But I prayed that God would renew my heart and give me a fresh wind. No sooner had I prayed that prayer when Nell came into town to visit her cousins. One look at her and she swept me away." He stroked his long white beard. "I'm not saying it's the same. A part of my heart will always long for what might have been with my Annie. But Nell has been God's good gift to me."

"Nell's a fine woman, Isaac."

Isaac nodded. "It isn't good for man to be alone. Marriage had always been God's intention." He started to walk back toward the buggy, hands linked behind his back, and Cal matched his stride. "God's ways are mysterious, and I'm not denying they can be hard to understand and accept, but they are always best.

We don't trust God because we *should*. We trust God because he is *good*." Isaac paused and crossed his arms across his big chest. "Give some prayer to the notion of marrying again, Caleb. Or maybe reconsider Sylvia's offer to care for Maggie."

"I just need a little time to sort things out."

The barn door blew open and out ran Maggie, then Ephraim, who scooped and picked up snow to toss at her. Maggie gave a yelp when the snowball hit, then scooped up one of her own. She aimed it for Ephraim, but he was too quick for her and ducked. The snowball hit the bishop on the back of the head and knocked his hat off.

With big eyes, Maggie said, "Oh no! I'm sorry, Bishop Isaac!"

"Maggie," Cal said in a voice of dismay. He bent down and picked up Isaac's hat.

Isaac shook the snow off his hat, placed it on his bald head, and said, "Maybe not too much time, Caleb."

That afternoon, Cal took Maggie and Ephraim to the hardware store to ask Lizzie Glick if she'd be willing to come work for him. She said yes before he even finished asking and said she would give Ron Harding two weeks' notice starting today.

Afterward, when he returned home, he packed up all of Mary Ann's belongings—her letters, her Bible, her clothes, even her recipe box in the kitchen with her handwriting on those recipes—and put them in a box in the attic.

Remembering Mary Ann was just too hard. So he decided to try to forget her, to fill his life with new memories. It was time he stopped living in the past and face the future, whatever it would hold.

The morning frost crackled beneath Cal's boots as he crossed the yard, passing under the deep shadow cast by the barn. It had been over a week since Jorie had asked him to look over the Kings' cottage and make a list of needed repairs, but this was the first morning he could spare the time.

He was pleased to see there weren't too many repairs to be made. A few new shingles were needed to patch a hole in the roof, and there was evidence of mice. He pulled the cottage door tight, checking to see that the lock still worked. The cottage wasn't large, but the water worked, the electricity and heater could be turned on, and it would suffice.

Cal walked through a field to reach the Kings' farmhouse. He came from the back side of the farm, past the barn, and noticed that Atlee's buggy was missing. He was bending to slip the list under the mat at the kitchen door when a flash of fire caught his eye through the window. Sitting in front of the fireplace was Jorie, brushing out her wet hair to dry by the fire's heat. It was long and thick, curling down to her hips, the color of burnished copper. He was transfixed; for a moment, he allowed himself to drink in the sight of her. He'd never seen anything so lovely in all his life. No wonder the Bible said an uncovered woman ought to be shorn. He quickly turned away, trying to keep his thoughts focused on the Lord. He slipped the list of repairs under the doormat and left, before Jorie knew he was there.

A soft smile touched his lips as he walked back home. He felt the stirrings of a faint breeze, the hint of a fresh wind in his spirit.

In the middle of the night, Ephraim woke with a start. He heard the bawling of his favorite heifer, Gloria, and knew her time had come to deliver her first calf. She had been off her feed at dinner and her eyes had a glazed look. He threw on his clothes, grabbed a flashlight and blanket, and ran downstairs and out to the barn. There, he waited for another hour or so, but he had watched plenty of birthings before this one, and something wasn't right. She was pushing but nothing was happening. He rubbed his head with his hands, and then he jumped up and ran for the house.

Ephraim took the stairs two at a time and burst into Cal's bedroom. "C-Cal, Cal, w-wake up," he said as he shook his brother's shoulder. "I think s-something is wrong w-with G-Gloria."

"Hmmm?" Cal mumbled, then sat up. "I'll be right out."

When Cal got out to the barn, he checked Gloria. "I don't see the calf's legs." He reached into her. "And I don't feel the feet. Could be it's twisted up inside there." He checked the clock on the wall. "It's three in the morning, Ephraim. Run over to Bud to call the vet."

Ephraim practically flew over fences and through a dark pasture to get to Bud's. He pounded on the door until a sleepy-eyed Bud answered it.

"C-could you c-call the v-vet?" Ephraim's voice caught in his throat, and he had to swallow hard.

"Slow down," Bud said. "What's wrong?"

"It's G-Gloria," Ephraim said. "She's c-calving, but we c-can't s-see the c-calf."

"Okay, Ephraim, you head on home. I'll call Doc Williams. I'm sure he'll be right along."

Ephraim ran back to the barn and stood by Gloria's stall. "It won't be long now," he soothed her. He waited for twenty anxious minutes until he heard the sound of the car coming up the drive. He ran to the barn door, but it wasn't Doc Williams's car, it was the new vet's.

"I'm Dr. Robinson," he said to Cal as he strode into the barn.

127

He gave a nod to Ephraim. "I understand you've got a heifer in trouble."

"She's been pushing for hours now," Cal explained. "Nothing's happening." He led the doctor down the aisle to reach Gloria, laboring in a straw-filled stall.

After examining the heifer, Dr. Robinson said, "Looks like that calf is just too big for her."

Ephraim drew in a sharp breath.

Cal noticed the look on his face. "Not to worry, Ephraim, I'm sure the doctor has seen this plenty of times."

"It's pretty common," Dr. Robinson said, smiling, "but I'll need some help."

Ephraim watched as the doctor took some chains and a large metal frame out of the back of his station wagon. Dr. Robinson and Cal put Gloria in a frame with a clamp that caught her across the hips. Dr. Robinson reached inside of Gloria and attached chains to the calf's small hooves so he could pull it out. He ratcheted the handle to keep the chains tight. Despite the cold winter air, sweat was running down his face and arms as he tried to manipulate the calf. Finally, relief covered his face as placenta water started to flow from Gloria, in drips and drabs, a sign that things were starting to happen.

"Steady and gentle," he told Cal and Ephraim, who were pulling the chains.

As Gloria bawled, distressed, the other cows began to stamp their hooves and stir in their stanchions, aware that something was happening.

Ephraim blew out a long breath when the calf finally emerged, a dark brown slippery mass on the straw bed.

"Here," Cal said, and he handed Ephraim a straw. "Tickle its nose."

Ephraim put a piece of straw up the calf's nostril and it half snorted a breath as its lungs filled up with air for the first time. Ephraim's eyes met Cal's; they both smiled at the sound. It meant all was well. They took the frame off Gloria, and it wasn't long before she pulled herself up and looked at her calf, surprised.

"You did g-good, Gloria," Ephraim said. "I knew y-you would." He stroked the cow's neck and scratched under her chin where she liked it best. "You're n-not a heifer anymore! Y-you're a real c-cow. I promise having a c-calf will n-never be that hard again."

The three of them stood for a while, mesmerized, watching the calf try to stand on its wobbly legs. When it began to nurse, Dr. Robinson packed up his bags.

"How is business going?" Cal asked.

"Little by little, it's building up," Dr. Robinson said. "I expected it to take time."

Cal nodded. "It's good you're here. Gloria's glad too."

"I'm just glad Gloria didn't wait any longer to go into labor," Dr. Robinson said. "My wife is due in just a few weeks." He turned to Ephraim. "Ever get a chance to go to that circus?"

Ephraim shot a horrified look at Cal, who spun around, curious. Ephraim gave Dr. Robinson an infinitesimal shake of his head, which he read perfectly.

"I meant, uh, I wondered if you heard what happened at the circus in town? When they were getting ready to move out, a cougar broke free from her cage. She's loose."

On Sunday, Cal closed the service with a prayer, then announced where church would be held, two weeks' hence. Standing in between the men and the women, he had been preaching mostly to the men, but as he finished up announcements, he turned to face the women. "And we'll meet again in two weeks at—" His eyes caught Jorie's and his mind was suddenly filled with the sight of her brushing out her long coppery red hair in front of the fireplace. Her hair almost *looked* like it was on fire. "At, uh . . ." Where *was* church to be held? For the life of him he couldn't remember. "Uh . . . um . . ."

"The Eli Stutzmans'," called out Eli Stutzman.

Cal spun around to face Eli, who was peering at him as if he might be a little touched in the head. Cal's cheeks stained red. "Thank you, Eli." He then dismissed everyone with a final benediction.

A squirrel scampered in front of Ephraim, its tail and whiskers twitching, and then disappeared into the trees. Ephraim spotted a downed log cushioned with moss, and he sat on it. He loved these moments, when chores were done and he could have some time to be off in the Deep Woods by himself. He didn't mind school so much, not since Jorie was his teacher, so long as he didn't have to open his mouth and talk about anything. Answering questions aloud made Ephraim's school day a misery. But as hard as speaking aloud was, nothing made his day worse than Esther Swartzentruber. He knew it was a sin to hate, but Esther Swartzentruber made it hard. Esther mocked him for his stammering nearly every day. When he had to stand in front of the class and he saw Esther's face just waiting for him to get caught on a word, the words jammed in his throat and wouldn't come out. Then Esther would start snickering and the rest of the kids would join in. She was clever enough to wait until Jorie's back was turned, occupied with another child. Maggie told him not to pay any mind to Esther, even if she was kin.

"Don't let her know she bothers you, Ephraim. That's what Dad tells me to do when Matthew teases me."

But Matthew's teasing wasn't mean-hearted, not like Esther's.

Ephraim walked down a trail he hadn't been on since Ben had left for Vietnam. It seemed like some days, like today, everything reminded him of Ben and Mary Ann. Then he was stabbed, suddenly and unexpectedly, by grief for the parents he hardly remembered. He tried to swallow down the wad of tears building in his throat. It just hurt so much to think of the people he loved who had passed.

The brush rustled behind him.

Ephraim whirled, nervous. He let out a shaky breath. It was only the wind.

He started walking again, quiet as a cat in felt boots. Then he heard the crackling, rustling noise again. Ears straining, he scanned the woods before he saw it. Standing high up on a rocky ledge was the cougar. She looked at Ephraim with a wild cat's insolent stare. His heart missed a beat. She was the same one from the circus, he knew for a fact. Short ears and a ringed bobbed tail. He knew he shouldn't move a muscle, but he didn't think he could have, anyway. She and Ephraim exchanged a long look, underscored by his shallow breathing. Then she turned and walked away in the opposite direction. He released a shaky sigh of relief.

As soon as Ephraim was satisfied that the cougar had gone a distance, he took a peanut butter and honey sandwich from his pocket, unwrapped the wax paper, and placed it carefully on the rock . . . just in case the cougar returned that way. Then he backed away slowly, and after he broke out of the woods, he took off for home at an all-out run, holding on to his black hat.

On a gloomy, gray morning with drizzling rain, Cal, Bud, Ephraim, and Maggie filled the wagon with tools and went to the cottage on the King property. Jorie and her grandparents were inside, sweeping and cleaning and dusting.

"The electrician came yesterday," Jorie told Cal when he found her. She flipped on the switch and an overhead light went on.

A blush pinkened her cheeks, he noticed, either from the chill in the air or excitement. Maybe both. She looked happy.

"I'm a little surprised that there aren't more neighbors here to help," Jorie said.

"It's still early," Cal said, sparing her feelings. He knew that there would only be a few helpers showing up today. During the week, many neighbors came by to privately tell him they wouldn't be coming. They didn't think they should be getting involved in English problems. It was one of the first times he felt truly like a minister. His job was to shepherd a flock of helpless sheep; except that these were not witless animals, they were his neighbors, and he loved them.

"It's our problem too," he told each one. "If you have trouble with a horse with colic or a breech calf one night, Dr. Robinson won't be asking if it's Amish or English."

By the end of the day, the cottage was in move-in condition. Dr. Robinson insisted on paying rent to the Kings, but Atlee preferred a barter arrangement: free veterinary care for his beloved Percherons in lieu of rent. Dr. Robinson told him, under those generous conditions, he would throw in consulting too, when they were considering a stud or an addition to their brood stock. Atlee was delighted with the arrangement. This way, he whispered to Cal and Bud, he could avoid having to pay taxes on rental property, and it suited him just fine to have a vet on the premises for his beautiful horses.

As Cal packed up his tools, he smiled at the sight of Jorie and Lisa Robinson talking together in the kitchen. An unlikely pair: a petite, bonneted Plain woman in a green dress with a white apron and black ankle boots, facing a tall, dark-skinned woman wearing bell-bottom pants and a brightly flowered maternity smock, with large hoops hanging from her earlobes. Despite their obvious differences, he could tell the two would become friends. They shared an interest in flower gardening, and he saw Jorie's eyes lit up in that animated way she had, as she described which flowers would attract butterflies.

It was a good thing—the *right* thing—to offer a home to the vet and his wife, especially with their baby soon to come. Cal just couldn't rid himself of a nagging feeling that, by doing so, they had poked a hornet's nest.

6

The first day that Fat Lizzie started working at Beacon Hollow, Ephraim came in from the dairy with Cal and thought he'd died and gone to heaven. The scent alone was overwhelming. Breakfast was fresh eggs, a mountain of potatoes, sausages, salt-cured ham, and hot biscuits. By dinner, he found a clean white shirt laid across his bed. Another ironed shirt was hanging up on a peg in his room. He brought the shirt to his nose; for the first time in his memory, he was conscience of the sweet scent of laundry detergent. Maggie's hair had been properly combed and pinned, and even Cal's weary eyes lit up with delight when he caught a whiff of Lizzie's chicken pot pie.

Matthew had a day off in the middle of the week and came home to see Ephraim and Maggie perform in the Christmas school play. He arrived early, in time for breakfast, and seemed surprised—annoyed, actually—to find Lizzie in the kitchen. Cal explained that he had hired Lizzie and she was doing a fine job. Matthew scowled, as if Cal should have spoken to him first, and Ephraim caught the look of abject disappointment on Lizzie's face. Matthew helped himself to breakfast and pointed to a pillowcase full of dirty laundry he had brought with him from Lebanon that he wanted Lizzie to wash.

All of the parents crowded into the schoolhouse to watch the scholars perform the Christmas story from the book of Luke in the Bible. Ephraim had memorized his lines with Jorie's help and didn't even stutter when he delivered them. Matthew felt like cheering, though it wouldn't be appropriate to single out one child's performance over another. He looked over at Cal and had to swallow hard when he saw tears burning down Cal's cheeks like a mini-fountain.

Maggie and the other first graders were given the job of moving props on and off the makeshift stage by Jorie's desk. Afterward, cookies and punch and coffee were served, and parents had a chance to look around the room and appreciate the scholars' artwork on the walls.

Matthew saw Cal sidle up to Jorie and whisper, "Did you hear him? Did you hear how smooth he spoke?"

"As smooth as syrup over pancakes," Jorie whispered back, smiling, interrupted by Maggie, who dragged everyone over to look at her pictures on the wall.

"And there's Ephraim's cougar," Maggie said, pointing to a pencil drawing of a mountain lion.

"How could he have captured such detail?" Cal asked aloud.

"It's amazing, isn't it?" Jorie said, stopping to admire it. "Like he's seen one close up."

"He did!" Maggie said, her face lifted high to peer at the drawing. "At the circus!" As soon as she realized what she said, she slapped her hands over her mouth as her eyes went wide as silver dollars.

"So *that's* where you both were when . . . ," Jorie began to say, then she, too, snapped her mouth shut.

"*That's* where Maggie and Ephraim were on the day they skipped school," Esther finished Jorie's sentence. "I knew it! I knew it!" She gave everyone a sweet-as-pie smile before she turned, yanked her mother's sleeve, and pulled Sylvia into the conversation. "I told my mother that Ephraim and Maggie weren't sick! I knew they were playing hookey!" Esther pointed to Ephraim's picture. "Look! He went to the circus and saw a cougar!"

Completely confused, Cal looked from Esther to the drawing to Ephraim, who was turning the color of beets. Sylvia grabbed Esther's hand and went to find Jonas.

Even though Ephraim's instinct was to bolt and run, he knew better. As they walked home, he tried to explain to Cal about the circus tickets that Dr. Robinson had given to him. "I j-just wanted to s-see the animals," Ephraim told Cal. "N-nothing else." That was the truth. Maggie was the one who wanted to see the two-headed man, but he was too loyal to say. He should admit it, though, because she was the squealer. She kept looking at him out of the corner of her eyes, biting her lip. He ignored her.

"Aw, Cal. Don't be too hard on 'em," Matthew said. "You and Ben would have done the same thing in your day. Probably did a heck of a lot worse than that, knowing our Ben." He grinned. "Remember the time when you and Ben 'borrowed' Amos Esh's rowboat to fish at Blue Lake Pond and it sunk?" He elbowed Ephraim. "It's still down there."

Ephraim flashed Matthew a grateful look.

Cal frowned at Matthew. "It's the lying I don't like," he said. "Lying is a terrible habit to start. One lie leads to another." He stopped and looked right at Maggie and Ephraim. "You have to promise me you won't lie to me, ever again."

Maggie promised and ran ahead home, to help Lizzie get dinner ready she said, but Ephraim thought she was smart enough to vanish before Cal changed his mind and decided to dole out punishments. Unsure of the ground he was on with Cal, he stayed by his side. He almost wished Cal would have just inflicted him with an added after-school chore for a month or forbidden him to go to town. Disappointing him felt worse.

Before they even reached the kitchen, a delicious smell drifted out to greet them: Lizzie's pot roast. It was made with beef and onions, and it smelled heavenly. As they walked inside, all thoughts of the circus vanished, replaced with a hearty appetite of sweet and savory expectations. Maggie was setting the table and Lizzie was at the stove, frying potatoes.

Over her shoulder, Lizzie said, "Hope you're all hungry. I've been waiting dinner for you and just kept adding things to the pot. I'm going to call it 'Late for Dinner Because of the Christmas Program Pot Roast.'"

Matthew tossed his hat on the wall peg like he was playing a game of horseshoes. "Ha! You should change the name to 'Found Out Maggie and Ephraim Ditched School and Went to the Circus Pot Roast.'"

A smile spread across his face at the scowls he was getting from Maggie and Ephraim. Then his smile faded. Behind them, he noticed the bag of dirty clothes in the same spot that he had left it in the morning.

When Matthew asked Lizzie about it, she froze, spatula in the air. Then, cucumber calm, she stepped away from the frying pan and let the potatoes sizzle. She put her hands on her hips and squinted at him. "Caleb Zook hired me to care for him, Ephraim, and Maggie. He never mentioned cleaning up after the high and mighty Matthew Zook."

Matthew looked to Cal, who only shrugged his shoulders. From that point on, Lizzie pretended Matthew didn't exist, which Ephraim thought was pretty smart, especially for a girl. It made Matthew crazy.

It was the Kings' turn to host church. The bench wagon had been brought over a few days before, and the men who delivered it helped move the downstairs floor furniture into the barn. The large interior doors in the kitchen were opened wide so the benches could be set up, facing each other, taking up the footprint of the entire first floor.

Early Sunday morning, as more and more buggies started to arrive, Jorie hurried down to the barn to lead Big John out to the farthest paddock before meeting started. Last time the Kings hosted church, when the hymn singing started up, Big John started to stomp and snort and carry on as if he wanted to join them. His noise stirred up all of the horses to whinny and neigh until they practically drowned out the singing.

As if triggered by an invisible signal, the men and women, huddled in tight little knots to keep warm, began to file toward the house just before eight. The children came running up from the barn; the girls joined the women, the boys joined the men. As soon as the older women, wives, and widows filed inside, the young bachelors flanked the doors to watch the young girls walk through. The girls' eyes stayed straight ahead, but their lips curled into pleased smiles and blushes pinkened their cheeks. Jorie's eyes suddenly blurred with tears. Sometimes if she just held her breath and concentrated really hard, she could almost see Ben standing beside the other young men, one booted foot hooked over the other in that way he had, watching her.

Jorie followed behind the unmarried girls, but she felt, with Ben's passing, as if she didn't know where she belonged anymore.

As soon as school ended each day and before he was due home for milking, Ephraim ducked out and went into the Deep Woods, cougar snooping. He found coyote tracks, bobcat tracks, and lots of deer tracks, but no cougar tracks.

One day, after a light snowfall, he found a trail of large paw prints. He followed the trail as long as he could. His concentration kept slipping because he had the feeling that he was being watched. It was a foolish notion, he thought, because of course he was being observed: by the deer he passed by, by birds in the trees, and probably a host of critters he couldn't even see. Suddenly, the birds stopped singing. The feeble winter sun that had been shining fitfully through the dense treetops disappeared. The forest grew silent and a chill went down his spine.

He paused for a moment to get some water out of his thermos. As he lifted his head to drink, his eyes caught sight of the cougar. She had already spotted him. She crept slowly out of the shadows, her round belly low and brushing the rough edge of a rocky ledge, high above him. When their eyes met, she went still.

Ephraim stayed motionless as a held breath. The cougar moved first. She whirled and dashed along the top of the ledge, her body floating against the shafts of sunlight that lit the rocks like streaks of fire. He watched her poise for a leap and then disappear into a crevice in the ridge.

Now he knew where she lived.

It had snowed so much during the night in Lebanon that cars weren't able to get out of their driveways. Matthew wasn't expected at work until nine, so he grabbed the shovel he had seen at the side of Mrs. Flanagan's garage and started to clean the snow off of her sidewalk, then her driveway. The feel of the shovel in his hands, the way his shoulders and back muscles ached after a while—it felt good. A good ache. This was the work he was used to. It surprised him to realize how much he missed hard labor. Even though he worked long shifts at the hospital, most of what he did was push patients around in wheelchairs or run errands for the staff.

He was enjoying himself so much that he got a little carried away and kept going. He shoveled Mrs. Flanagan's neighbor's sidewalk and driveway, and then the neighbor after that. When he got back to the house, cheeks chapped red from the cold, Mrs. Flanagan stood on her glassed in porch with black thunder on her face.

"What do you think you're doing?" she asked him, holding the door open for him as he stomped snow off of his boots.

"Just shoveling."

"Why did you shovel those neighbors' sidewalks? Especially two houses over?" She sounded mad.

"I was just enjoying the work." He pulled off his coat and scarf and gloves and hung up his coat. "Is there a problem?"

She stood there with her hands on her hips, angry. "Yes, there's a problem! I don't like that neighbor!" She marched into the kitchen.

Matthew was stunned. Part of being Amish was helping your neighbor. They didn't decide first if they liked someone or if that person deserved help. Helping each other throughout the year—loading the silos, shocking cornstalks in the fields, building barns—well, it went without saying. It was as much a part of being Amish as driving a buggy.

He couldn't even imagine a single person in his church who wouldn't agree to help if someone asked. Not one. Often, a person didn't even need to ask. Like after Mary Ann passed, the neighbors stepped in and helped Cal with his third cutting of hay, stacking it neatly in the hayloft to help them get through the winter. Cal didn't ask for help; he was too careworn to even know what was needed on the farm. But one day, they just arrived and went to work.

It took leaving that community for Matthew to realize all it meant to him. He remembered a time when a photographer came to the farmhouse to try to sell his father an aerial shot taken of the entire neighborhood. His father called all of his sons to come see as the photographer spread out the photograph on the hood of his car. His dad pointed to Beacon Hollow's fields and the dark section of the Deep Woods that bordered it. Matthew remembered looking at the map and marveling at the landscape from the air: the view the turkey vulture had when it soared high over the fields. The creek, meandering through the pasture fields, where he and his brothers fished and swam on hot summer afternoons. He saw things in that photograph he had never noticed before, just by seeing it from a different vantage point.

Living here in Lebanon, he felt like that man in a quote by Emerson: "A man standing in his own field is unable to see it." His nose was too close to the picture. He didn't realize what he had until it was gone.

Late one evening, Jorie King was working in the schoolhouse. She heard a knock at the door, went to answer, and peeked her head out, then opened it wide. "Cal, what are you doing here?"

He came inside and stamped the snow from his feet. "I could see the light on from the barn and thought maybe you'd forgotten to turn it off," he said. "What are you doing here so late?"

She closed the door behind him. "Getting some work done," she answered.

Cal walked up and down the center aisle of the classroom, looking at the walls. "Is Maggie behaving for you?"

"Of course. She's a bright girl."

"She prefers out of doors to being inside, in the kitchen."

"I was like that. Still am. My biscuits could break a man's tooth."

She saw a smile crease over Cal's face, then it faded. He seemed to have something on his mind. He looked up at the artwork hanging on the walls, his hands clasped behind his back.

"Is Lizzie working out?" she asked, hoping he would relax. He seemed nervous, jumpy, almost. She had never seen him like that.

"Yes. She's a big help, just like you said she'd be. But Maggie needs a mother."

"I know how she misses Mary Ann. She'll never forget her, Cal, if that's what you're worrying about." She noticed that he winced slightly when she said her name.

Cal put his hands to his temples and rubbed. "I'm asking if you would consider becoming her mother."

Jorie stopped in her tracks. She had not expected *that*. Her mouth dropped open, then she closed it tight, nearly laughing. "This is about the aunties' list."

His cheeks colored up just like the boys in her classroom did when she caught them. It touched her heart—she was discovering that Cal couldn't mask his feelings. He looked down on the ground, avoiding her eyes, as the awkwardness between them widened into a large gulf.

"It's only been a few months," Jorie said softly. She put the books on the desk. "I'm sorry, Cal. I can't be a substitute for Mary Ann. No one can." She walked up to him. "There's not a girl in the county who wouldn't jump at the chance to marry Caleb Zook. But I think you should wait. Mary Ann is still in your heart. You just need some time. Sometimes the heart takes longer than the body to mend."

She wanted to smooth the dark hair off of his pale forehead like she did with one of her scholars when he had fallen down and hurt his knee or elbow. To let him know he would be all right. But, of course, she didn't dare touch him and Cal turned to leave.

He was almost at the door when he turned around to say, "I can't remember the color of her eyes. I lived with her for eight years and I can't remember what she looked like."

He started to open the door but stopped when Jorie called out, "Brown. They were dark brown." She walked up to him. "I loved her too, Cal."

He lifted his head to look at her. "How much time? How long until life feels normal again? Until the house doesn't seem cold and empty? Losing Mary Ann was like losing . . . light and warmth and joy. Have you ever loved someone enough to feel as if a limb has been torn from you?" As the impact of what he just said dawned on him, he covered his face with his hands. "I'm sorry, Jorie. Forgive me. I don't know what's wrong with me tonight. I shouldn't have come. Please . . . forget what I said, what I asked."

She leaned against the doorjamb, watching him walk down the lane. "Yes, Cal. I loved someone like that."

She said it so softly that he couldn't have heard. Yet he stopped and turned, locked eyes with her briefly, before turning around and picking up his stride.

7

Cal didn't see Jorie again until Sunday meeting, which happened to be Christmas morning. After services, he gave her a crisp hello, trying not to remember how soundly she had turned down his foolish, bumbling, impulsive marriage proposal. He still couldn't *believe* he had proposed marriage to her. What had he been thinking?! He supposed it had to do with walking home on a cold night and seeing that warm buttery glow in the schoolhouse windows. He had suddenly felt a desperate longing, as if the blaze of the lanterns was a beacon, a sign of hope, to him. The next thing he knew he was knocking on the schoolhouse door and proposing marriage! Every time he was reminded of it, like now, he felt his cheeks grow hot with embarrassment.

But Jorie seemed, or at least acted, as if she didn't even remember it had happened. She caught up to him as he walked to his buggy. "Did you hear that Dr. Robinson's wife had her baby last night? A little boy. A Christmas baby!"

He started to say something, then changed his mind. He couldn't help but smile as she told him the news. "No, I hadn't heard. Maggie and Ephraim will want to know." She was wear-

145

ing a bright blue dress that made her eyes look bluish-green. How would he describe that shade? Turquoise? Jewel blue? He wondered if that's what the color of a sea surrounding a tropical island might look like—mesmerizing and endlessly deep. They were incredible eyes.

Were her eyes as blue as the sky? He looked past her to study the sky.

"And I've been meaning to tell you that Ray Smucker is starting to speak English in the classroom. He's still far behind where he should be, but he's making quick progress. Thank you again, Cal, for talking to Gideon that day. I couldn't persuade him, but you seemed to know just the right thing to say to make him change his mind. It's a miracle."

"It was God who worked the miracle," he said, reminding himself as well as Jorie, so that he would not be tempted to the sin of pride.

She smiled slightly, before turning to go speak to someone else.

Those eyes, Cal realized. They were definitely bluer than the sky.

During the first week of January, the weather was so cold that an icy crust formed on top of the snow. Jorie told the scholars they could bring sleds to school. Some had real sleds, Lightning Guiders with shiny runners and handles to steer by. Others had homemade wooden sleds with cast iron runners. Those sleds couldn't be guided and the children always landed in a ditch. A few brought whatever they could find that would do the job: an old dishpan or a scoop shovel. Ray Smucker had a twenty-inch square board that he sat on to slide down the hill. It worked a few times and Ray was feeling pretty pleased with himself. He started down the hill a fourth time and—about halfway down—the edge of the board dug into the crust. The board stopped, but Ray went on for quite some distance. When he stood up, the seat of his pants had been worn to a thread, showing off a sizeable portion of his long underwear. He backed down the hill away from the laughing children, jumped over the fence, and ran home. He didn't return for the rest of that day.

On a bitterly cold Saturday afternoon, Matthew sat at the kitchen table while Lizzie ironed Maggie's prayer caps. The iron hissed as it glided over the damp cap and the smell of hot starch filled the kitchen. Matthew told her stories about the kinds of people he met working in the hospital.

After he finished, Lizzie gave him a look of mild interest as she carefully placed the cap over a roll of toilet paper to keep it stiff as it cooled. "After working in that hardware store for the last two years, I came to realize that—English or Amish—people are people. There are plenty of good English out there and plenty of bad ones. We Amish, we're not so different. Good ones and bad ones."

Matthew took a long sip of coffee, mulling over Lizzie's remark. She wasn't much for book learning, but he thought she had plenty of common sense and a knack for sizing up people.

Carefully, she set another freshly ironed prayer cap on the counter next to the two she had finished. "So, how do you like city living?"

"I like everything about it but the sounds," Matthew said. "Sounds in the country are soft and gentle. City sounds are harsh: tires squealing, shouts in the night, constant wailing of sirens.

Fires, police, ambulances. Even when I'm working, the patients in the ward make weird sounds. Almost like they're moaning."

He wasn't really sure if she was interested in his thoughts or just being polite—as she ironed she hardly threw a glance his way—but he kept talking. "And the people—they're different. City folks constantly complain about the weather. It's either too hot or too cold or too wet. Even if it's dry and the crops and garden desperately needed moisture, the weatherman would say that the weekend would be miserable because of the threat of rain. For me, coming from a farm that's tied to the weather, that way of thinking is crazy talk. Whoever heard of an Amish man complaining about the weather?"

"That's because we know that God controls everything," Lizzie said quietly. "The sun, the clouds, the wind, and the rain. We know that complaining is finding fault with God."

Matthew tried to hold back a grin. Lizzie Glick was finally talking to him.

The next morning, Matthew poured hot coffee from a chipped white enamel pot into two mugs. He handed one mug to Cal. A pot of oatmeal sputtered on the stove. It was a cold, snowy morning and the wind was blowing hard enough to take the bark off the trees. So cold that Cal let Ephraim and Maggie sleep in while he and Matthew milked the cows and fed the animals.

"I'm starving. Shouldn't Lizzie be here by now?"

Cal gave him a questioning look over the ridge of the mug. "It's Sunday."

Matthew frowned. That meant breakfast was going to be pretty slim pickings. He took a bowl from the cupboard and spooned oatmeal into it. "Want some?"

Cal shook his head.

"Suit yourself." He sprinkled brown sugar on top of his oatmeal and sat down at the kitchen table to eat.

Cal sat with his hands wrapped around the mug of coffee, watching the steam rise. "Matthew, I think you are the only person in this town who isn't trying to tell me who to marry and when."

In between spoonfuls of oatmeal, Matthew asked, "Want me to?" He grinned, knowing what was on Cal's mind this morning.

Last night's Supper List prospect, Katie Miller, had been particularly disappointing. Not only was Katie a poor cook, which dismissed her immediately in Ephraim's mind, but she started to cry when everyone refused second helpings of her overcooked moon pie. She didn't stop crying until they finally ate more, just to appease her. Matthew wasn't sure he could ever stomach another piece of moon pie again, as long as he lived.

One of Cal's dark eyebrows arched at him. "No, I don't."

"Want to hear how the odds are running?"

Cal gave him a look of disbelief.

"Half the town thinks you're going to marry Laura Mae Yoder because you ate two pieces of her chocolate cream pie."

Cal rolled his eyes.

"And the other half thinks you're going to marry Susan Stoltzfus because she signed up for two Saturday nights in a row."

Cal sighed. "Where are you getting this information?"

"Lizzie told me."

Cal eyed him. "Thought you didn't care much for Fat Lizzie."

"Oh, she's not so bad," he said with a careless shrug. "Not so fat anymore, either. Then there are a few stragglers who are rooting for Jorie King." Matthew glanced at Cal to see his reaction but there was nothing. "Folks are saying that since you're

149

a minister and all, you've probably been told to hurry up and get hitched."

Cal clenched his jaw. "I will not marry just because I've been told to."

"*That's* what I told Lizzie," Matthew said, eyes twinkling. "And besides, even if you were to consider Jorie, you'd have to get in line behind me." He picked up a banana and started to peel it. "I've given some thought to marrying her myself."

"You've given some thought to marrying most every girl in town," Cal said. He glanced at Matthew. "What, you're serious? You? You're nearly six years younger than her."

"Quit looking at me as if you think I'm addle-brained." Matthew broke off a piece of banana and popped it in his mouth. "Dad was ten years older than Mom. And Mary Ann was older than you, big brother." He grinned. "It could work."

"And what makes you think a woman like Jorie King would be interested in an eighteen-year-old boy?"

"Well, brother Caleb, I never thought I'd see the day." Matthew laughed. "And here I thought you were immune to women."

"What are you saying?"

"You're a little sweet on Jorie King."

Cal stood up abruptly, walked to the sink, and poured his coffee down the drain. "I never said such a thing."

"No? Well, then, you're blushing like a ripe summer tomato for no good reason."

Later that afternoon, Cal had just finished milking the cows when he saw Jorie walk up the long incline to Beacon Hollow. A smile crept over his face, then he remembered Matthew's teasing and quickly sobered up. His mind wandered to Katie Miller weeping over the moon pie; that pie still sat like concrete in his stomach. He just didn't think he could stand one more evening of the aunties' Saturday Night Supper List.

Jorie waved to Ephraim, who was cleaning out the metal milk cans. "Where's Maggie?" she asked as she slid the barn door shut.

"In the house with Fa—" Cal caught himself. "With Lizzie. I have *got* to stop calling her Fat Lizzie."

Ephraim snorted and Cal tossed a rag at him.

"Lizzie dropped by this afternoon to play a game with Maggie," Cal added.

"With M-Matthew, you m-mean," Ephraim added, grinning.

Jorie smiled. "I stopped by to ask if you heard that cougar scream last night. Sounded close by."

Ephraim's grin faded. He tucked his chin to his chest.

"I did," Cal said. "No stock was hurt last night. Same for you?"

"No, none hurt. But I worry about it scaring my pregnant mares into early labor. Not to mention what a cougar could do to a foal."

"If you're worried, I'll get a few neighbors together to hunt for it."

With that, Ephraim dropped the metal can and ran out of the barn. Jorie and Cal watched him go, a puzzled look on their faces.

"What's troubling him?" she asked.

"It's that cougar. Any time someone brings it up, he jumps like a jackrabbit." Cal closed the door behind him. "Not really sure why he's so frightened by it."

"He bolted when you said you would hunt it."

"You're right. He did." Cal cocked his head. "But you've always understood him better than the rest of us."

"Ephraim has a tender heart. And a soft spot for animals. He's like you that way." An awkward silence spun out between them. "I'll go say hello to Maggie before I leave for home." She turned and reached for the handle of the barn door.

Cal put his hand over hers to stop her from sliding open the door. "Jorie, I was hoping someday, maybe before too long, you'd be thinking of Beacon Hollow as home." *Lieber Gott, did I really just say that?* He felt his face grow warm, but he kept his hand on hers.

Jorie seemed to be studying his hand. She was quiet for a long moment, as if gathering her thoughts. Finally, she lifted her head. Their eyes locked, hers as dark as the sea. "Men seem to ask women to marry them for all the wrong reasons. Daniel Riehl asked me to marry him to combine our land, which basically meant he wanted Stoney Creek because his land is a sodden marsh. Jacob Schwartz wanted me for my fine features. Said it would be nice to look at me each day. Never mind that he's thirty years older than me and I might not be as interested in looking at him. And never mind that he talks so much and in such a loud voice that he can burst a person's eardrums." She released a sigh. "Ben wanted someone waiting for him back at home, whenever he was *ready* to come home." She pulled her hand out from under his. "And you want me to raise Ephraim and Maggie."

Cal turned her shoulders so she would face him. "So what is it *you* want, Jorie?"

She looked at him. "I don't want to be just a convenience to someone. There's got to be more to a marriage than that. I want a marriage . . . ," she gently rapped her fist against her chest, ". . . from the heart." She stepped back from him and slid the door open, avoiding his eyes as she closed it behind her.

"She said no. Flat out, no doubts about it. No." Cal walked over to Bud's house on the pretext of borrowing a tool, but it was really to talk. He still couldn't believe he had asked Jorie to marry him, *again*. And again, she said no.

"How did you ask?" Bud asked, sitting in his favorite easy chair by the fire. The Sunday newspaper was spread around him on the floor, as if he hadn't moved all day. He had been working on a crossword puzzle when Cal interrupted him.

Cal moved some newspapers off the sofa and sat down across from Bud. "I said I was hoping she'd start to think of Beacon Hollow as her home."

"Hoo-boy! And that didn't sweep her off her feet? Imagine that. It's right up there with your first winner, when you told her Maggie needed a mother." Bud shrugged his shoulders. "Well, maybe this aunties' list will get your mind on some other gal."

Cal jerked his head up. "No."

"So she's the one you want?"

"Yes." Yes, she was. Yes! He suddenly realized that Jorie was the only one for him.

"Tell me again what she said."

Cal repeated the conversation.

"Sounds to me like she wasn't saying no at all. Sounds to me like she was giving you another chance by telling you what she *didn't* want."

Cal felt a pang of regret. He leaned back on the sofa. "It wasn't so hard with Mary Ann."

"Aw, you were just kids. You grew up together. This time, Cal, you're going to have to woo her."

"What?" Cal asked, mild panic rising in him.

"Woo her! She's a woman, Caleb. What does she like?"

"We're Amish," Cal said, as if that explained everything.

Bud rolled his eyes to the ceiling.

"I guess I don't know that much about her," Cal said.

"Try to think of something," Bud said in a longsuffering voice.

Cal exhaled, resigned. "She likes reading books. She likes taking walks in the Deep Woods. She loves her horses. She likes teaching. And children, even the difficult ones. She's able to find the good in people." He leaned forward on the sofa. "She's got a flair for drawing, especially things she spots in nature. She loves church—I can tell by the look on her face. In fact, it's usually pretty easy to tell what she's thinking or feeling. If you can't see it written on her face, she'll tell you. She speaks her mind, that Jorie. She's not much of a cook—"

"Well, well, well," Bud said, interrupting, folding his hands behind his head as he leaned back in the chair.

"What?" Cal asked.

"Thought you didn't know her."

8

After church one Sunday, Isaac asked Cal to stop by his farm on Tuesday for an informal meeting of the ministers. Cal braced himself for some kind of sticky problem with a church member. Hardly a few weeks went by without some kind of need arising. Being a minister was harder than he could have imagined. It wasn't the time he gave to sermon preparation—that he found nourishing to his soul. It was knowing so much about the inner life of his people. In the last few months, he had learned things he would rather not have known: Petty quarrels. Flirtations with worldly temptations. Young couples who got ahead of their wedding night. It was hard for him to shake off.

After Isaac's wife served the men coffee and pie, Jonas jumped right in to explain the reason behind today's gathering. "There's concern brewing about Jorie King," he said. "About her teaching methods."

Isaac crossed his arms against his chest. In his slow, meditative way, he asked, "Caleb, Samuel, what do you think?"

A short, stocky man with a kind heart, Samuel Riehl shifted in his chair as if he felt uncomfortable, then shrugged his rounded shoulders. "Maybe I've heard a few things."

Then all three men looked to Cal for his opinion. He felt his stomach tighten into a knot. "She might be a bit unconventional—"

"A bit?" Jonas sneered. "Her class spent the better part of December counting birds over by Blue Lake Pond."

"There's a reason, Jonas," Cal said. "That bird count helps the government keep track of bird populations. Birds are an indicator species. They reveal a lot about the health of an ecosystem. If their numbers are down, there is a problem somewhere."

Jonas leaned back in his chair. "Her job is to teach those scholars how to read and write. That's all."

Cal stole a sideways glance at Jonas, a man he had always considered a friend. He wondered how much of Jonas's complaint toward Jorie had to do with the fact that he had chosen her to teach over Emma, Jonas's eldest daughter, who didn't have an interesting thought in her head. Cal knew what kind of teacher Emma would make. He had plenty of those kinds of teachers when he was in school. He had decided that he would have to risk disappointing Jonas; he just couldn't foist Emma Lapp on those scholars.

"First things first, I always say," Jonas continued. "We need to make sure those scholars are getting their basics in, before they go traipsing off to the woods to count birds."

"Counting those birds is a lesson in arithmetic," Cal said, trying to keep his voice calm. "And science too. Maggie said they had to memorize the birds' names in Latin so they could identify the species. That's a language lesson, right there."

Jonas leaned forward. "That state exam in May has two hundred questions on it and I don't think there will be any questions in Latin."

Cal lowered his head. He didn't know why he felt such a strong need to defend Jorie, but he knew he would do anything for her.

"Maybe you could talk to her, Cal," Samuel said.

Isaac stroked his long white beard, a sign he was thinking. "Samuel has a good point. Perhaps, Caleb, you could speak to Jorie. Just to remind her to get the basics in, *before* the bird counting."

Cal folded his hands together. He couldn't say no to Isaac. "I'll talk to her."

Later in the week, Cal stopped by the schoolhouse as Jorie was locking up the door for the evening. "Hello, Jorie."

She spun around. "Hello, Cal. What are you doing out tonight?"

"Earlier today, old Eli Stutzman stopped by to say his wife was done."

"Done what?"

"That's just what I asked him. 'Done living,' he said."

"Clara's passed?" Jorie's eyes went wide.

Those eyes of hers, they kept changing colors, he realized. Tonight, in the dusk of winter, they looked as blue-gray as an ocean storm. "She did. Very peacefully. Her heart gave out on her. I'm just coming back from their place now."

Jorie locked the schoolhouse door. "Now she'll be seeing those sunsets from high above."

They stopped for a moment and looked at the setting sun. Its rays were casting long shadows that appeared blue on the pure whiteness of the powdery snow.

"E. B. White once wrote, 'I am always humbled by the infinite ingenuity of the Lord, who can make a red barn cast a blue shadow,'" Cal said softly.

Jorie caught his eye, smiled faintly, and looked away, as if she was a little embarrassed he caught her looking at him. He noticed a couple of tendrils of hair, loosened by the breeze, curl about her ears.

The wind kicked up hard as they started walking up the road that led to their homes. Cal's hand flew to his head, barely snatching his hat before it went sailing.

She pulled her cape around her, shivering. "How does Matthew like living in the city?"

"He hasn't said. Probably means that he likes it very much."

"I can't imagine why anyone would choose to live in a city. Out here, most everything around us has been made by God: the grass and trees and birds. But in the city, so much is made by humans: those hideous electric wires, telephone poles, asphalt, cars, pollution."

Cal half listened to her, looking for a segue to broach the real reason he had stopped by. To talk to her about the scholars, like Isaac wanted him to. "Jorie, I know you like taking the class out on nature hikes . . ." He swallowed hard.

She stopped and turned to him, her blue eyes wide with happiness. "Oh, I do. I do! And you understand why, don't you, Cal? Do you see how knowing about God's earth only brings us closer to him? How it helps us to feel the awe and majesty? That's what I want the scholars to discover. So that all of their lives, they know to look around them, at nature and up at the heavens, and they remember God."

Her face was so lit up with joy that the sight of it took his breath away. Imagine what it would be like, having a teacher like her to open scholars' minds and point them to God's majesty.

"Well, I'll be on my way," she said, when they reached the turnoff to Stoney Creek. She turned and started down the long drive.

"I'll walk you to the farmhouse," he offered, falling into step beside her. "Don't want you crossing paths with that cougar."

She glanced at him, alarmed. "Do you think it's still a danger? I haven't heard of anyone losing stock."

"Samuel found the remains of a deer carcass near his field. Thought it looked like a mountain lion had taken it down."

A worried look passed over her face.

"Don't you worry about that cougar," he said in a voice of gentleness. "It's probably moved on by now. Cougars don't want to tangle with people."

Her mouth curved into a smile. "Well, come springtime, it had better not try to tangle with my new foals."

"How many are you expecting?"

"Four, Lord willing."

As she described each mare and what traits she had been looking for in the studs and what she hoped to get from the pairing, Cal watched her. He thought her face was even lovelier when it was animated by excitement. The intensity of her look, the sparkle of eagerness in her eyes, made him lose track of what she was saying. In the fading sunlight, he noticed a light sprinkling of freckles over her nose. He had never noticed those before.

Too soon, they arrived at her farmhouse. He saw that the moon was rising, yellow as a wolf's eye. Somehow, they had stopped walking and were facing each other. Without thinking first, he reached out, and pushed a loose strand of her hair back under her cap. Then he stepped back, worried that he offended her. But she only smiled and said, "Good night, Cal."

On the way home, Cal slapped his forehead when he realized he never did get around to the subject of sticking to reading and arithmetic in the classroom.

Oh well, he thought. Another time.

Caleb Zook kept surprising Jorie. Tonight, he seemed genuinely interested in what she was trying to inspire in the scholars. Maybe she shouldn't have been surprised. Cal was known to plow a field with a book in his coat, so that when the horses rested, he could read. After hearing his sermons, she could almost imagine him more as a professor at a fancy English university than as a dairy farmer. Yet he loved his dairy and his farm. And more than anything, he loved being Plain.

Last week, he surprised her another time with that marriage proposal, said in his roundabout way, with a stain of flush brushing his cheeks. She knew he was getting pushed by the aunties to remarry. Probably others too. As fond as she was of Cal—and she couldn't deny she felt a little flutter of pleasure in her chest when he asked—something held her back.

Sometimes, Jorie wondered if something was wrong with her. Most of her friends were keen to get married. If they were still single, as she was at the age of twenty-four, they were more than keen. They were desperate. Half the girls in Stoney Ridge would like to marry Cal. Maybe it was vain and foolish, but Jorie wanted more out of marriage than to be a poor substitute to the memory of a first wife, especially to dear Mary Ann.

Her grandmother complained that her grandfather had spoiled Jorie for marriage by expecting too much. By that she meant the conversations Jorie and her grandfather would have about the Bible and other books they'd read, plus their late-night discussions about breeding and training Percherons. Marge was never especially interested in the horses, and Atlee preferred she not go near them, anyway, after she nearly killed one with an herbal remedy for worms. But he would always ask Jorie's opinion before choosing a pairing. Jorie would spend hours poring through files, with measurements, notes, charts, cross-references—going back five generations into the horses' lineage. Atlee grumbled that all she did was point out a horse's fault. "But the first question about any potential pairing," she would insist, "is not how great the offspring will be but what problems it might produce."

Ben never understood her love of horse breeding. She tried to teach him about the mysteries and complexities of genetics. "Just put two horses you like together and they'll make a horse you love," was his response.

"It isn't just one or two traits we're looking for," she tried to explain to him, "but how the horse combines all these things. The whole of every horse is always greater than the sum of its parts." Ben would listen for a while but soon lose interest. Anything that smacked of farming bored him.

But he did like book reading. He was a Zook in that way. Their shared love of books was one quality that had drawn her to Ben. Her grandmother often said that Ben was charming, gregarious . . . and handsome as the devil. "That man could charm the spots off a leopard and sell them to a zebra," Marge would say, though she was fond of Ben. Everyone was fond of Ben. And the weaknesses in him—his wild streak, his fiery temper, his tendency to be a fence jumper—Jorie had hoped those would change in time as he grew into manhood.

But Ben was gone now. And she had never imagined herself married to anyone else.

Before going inside the farmhouse, Jorie stopped to make sure the barn doors were locked tight. The wind blew her apron up against her face. As she smoothed it down, she thought again about changing her apron from white to black, from unmarried to married. It would be a significant step, a message to others that she was choosing to remain single. At least she had been thinking about it . . . until yesterday. She had dropped by the Robinsons' cottage with a meal and a baby quilt. Lisa let Jorie hold the baby—a warm little Easter egg of a body. With his tiny belly full of milk, he fell sound asleep in her arms. A pang of longing pierced her heart as she realized she might not ever have a child of her own. Yet for all that was hard about it, remaining single might be what the Lord wanted for her. And the Lord knew best.

Maybe she would wait to change her apron, though. Just in case.

9

On a cold and sunny afternoon, Ephraim went cougar snooping, hoping he might spot her. Every few days, he left a big chunk of raw meat for her on that rocky ledge where he first saw her. When he returned, it was always gone. He hoped Cal hadn't noticed that the meat packages in the freezer might be diminishing faster than usual, but he wasn't too worried. Cal still seemed pretty distracted and wasn't paying attention to details the way he used to. The way Ephraim reasoned it out, if he could make sure the cougar could get food, she wouldn't be as tempted to kill their stock or their neighbors'.

When he reached the ledge, he took out the frozen meat, a roast, from his sack, unwrapped the paper and laid it out in the sun to thaw. Then he hid in a small crevice in the rocks. Out of his sack, he took the charcoal pencils and sketch pad Jorie had given him. He settled down to wait, hoping to see the cougar. He wanted to try to draw her, not from memory, but from real life. While he was waiting, he went ahead and polished off his lunch.

He didn't mean to doze off, but the winter sun was shining

down on him, the rocks were warm, he was sheltered from the wind, and Lizzie had made him an enormous lunch. He startled awake when he heard a man's voice, then another. He crouched down low and hid until the men passed by him. He heard one say, "We warned him. We told him what to do—what to *not* do. I think we need to teach them a lesson so they'll all take notice."

Ephraim didn't see their faces but he did see Rex, Jerry Gingerich's dog, trotting along behind them. Rex spotted him and let out an earbusting woof, but Jerry whistled and Rex ran off to join his master. That dog was too good for the likes of Jerry Gingerich, Ephraim thought. He wondered what warning they were talking about. And why. He thought he might ask Cal. His brother had a way of fitting things together, like the last piece of a tricky jigsaw puzzle. He made things Ephraim couldn't understand seem so clear. But then he thought better of it. Cal would ask why he was out in the Deep Woods when he should have been home, choring. And that might lead to questions he didn't want to answer about cougar snooping.

Remembering why he had come in the first place, Ephraim eased out of the crevice and walked over to the ledge.

The meat Ephraim had left for the cougar was gone.

After Maggie and Ephraim were sound asleep, Cal took out all of his books and spread them on the kitchen table. Matthew, home for the weekend, had gone out with friends and wouldn't be home for hours. Cal had been looking forward to this evening of quiet study. He needed to infuse himself in the Word of God, like steeping a tea bag in hot water. He shook down the ashes in the woodstove and added new wood. The new wood settled into the fire with a hiss and pop. As he sat down at the table, he released a contented sigh, opened his Bible, and prayed for God's Spirit to give him understanding.

He was engrossed in a passage of Scripture and didn't know how much time had passed when a noise of hooves outside interrupted him. The kitchen door blew open, bringing in a swirl of frigid air. Matthew stood, feet planted, at the open door threshold.

"Was fehlt dir denn?" Cal jumped up to pull Matthew in and closed the door tightly behind him. *What's the matter with you?* He was alarmed by the angry look on his brother's face.

"It's Lizzie Glick. You've got to fire her."

Cal gazed steadily at Matthew. He had to work to keep a grin off of his face. "Do I?" He went to the stove and picked up the teakettle. "Any particular reason?"

Matthew pulled the kitchen chair out and sat down, leaning on his elbows, hands clasped together. "I'm sorry to say I have discovered a serious moral lapse in Lizzie Glick." He had a very earnest look on his face. "It's Maggie I'm worried about. Lizzie could be a bad influence on our Maggie."

Cal pulled out two mugs, dropped a tea bag in each one, then filled them with steaming water. "And what seems to be the cause of this moral lapse?" He handed a mug to Matthew and sat down beside him.

"She went home tonight with Mose Riehl." When Cal didn't seem to look shocked, Matthew leaned closer. "He is *seven* years older than she is."

Cal had to swallow a retort about how age didn't seem to matter when *Matthew* was doing the considering. He took a sip of tea and tried to look as if he was giving the matter serious reflection. "Did you happen to ask her home?"

"I did," Matthew said, leaning back in his chair. "Out of kindness."

Cal felt a smile tug at his mouth and fought it back. "Kindness?" He knew his brother wasn't used to putting himself out to make a girl notice him. When it came to girls, Matthew rarely, if ever, met with failure.

"Yes. Kindness. I thought she might be needing a ride home after working all day here. And that was when she told me she was going home with Mose Riehl. I pointed out the age difference between them, and she said she *prefers* mature men." He pointed his finger at Cal. "Now that is just what I mean by being a terrible influence on our Maggie." He shook his head. "There's no telling where that thinking will lead." He blew on the top of the tea, cooling it. "So, you should fire her."

"Lizzie has done a fine job for us, Matthew. She runs this house like a tight ship." In fact, he had noticed that having Lizzie in the house gave the place a feel of ticking along to a natural clock. Life had some semblance of order again.

"It's only Maggie I'm thinking of, Cal."

"I haven't seen this serious moral lapse affect our Maggie yet, Matthew." Just the opposite, Cal thought.

Maggie enjoyed Lizzie so much that she spent more and more time with her in the house. That meant less time shadowing Ephraim, which was probably for the best. Maggie could be pesky, he was aware, and Ephraim required more and more time to himself lately, to wander in the woods and think out the troubling thoughts that plagued a thirteen-year-old boy. Lizzie Glick was the best thing that had happened to them in the last few months. Why, just the other afternoon, he had walked inside and found Lizzie and Maggie in the living room, heads bent together over a quilting frame, with the midday sun streaming over them. The sight would have pleased Mary Ann, he was sure.

166

Still, Cal knew enough not to say those thoughts aloud to Matthew. "Well, I'm thinking there might be another option than firing Lizzie."

Matthew looked at him, confused.

"You could try being a little more mature yourself."

Insulted, Matthew pushed away his teacup, stood, spun on a booted heel, and headed out the door to put away the horse and buggy, leaving the door unlatched so the wind blew in again. Cal got up, closed the door tight, and sat down at the table again. He couldn't stop grinning.

Jorie arrived at the schoolhouse on Monday morning to a door flung wide open. She heard voices and stepped inside with caution. Her eyes went wide when she saw what had happened: the schoolhouse had been vandalized. Desks were knocked over, profane words were scrawled on the blackboard, her desk was turned upside down. In the center of the room stood Cal, Ephraim, and Maggie, looking just as stunned as she felt. "Was is do uff?" she asked. *What happened here?*

Cal spun around when he heard her voice. "I don't know. We just got here ourselves. Ephraim remembered that it was our turn this week to refill the coal bucket, so we came early and found it like this."

Jorie fought back tears as she read the abusive words written on the blackboard. At first, she felt defeated. Then, a new feeling swelled up within her. She wasn't going to let whoever did this triumph. "Ephraim and Maggie, would you mind running to Stoney Creek? Ask Atlee for black paint and a brush."

"It'll be quicker to get the supplies at Beacon Hollow," Cal said. "Ephraim, you know where they are."

Working silently, Cal started righting desks on one side of the room, Jorie on the other.

"Once or twice," she said quietly, "when I arrived in the morning, I had the feeling that someone had been inside."

He stopped working and turned toward her. "Why didn't you say something?"

"I couldn't be sure. It was more of a feeling."

He hooked his hands on his hips. "I don't want you working here at night anymore. Not as long as it's dark so early."

"Cal, do you have any idea who would do this?"

He took the broom off the wall hook to sweep up broken glass. "Es macht nix aus." *It doesn't matter.*

"Es macht aus." *It does matter.*

"What would be the point of knowing? It's not our way to seek confrontation with outsiders who seek to do us harm."

"All I'm wondering is *why* this happened." They stood looking at each other for a long moment, a standoff. Then Jorie tucked her chin to her chest. "It's because I rented the cottage to Dr. Robinson."

Cal leaned the broomstick against a desk and walked over to her. "You did what you felt God led you to do. Our people have always faced persecution because we have tried to do what God asked of us. This is no different."

Tears prickled her eyes. "I'm not so sure the parents of twenty-five scholars will see it the way you see it."

She wasn't sure how it happened—did Cal reach for her? or did she lean toward him?—but suddenly she was in his arms and he was gently telling her not to worry herself about those parents. Her face was buried in his shirt, the top of her head under his chin. And oh, he felt good. He smelled good and felt so good.

When they heard the thundering footsteps of Ephraim and

Maggie approaching, Cal pulled back, but before he released her, his fingers barely brushed her cheek, sliding softly down her neck. She felt his touch all the way to her toes. She turned away, suddenly shy.

The door burst open as Maggie and Ephraim came in with a can of paint and a brush. The four of them went to work cleaning up the schoolroom. She overheard Cal tell them that he thought it might be best not to tell the other scholars about the vandalism. She was grateful for his decision to keep it quiet. Ephraim wouldn't tell, she knew, because he didn't like to talk, but Maggie had a tendency to talk first and think later. By the time the scholars started to arrive, all that was left was a broken window to repair. Jorie decided that even though it was Monday, it would be a good day for a field outing to see if there were any signs of an early spring in the Deep Woods. That way, she reasoned, the blackboards could dry, undisturbed, and Cal could quietly replace the broken window. She just couldn't stay inside the schoolhouse today. Not after *that*.

A few nights later, Cal sat at the kitchen table, studying the Scriptures for Sunday's sermon. He was reading about the ark of the covenant and the symbols placed inside—a jar of manna, Aaron's staff, the stone tablets of the Ten Commandments. He knew the Lord wanted the Israelites to remember these signs as evidence of his faithfulness, but he kept feeling as if there was something else he wasn't quite grasping from the text. He heard a soft humming and looked over to see Maggie, standing at the foot of the stairs. He held out his arms and she ran into them. He scooped her onto his lap.

"Have a bad dream, Maggie?"

"No," she said softly. "A good dream."

He tucked his chin on the top of her small head. "Want to tell me about it?"

She screwed up her nose and concentrated on remembering her dream. "I dreamed that I saw Mom in heaven. She was holding baby Sammy in her arms. He was looking up at her and trying to pull her cap strings. And she was laughing. She looked so happy."

Cal took a sharp breath. He didn't realize Maggie remembered little Sammy. She had only been a toddler when he was born.

"We don't talk about Mom very much," Maggie said, stroking his beard gently with her small fingers. "Have you forgotten her?"

"No," he said quickly. "Of course not. I could never forget her." But the truth was, he *was* trying to forget Mary Ann. That was one of the reasons he didn't bring her name up very often.

"Jorie says that sometimes remembering Mom can hurt, but it's still good to do. She says that remembering is part of who we are. That remembering Mom helps make me Maggie." She yawned loudly. "She told me I'm the keeper of Mom's song." Maggie slipped off of his lap. "Mom is happy now, Dad."

Cal listened to her light step climb up the stairs, accompanied by a sweet, tuneless humming, and the sound lifted his spirits. He gave up a silent prayer of thanks for his Maggie.

The keeper of Mary Ann's song? He sat there for a while, pondering that, then glanced at the grandfather clock against the wall. He closed his Bible, grabbed his hat, coat, and gloves, and went to Stoney Creek to see Jorie.

As he strode up the gentle rise that led to the Kings' farmhouse, his feet crunching through the half-frozen mud, Cal noticed a bobbing lantern crossing from the house to the barn. He knew the lantern would be held by Jorie, checking on the horses one last time. He called out to her and picked up his stride to reach her.

"What are you doing out so late, Cal?" She held a shawl tightly around her and her hair was covered with a bandanna. Her voice was quiet, practically blending in with the inky night.

"I . . . was hoping to talk to you," he said. "But don't let me stop you from checking the horses."

Cal followed her into the barn and watched as she walked past each horse, checking the locks, looking in each stall to make sure each one was safe and sound for the night.

Satisfied, she turned to face him. "Now you've got my full attention. What's on your mind?"

He took one step closer to her. "What did you tell Maggie about being the keeper of the song?"

"The keeper of the song?" She looked confused, then understanding flooded her eyes. "You mean, Mary Ann's song?"

Cal winced when he heard Mary Ann's name spoken aloud, even though he was aware he was doing it. She noticed too.

He looked around and pointed to hay bales, lying side by side. He sat down on one, leaning his back against the wall. She followed him over and did the same. It was easier this way, he thought, not having to look right at her.

"Maggie has been staying after school to help me clean off the blackboards and sweep up. She's been asking me questions about her mother. She wants to remember her, Cal."

And he wasn't helping her do that, he knew Jorie was thinking. He kept his eyes on the hay-strewn floor. This was hard, so hard.

"I think it's a good sign, that Maggie is working through her grief. I told her that by remembering her mother, she was the keeper of her mother's song." Softly, she added, "I'm the keeper of my grandfather's song, here at Stoney Creek. You're the keeper of your folks' song, by caring for your brothers and Beacon Hollow."

Cal looked away. "Memory can be a curse too."

"It's true, memories can be painful. But it's what makes us unique in all of God's creation. Animals run by instinct, but they can't call things to mind the way God tells us to." She turned her head to look at him. "Why, you mentioned it yourself in a sermon just two weeks ago. About how the Israelites were told to gather stones as a means of remembering."

Cal's gaze lifted to the barn rafters. "'That this may be a sign among you, that when your children ask their fathers in time to come, saying, What mean ye by these stones? Then ye shall answer them, That the waters of Jordan were cut off before the ark of the covenant of the Lord; when it passed over Jordan, the waters of Jordan were cut off: and these stones shall be for a memorial unto the children of Israel for ever.'" He dropped his gaze. "Joshua 4:6 and 7."

She smiled. "Sometimes I think you and Samuel and Isaac have the entire Bible memorized." She tucked a strand of loose hair back under her bandanna. "The stones were meant to remind them of how faithful God has been to them, but also to remind them of their dependence on him. It's like keeping that jar of manna in the ark of the covenant. God wanted them to remember their hunger too. That hunger drove them to God for his mercy."

Cal felt his heart miss a beat. That was the *very* section of Scripture he had been puzzling over when Maggie came downstairs, not thirty minutes ago.

"Our memories, good and bad, they shape us. God uses them all for his purposes. He wants us to embrace our past, not forget it. That's what I've been trying to tell Maggie." She searched his face. "I hope that's all right with you."

He nodded. He rose to his feet and walked to the barn door to slide it open, then waited for Jorie. "She's humming again, our Maggie."

She picked up the lantern she had set on the floor and followed him to the door. "I know. Esther complains about it on a daily basis. Says no one can concentrate with all that racket going on." She slid the door shut and latched it. "But no one else seems to notice the humming."

A big grin spread over Cal's face.

On Sunday, Cal woke to a sky filled with low iron-gray clouds, so close they almost seemed to touch the earth. When it was time to leave for church, Cal, Maggie, and Ephraim ran to the buggy with their heads covered to keep the driving rain off their faces. But as the horse turned into Walter Schlabach's farm, where church would be held that morning, the rain tapered off and sunbeams broke through the clouds.

How fitting, Cal thought, as he handed the reins of his horse to Walter's eldest son, Eli, to stall in the barn during the service. The sun streaming through the heavy clouds was a symbol of the morning, rich with the promise of what was to come.

It was not as if Cal felt God more on these church mornings, for he knew God was everywhere and with him always. But when he heard the rustling of members filling up the benches, he never failed to be filled with a sense of the glory of the Lord. It was all done in silence, in quiet expectation, a time of waiting.

Then Amos Esh, the vorsinger, slowly rose to his feet. He lifted his head and opened his mouth in a big *O*, releasing a perfectly pitched note to begin the first hymn. The men's deep baritone voices joined in, filling the room with slow waves. The women's voices, an octave or two higher, blended sweetly with the low tones of the men to create one voice, an embodiment of their unity, making the church one with God. For three hundred years, the Amish have sung their beloved hymns in just that way. Slow, unrushed, almost chanting.

When the time came for the first sermon, Cal and Samuel and Isaac each tried to defer to the other. "I'd prefer if you spoke, Samuel," Cal said.

"And I'd prefer to have you speak first, Caleb," Samuel told him.

Cal and Samuel turned to Isaac, but he preferred to have the others begin. It wasn't a show, it was a sign of sincere humility.

After a few more preferrings, Cal rose to deliver the sermon. He looked around the room for a moment, catching as many eyes as he could, making sure he had their concentrated attention. He started preaching from Joshua 4, about gathering stones of remembrance. A baby cried out and Cal turned toward the women's side, still preaching, when his eyes met Jorie's and his heart missed a beat and his mind went completely blank. He turned back to face the men, quickly recovering his train of thought.

What was happening to him? He was starting to act like Matthew around Lizzie.

A few hours later, after returning home from church, Cal went up to the attic and brought down the box of Mary Ann's things. Her Bible and her recipe cards and her letters from her father. He found Maggie in her bedroom, reading a book on the bed. He set the box down on the floor and opened it.

"Maggie, these are your mother's belongings. I think she'd want you to have them." He picked up the recipe box and sat next

174

to her on the bed. "They'll help you remember her." He opened the recipe box. Leafing through the index cards, he pulled out one and smiled. "Now, here's one. When we were first married, your mom wanted to make this cake just like my mother used to make it. But she forgot to add the sugar!" He pointed to it. "See how she's underlined 'two cups of sugar'? So she wouldn't forget, next time."

Maggie took off her glasses and held the card up to her nose to read it up close.

Cal reached down in the box and picked up the Bible. "Your mom made little notes in the margins when she read a verse that meant something special to her." He opened it to Psalm 139 and ran his finger along the text until he found verse 14. "'I will praise thee; for I am fearfully and wonderfully made: marvelous are thy works; and that my soul knoweth right well. My substance was not hid from thee, when I was made in secret, and curiously wrought in the lowest parts of the earth.'" He pointed to Mary Ann's small margin note: "'Went to midwife today and heard baby's heartbeat with a stethoscope.'" He put a hand on his daughter's head. "That was you, Maggie. That was your heartbeat."

Maggie reached over and threw her small arms around Cal's neck, hugging him tightly.

10

*J*orie brushed out her long, thick hair and rolled it into a bun, then carefully pinned her prayer cap into place. Any minute now, she was expecting to see Ephraim and Maggie run up Stoney Creek's drive, eager for their planned hike to a golden eagle's nest by Blue Lake Pond. When she looked out the window and saw Ephraim and Maggie, she was surprised to see that Cal had tagged along, uninvited but welcome. She smiled.

The day was cold, even for February, though it was bright and clear. Lizzie had made a snack for them that could have fed half the town of Stoney Ridge. After spotting the eagle's enormous nest, six feet wide, made of sticks and branches, Jorie led them to a sheltered spot overlooking the pond. They leaned against rocks that were warmed by the winter sun and shared Lizzie's picnic. Through his binoculars, Ephraim saw the mother eagle return to the nest with food in her mouth, so he and Maggie took off to see if they could get high enough to catch a glimpse of how many eaglets were in the nest.

Cal smiled as they scrambled up the hill. "I thought we'd have leftovers, but Ephraim eats more than all of us put together."

Jorie looked out over the pond. "This is my favorite place on earth. I used to spend hours here with my brothers in the summers."

"What do you hear from your folks?" Cal asked, stretching out his long legs.

"The settlement is doing well. Good farmland and opportunities for growth." She took an apple out of the basket and tossed it to Cal. He shined it on his shirt and took a large bite out of it. "They want us to come and join them."

Cal stopped chewing and looked at her. "You're not thinking of going, are you?" His cheeks reddened slightly. "I mean, the Percherons. We farmers need those horses. You can't breed them fast enough for us." He swallowed.

"How well I know. We have a two-year waiting list." She looked up at the mother eagle, soaring in the sky. "I don't want to go, but my grandfather has been talking about it some. He's getting older, and Mammi is not . . ." Her voice tapered off.

"Not quite herself?" Cal took another bite of apple and chewed. "I've noticed. I brought her home from town awhile back—she had forgotten to tie her horse and buggy to the hitching post—and she was determined to have me turn right on the main road when she knew the way to Stoney Creek was left."

"Oh," she said flatly. "I hadn't heard about that." She wondered if her grandfather was aware of it and just didn't tell her.

His dark brows lifted. "If you need extra help with her, all you need to do is ask."

She smiled. "For now, we're doing all right. She takes a little extra watching."

"Seems like something the aunties would take to. They love a cause. And I would love to direct their attention away from getting me married off." He slapped his hand against his forehead. "Judas Iscariot! Tonight is another Saturday Night Supper. I completely forgot."

She laughed at the stricken look on his face. "How are those suppers going?"

"Depends who you ask." He took another bite out of the apple. "If you ask Ephraim, they are heaven on earth. Mark my words— his future bride will win his heart through his stomach."

"So the aunties haven't located your perfect match yet?"

"Not yet. But they won't give up. They're moving into the next district over now. Six weeks ago, they brought a widow lady who was rather . . . long in the tooth. And that's putting it kindly. Four weeks ago, they found a gal who sneezed her way through dinner. At the end of the evening, she confessed that she was allergic to cows."

"Oh, that would *never* do for a dairy farmer." Jorie drew a line through an imaginary list in the air.

He grinned and rose to his feet, stretching. "Two weeks ago, it was a stern woman who felt children should be seen and not heard. Matthew happened to be home, and you know what a relentless teaser he is. He got Maggie giggling so hard that milk came out of her nose. That did not sit well with Miss Manners. She left early, in a huff." He reached a hand down to help her up.

Jorie laughed as she took his hand and let him pull her up. "Well, maybe tonight will be the night."

Cal didn't release her hand; instead he reached for her other hand and entwined their fingers together. Jorie thought she could hear her heart beating and wondered if he could hear it too. His eyes locked with hers, watching, waiting, when suddenly a loud whoop from Ephraim burst through the tree branches. Cal dropped Jorie's hands and took a step back as Ephraim and Maggie scrambled through the brush to join them.

"We s-seen 'em with our own eyes!" Ephraim said. "Three eaglets!"

Jorie was surprised to feel a twinge of disappointment. She couldn't help but wonder what might have happened next, had Ephraim not swooped in when he did.

On the way back to Beacon Hollow, the shadows were growing long and Cal was getting anxious to get home in time for milking. Ephraim led the way through the endless woods. He was at that age when boys have more energy than they know what to do with, so he was usually one hundred yards or so ahead of them. But Maggie was wearing out. Her small legs were made for playful scamper, not for a long hike, and she dropped behind constantly, so that Cal and Jorie had to stop and wait for her to catch up. Finally, Cal swung Maggie on his back and picked up the pace.

Ephraim was far enough ahead that they couldn't see him. As they came around a bend, they stopped abruptly. They hadn't seen the three men until they had nearly run right into them. One of the men had a hold on Ephraim's jacket collar like he was hanging him on a wall peg. The men's faces were haggard with rough growths of beard, their eyes red-rimmed. Jorie recognized one face: Jerry Gingerich. He was the one holding on to Ephraim.

"Well, what have we here?" Jerry asked, his words thick and slurred. "Hey, Pete, Jim. I think we got us some Plain folks!" In one hand, he held a bottle filled with amber-colored liquid. He started to bring the bottle back up to his mouth, then let it fall as recognition filled his bloodshot eyes. He knew Cal. A satisfied look covered his face, as if he couldn't believe his good luck.

"Let us pass," Cal said in a calm, relaxed voice, but Jorie could tell by the stillness of his features that he was dead serious.

Another man circled around Jorie. "This here is that uppity red-haired gal. I've seen her in town." A few bits of spittle from his mouth careened through the air.

Jorie met his animosity in the way her people always did: by turning silently away from it, but her heart was thumping wildly in her chest.

"Oh, you think you're too good for me!" He reached up a hand to pull her prayer cap off, but Cal quickly sidestepped between Jorie and the man, causing the man to lose his balance and stagger back a step.

"Let us pass," Cal repeated, lowering Maggie to the ground.

"Or else . . . what, Plain man?" Jerry said, waving his bottle in the air. He took another gulp straight out of the bottle. "What are you going to do about it, huh?"

He dropped his hold on Ephraim and pushed Cal. Cal swayed back a little but his feet didn't budge.

"We warned you. We told you not to let that colored man move in, but you went ahead and ignored us."

"Jorie, take Ephraim and Maggie," Cal said, "and run on back to the house." His voice was flat, quiet, and he stood with his hands loose at his sides, his head a little bent. But the air around him pulsed and thrummed.

"Hold it," the third man said, talking around a thick wad of chewing tobacco that puckered his mouth. "You don't give the orders around here." He spewed a thick glob of tobacco juice onto Cal's boots.

"Let my family go," Cal said. "It's me you've got the quarrel with." He turned his head toward Jorie. "You heard me. Go, now."

Jorie grabbed Ephraim's arm, but he pulled away from her. She grabbed him again, more firmly. Leading Ephraim and Maggie by the hands, she backed away, then turned and started running the way they had come. She heard one of the men object, but Jerry said, "Let 'em go. He's the one we want."

As soon as they had gone a distance, she stopped. "Ephraim, lift Maggie onto my back. I know a shortcut to Bud's."

Ephraim linked his fingers together to give Maggie a leg up.

"I'm scared," Maggie whispered into her ear.

"Then say a prayer, Maggie," Jorie said in as calm a voice as she could manage. She followed a chain of animal trails through the dense woodland until she found a narrow passageway through a bramble thicket that bordered Bud's field. She put Maggie down and grabbed her hand to run, not stopping until she reached Bud's farmhouse. He was passing from the barn to the house and saw them waving and calling to him.

"What's the matter?" Bud asked, looking alarmed. "Is there a fire?"

Jorie spilled out the story to Bud in big gulpy breaths as Maggie pulled on her dress sleeve. Bud told her to sit tight while he went in the house to get a gun.

"No, Bud! No gun," Jorie said. "It's not our way."

"But I'm not Amish," he said, then he turned and walked to the house.

Maggie kept pulling on Jorie's sleeve. Still panting, Jorie looked at Maggie. "What is it?" she asked.

"It's Ephraim! He's still in the woods. He didn't come with us!"

As Bud came out of the house with his shotgun and his hunting dog, Jorie told Maggie to go to Beacon Hollow and stay with Lizzie until they got back.

"You go on with her, Jorie," Bud said. "This is no place for a woman. Besides, Maggie needs you."

Jorie looked down at Maggie and knew that Bud was right. Maggie looked so small and scared. Jorie nodded. "Please hurry, Bud."

An hour later, Bud and Ephraim brought Cal, bruised and bloody but upright and walking, to Beacon Hollow. Relief washed over Jorie, and she was surprised at the strength of her own emotions. She had feared the worst. She couldn't bear to lose him—and with that sudden awareness came a rush of tears. Maggie ran toward her father, hugging his middle. Cal winced as her arms tightened around him.

"I'm fine, Maggie. I really am. Just a bump or two." He exchanged a look with Jorie and she knew he wasn't fine.

"Put him up in his bed," she told Bud and Ephraim.

"Wait," Cal said in a voice as dry as toast. "The cows need milking."

"Lizzie, Maggie, and I took care of it, Cal," Jorie said. It had helped keep them busy and their minds off of worrying about what those men were doing to Cal.

"And the aunties?" he asked.

"They came and left," Jorie said. "Lizzie said you weren't feeling well, which was the truth."

After Cal was settled upstairs, Jorie set about doctoring his injuries with calm efficiency. A solution of powdered golden seal and myrrh for his cuts, first boiled and steeped for twenty minutes. A lavender and almond oil infusion for his swollen eye. She took ice from the kitchen, wrapped it in a dish towel, and gently placed it on his sore ribs. "Hold it there," she said, placing his left arm over the bag.

When the ice touched him, his entire body went rigid, but he relaxed as the numbness set in. Within seconds, he closed his eyes and breathed deeply.

Jorie stayed for a moment, watching as he fell asleep. His face was so bruised and battered, it nearly broke her heart. She felt a strange tenderness toward Cal. She always had. Impulsively, she leaned over and kissed his forehead and quietly left his room.

When she went downstairs, Bud was sitting at the kitchen table with Ephraim. Lizzie had made dinner but no one was hungry.

"I think he needs a doctor," Jorie said. "He might have some broken ribs."

"I'll go home and call for a doctor," Bud said. "I'll let Matthew know too, but first I'm calling the police to report this."

"No!" Jorie said, more loudly than she meant to sound. "No, Bud. I'm sorry, but that's not our way."

Bud slammed a fist down on the table, upset and angry. "That's the very reason you folks get harmed. It never stops. Fellows like Jerry Gingerich know you won't fight back. You won't press charges. You Amish don't do a dadblasted thing about it!"

"Vengeance belongs only to the Lord," Jorie said in a shaky voice. She spoke those words and believed them to be true, but in her heart, deep down, she was struggling to accept them. She *wanted* those men to pay for what they did to Cal. It was a terrible thing that people felt they could do anything to the Amish and get away with it.

Bud seemed to realize her inner turmoil. His craggy face softened around the edges. He eased out of the chair and tousled Ephraim's hair. "Here's the hero, today. He stayed right by Cal until I arrived. By the time I got there, those yellow-bellied cowards were gone."

Ephraim didn't look like he felt like a hero. Jorie thought he still looked frightened. She wondered what he had witnessed of the beating Cal took.

"Don't worry, Ephraim," Maggie said, patting him on his arm. "Dad just has a bump."

When Cal woke, Jorie was sitting in a rocker by the window. "You shouldn't be here," were his first words. "It'll get people talking. It isn't proper."

"Well, good thing I've got an understanding minister." She stood and came to his bed. "I went home for the night and just came back a short while ago." She smiled. "Marge is working on a curative for you."

He laughed, a soft laugh that turned into a cough. He tried to sit up and moaned, then leaned back down.

"You've got broken ribs. And a concussion. The doctor said you're going to need to take things slow for a while." She pulled up the chair beside him. "Can I get you anything?"

"No." He closed his eyes for a moment. "Ephraim's all right, isn't he?"

"Yes. He's downstairs. He's quiet. But then, he's always quiet."

Cal opened his eyes. "It was the strangest thing. I remember seeing him come back, alone. I knew he was watching the men beat on me. Then, suddenly, there was a scream—one prolonged scream, and then another. I thought maybe it was you, but then I got hit and blacked out."

"It wasn't me," Jorie said. "While I was running to get Bud, Ephraim slipped away and doubled back."

"Maybe it was Ephraim, trying to distract them." He closed his eyes again. "Next thing I knew, Ephraim and Bud were standing over me."

He was quiet for so long that she thought he had fallen asleep. She went to his bedside to pull the blanket, slipping off the side of the bed, back over him. She gazed fondly at him. He was young, only thirty, and despite his battered face, he was a handsome man with his thick mane of dark wavy hair and his sparkling blue eyes. Though she was brought up believing that no man was better than another, Cal was an anchor in their community. How could anyone dare to lay a hand on him? The thought of what happened in the Deep Woods sickened her.

"Aw, Jorie. Quit looking at me like I'm such a pitiful sight."

She laughed. "Right now, you are a pitiful sight, Caleb Zook." Then she sobered. "I'm the one who brought this trouble on you."

"What's done is done. We're all in this together." He fixed his eyes on her. "But while you're feeling beholden, there is something you can do for me."

"What's that?"

He took a deep breath. "I've been lying here, thinking and praying. I feel, more than ever, that it's the right decision." He bit the corner of his lip. "I want you to marry me."

She stopped smoothing the blankets and stilled for a long moment. Then she straightened up. "Yes." This time the answer came from her heart.

"I'm going to keep asking you till you say yes."

"All the more reason I should say yes."

"Jorie, we're a good team, you and I. Maggie adores you, so does Ephraim. You belong here at Beacon Hollow."

"Cal, are you listening? I said yes."

He was just about to start talking again when he realized what she said and snapped his mouth shut. His left eye, the one that wasn't swollen nearly shut, widened in surprise. "You mean it?

You're not just saying that because you're feeling sorry for me?" His cheeks stained red.

"I mean it." She had no doubts. It just felt right, like lemonade and picnics by the lake on a warm summer day. There was another long silence where their eyes locked and they both knew they had an agreement. Silent, but there. She smiled and reached out to stroke the hair off of his forehead. "We can talk it all over when you're feeling better."

A tenderness came over Cal's face. He reached for her hand and brought it to his mouth, pressing his lips to the inside of her wrist, where the blue veins pulsed beneath her pale skin. "If I could sit up, and if I didn't look like I've been sent through a washer wringer, I would kiss you properly."

She felt breathless, the way she got when she was climbing the ramp to the hayloft. "Matthew is here," she said, suddenly shy. "He wants to see you."

"Not like this. I'll come downstairs."

She nodded and walked to the door. As she turned the knob, she heard him ask, almost in a whisper, "Jorie, do you really mean it?"

She kept her hand on the doorknob, though she did turn to look at him. "Preacher Caleb," she said in a lightly teasing tone. "My no is no, and my yes is yes."

11

As Ephraim saw Cal wince with every step as he made his way to the kitchen table, he felt his throat tighten. How could those men have hurt his brother like that? Cal was such a good and kind man. He didn't deserve that treatment. It disturbed Ephraim deeply to have seen those stupid, drunk men pummel Cal, over and over. Just thinking about it made his eyes start to prickle with tears, so he went out on the stoop and called for Maggie to come in to see her dad. He held the door open as Maggie raced inside, then practically bumped into her when she skidded to a stop, shocked by the sight of her father. She had seen him last night, but he looked even worse this morning, swollen and bruised. Cal spread out his arm so that Maggie would stand close and lean against him.

Jorie brought Cal a cup of hot coffee.

"How do you feel?" Matthew asked, handing Cal the milk and sugar pitchers for his coffee.

Cal stirred his coffee, then took a sip, carefully avoiding the cut on his lip. "Like someone dropped an anvil on my chest."

"Looks like someone dropped it on your face," Matthew said, peering at Cal's cuts and bruises.

Cal glanced over at Ephraim. "You should have stayed with Jorie, Ephraim. I'm sorry you had to see that. But I'm grateful for your concern."

Jorie sat down next to Ephraim. "What's troubling you?"

Ephraim looked at Cal. "You n-never th-threw a p-punch. You just s-stood there. You just s-stood there and l-let them hit you." He had never seen men so riled up, not even his brother Ben, who had a temper on him.

"If I had, Ephraim, I wouldn't have been any different from those men," Cal said. "I would become just like them. The rage and hate that lives in them would become a part of me. Vengeance belongs only to God."

Maybe, but Ephraim still wanted to hurt them back. Especially that Jerry Gingerich. He didn't recognize the other two men, but he hated them too.

"I sort of remember the sound of a scream," Cal started. "But then I blacked out. What was that all about?"

All of the eyes at the table turned to Ephraim. His eyes went wide and his mouth fell open, but no sound came out. A knock on the door diverted everyone's attention. Ephraim jumped up and opened it to Flora Miller, bearing a hot casserole. Flora gasped when she saw Cal's battered appearance.

After Flora left, Jorie said she should be getting home. "The news is out. Every woman in our church district will be bringing you a casserole, so I think I will be getting home to help Atlee with the horses."

Cal tried to get up, but Jorie shook her head. "Stay put. I'll stop back later to see how you're doing. Maybe my grandmother will have a remedy cooked up for you."

Matthew snorted. "Last time she gave me a remedy, I spent two days on the john. No, big brother, if you're smart, you will run for the high hills if Marge King tries to get anywhere near you with one of her curatives." He tipped his head toward Jorie. "No disrespect to your grandmother."

Jorie tried to look stern but broke into a laugh as she tied her bonnet under her chin. "None taken. He's right. Run for the hills."

Matthew was spreading blackberry jam on his toast. Maggie was stirring spoonfuls of sugar into Cal's coffee. Ephraim was sure he was the only one who caught the look that passed between Cal and Jorie as she turned at the door to wave goodbye.

Something had changed between them, something had been sealed.

When Jorie returned home, she found her grandmother in the kitchen making sweet rolls. As she hung her bonnet and cape on the kitchen wall peg, she braced herself, expecting her grandmother to drop everything and insist on going to Beacon Hollow. A few hours earlier, as Jorie left to see Cal, her grandmother had been poring over books to find just the right painkiller. She half-expected Mammi to have shown up at Beacon Hollow this morning, holding in her hands some vile-tasting liquid to force down Cal's throat. But Mammi stood at the kitchen counter, in the middle of a cloud of flour, kneading dough as if her life depended on it. Books were still open on the kitchen table, surrounded by all kinds of dried herbs in jars, but Mammi never even mentioned Cal, which struck Jorie as strange.

She went out to the barn to help her grandfather feed the

horses. She smiled when she heard the shuffling of the horses' feet in anticipation of their noon meal.

Atlee stopped pitching hay into a wheelbarrow when he saw her. "How is our Caleb?"

"He looks worse, with all of the swelling and bruises. But he was up."

Atlee grabbed a forkful of hay and tossed it in the wheelbarrow. "You're looking pretty chipper this morning," he said, in between heaving the hay.

"Oh?" she said. "I saw the first robin on my way home. A foretaste of spring."

Atlee gave her a look as if he didn't really think a robin alone deserved the credit for giving her that kind of happiness.

Briefly, Jorie thought about telling him that she and Cal were going to be married. If she were going to tell anyone, it would be her grandfather. But she thought better of it. It was hard not to spill her secret; she felt as if she was nearly bursting with the news. Her heart had almost stopped when Cal asked her. When it started up again, it felt like it was beating in unsteady lurches. It still surprised her, saying yes like that, but she found she had no doubts. For now, it would remain a secret, shared just between her and Cal.

Instead, she said, "Surprised me a little to see that Mammi had forgotten all about making a remedy for Cal. When I came home, she was making rolls."

Atlee lifted his eyebrows. "Guess she forgot about it."

"Doesn't it seem as if she's getting more than a little forgetful about things like that lately?"

Atlee continued to heave hay into the wheelbarrow. "What else?"

"She left the oven on all night the other day. And last week I went out to get a casserole from the freezer, and there was her knitting project, frozen solid."

"Well, she's getting older. We old folks get a little forgetful now and then."

"Maybe. But usually that's about insignificant things. Her doctoring has always been so important to her."

Atlee didn't answer, which meant that he didn't want to discuss it. Jorie grabbed another pitchfork and joined her grandfather as he wheeled the barrow down the corridor of the barn.

As soon as he finished helping Cal milk the cows, Ephraim tucked another frozen package of meat under his coat and took off for the Deep Woods at a fast run. It wasn't easy to get away this week. He felt bad about Cal, but a little sorry for himself too. Cal needed extra help, which meant a lot more choring for him and less time for cougar snooping.

The scream Cal had heard before he got whacked on the head was the cougar's scream. She was in a tree above them, her lithe body poised on a branch, peering down at the men beating on Cal. Then she spotted Ephraim, hiding behind a rock, and exchanged a long look with him. That was when she let out a scream that made the hair on the back of his head stand up straight. One of the men had been holding Cal up under his arms and the other two were taking turns pummeling him. When the cougar screamed, they stopped, looked up, and saw her. She screamed again. This time, they dropped Cal and ran.

After the men left, he ran to Cal's side, praying he wasn't dead. He also wanted to protect Cal in case the cougar decided to come down from the tree. Her expression was unmistakably belligerent. He threw his body over Cal's and covered his head with his arms, bracing himself for an attack. After a long wait, satisfied that Cal was still breathing, Ephraim stole a glance up at the tree. The cougar had gone.

Not a minute later, Bud arrived. Ephraim knew the cougar was a wild creature and that it couldn't really have known he needed her help. Even still, today he wanted to leave an offering, a thank-you for saving his brother's life. And one thing else Ephraim noticed. The cougar's belly was round with life.

"It's warming up some, don't you think?" Jorie asked Cal when he stopped by the schoolhouse on Friday afternoon.

He laughed, a sound rich and thick. "Only you, Jorie King, could find the good in a bitterly windy March day."

"At least it's not snowing," she said as a smile wreathed her face. She was so happy to see him up and around and looking like himself that she wanted to laugh and throw her arms around him in a big welcoming hug. Instead she stood before him, assessing his face, with her hands linked behind her back. His eye looked nearly normal; the swelling was almost gone. The bruising had gone from angry red to blue and yellow and purple. But she saw he still held himself stiff and upright, as if he couldn't bend over without fear of snapping in two.

Cal looked down at her and held her gaze. "If it's not making you feel rushed, I'd like to talk to Isaac on Sunday afternoon about how soon he could marry us."

"That sounds fine," was all that she said, but she knew her eyes were smiling. Ever since she had agreed to marry Cal, she was nearly floating with sweet anticipation. She felt lighter than air.

"Good. It's settled then. Sunday it is. And that will be the *end* of the aunties' Supper List."

She couldn't help but laugh at that. Cal's smile deepened, his eyes warmed. He took a step closer to her and reached for her hands. His calloused hands felt large and strong. He studied her face for a long moment, before he leaned into her, tilting his head, and his mouth came down onto hers. His lips were warm, his beard gently tickling. He kissed her with such sweetness it was almost unbearable. And when he pulled back, she had to look away because she had tears in her eyes. Something had become very clear to her: she loved him.

12

$\mathcal{M}$atthew's night shift was nearly over. He had finished up cleaning the bathrooms and stopped at the nurses' station to study the updated patient board. "Morning, Lottie," he said. "Did you just get here?"

"Hello to you, farm boy," Lottie said with a big toothy grin. "How'd you get stuck on night duty?"

"Only way they let me off on weekends is if I pull a Saturday night once in a while." He leaned his elbows on the counter and turned his head to look down the hall at a cluster of Plain People, hovering by a patient's door like bees over flowers. "What's going on?"

Lottie tilted her head. "Say, you speak German, don't you?"

"They're not speaking German. They're speaking Deitsch, a dialect. But yes, I do speak it."

"Well, if you can understand what they're saying, get yourself down that hall and make yourself useful. Those folks came in this morning to see a new patient. They seem upset, but no one on the floor can understand them."

"Sure. I'll go."

Matthew walked up to the group in the hallway. An older woman was crying. He spoke to the eldest man and asked, in Deitsch, if he could help him. The man looked at Matthew, startled to hear his own language coming out of a hospital worker. "Er is net mein Sohn!" He pointed to the door. "Er is net mein Sohn!" *He is not my son.* He gripped Matthew's shirt with his two hands and clung to him. "Warum is mein Sohn?" *So where is my son?*

Matthew spotted Dr. Doyle, the floor physician, coming out of the elevator. "Let me go tell the doctor what you've told me." He unclasped the man's strong fingers from his shirt and hurried to the elevator.

"You're sure?" Dr. Doyle asked the Amish farmer, after Matthew explained the situation. "You're absolutely sure?"

Matthew translated back and forth between the doctor and the Amish farmer. The farmer kept insisting, "Er is net mein Sohn!" *He is not my son.* "Warum is mein Sohn?" *So where is my son?*

The doctor looked through the charts. "This man had identifying dog tags. They sent him here to Pennsylvania *because* of those tags."

"Er is net mein Sohn! Warum is mein Sohn?" the farmer kept repeating.

"Why don't you folks go down to the waiting room with me and we'll see if we can get things straightened out." Dr. Doyle turned to Matthew. "You'll help with the translating?"

"Sure, sure," Matthew said.

"Then who *is* this patient?" Lottie whispered to the doctor. "How are we going to ID him?"

"Write him up as a 'John Doe,'" the doctor told her. Exasperated, the doctor blew air out of his cheeks. He led the family down the hall, but before Matthew went to join them, Lottie asked him to take the new patient his breakfast. Matthew balanced the breakfast tray in one hand and slipped open the door with the other. The patient, a young man with a nearly shaved head, sat in a chair, facing the window. He was entirely still except for his fingers, which drummed restlessly along the arm of the chair. How sad, Matthew thought, to be a John Doe. A no-name. To not belong to anyone. He felt a sweeping gratefulness for the family he had, the place at his table. Even Ben's spot had never been sat in.

He walked a few steps closer to the patient. "Can I get you anything?" Matthew asked him softly.

The patient didn't respond.

"Some water? Or juice? I know where Lottie keeps a box of candy hidden, if you like chocolates." Matthew's words fell into an empty silence. "Okay, then. I'll come back and check on you later. Maybe by then you'll want some of Lottie's chocolates. Everything's going to be all right. You'll see."

The patient had stopped his finger drumming. He had grown so still, so motionless, that it almost seemed to Matthew as if he had died. An eerie feeling crept up Matthew's spine. How could he explain a dead patient to Dr. Doyle? He took a tentative step closer to the patient, hoping to see his chest expand with a breath. He crouched down carefully in front of him and placed a hand on his knee.

The patient suddenly lifted his head and looked straight at Matthew with blank, empty eyes.

Matthew lurched back, nearly falling. "Judas Iscariot!" He felt his heart miss a beat. "Er is noch lewendich!" *He's still alive!*

All during meeting, Cal tried to keep his mind on the Lord and off of Jorie. Still, whenever he walked or turned around as he preached, he found himself searching for her face among the sea of prayer caps. He'd known her all his life, but lately, out of nowhere, the sight of her could snatch away his breath and make his chest hurt. As he closed the service, Cal made a few announcements: a barn raising would be held next week at the Reuben Yoders'. A comfort knotting would take place at Sylvia Swartzentruber's on Friday. "And next meeting will be held at the Roman Stoltzfuses'." He looked over at Jorie and they shared one of those special smiles that came only into their eyes. Maybe as soon as next meeting, he would be making the announcement that he and Jorie were planning to marry. This very afternoon, he would speak to Isaac about it.

Just as Cal opened his mouth to give the benediction, the door blew open and Matthew burst in, scanning the room until his eyes found Cal's.

"I found him! Cal! He's alive! Our Ben's alive!"

When Bud heard the news about Ben, he offered to drive the Zooks over to Lebanon in his station wagon. Maggie squeezed between Cal and Bud in the front seat. Matthew and Ephraim sat in the backseat. "Shall I stop by the Kings' and pick up Jorie?" Bud asked Cal.

"No," Cal said, firmly. He was still reeling from Matthew's discovery—that Ben was alive, in a hospital, just an hour from Stoney Ridge. It was all he could do to finish the church service and rush back to the farm to find Bud.

"She's not expecting to come?" Bud asked.

Cal's jaw clenched tight. "She doesn't know we're going to Lebanon."

"Think that's being fair to her?" Bud said.

Cal didn't answer.

Bud looked at him. "Or are you just being fair to you?"

Cal looked out the window. He couldn't think about Jorie right now. He just couldn't. He avoided her after church. He didn't even look at her, though he knew she was watching him as he grabbed Maggie's hand and hurried to the buggy. Right now, all he could think about was Ben.

Bud shrugged. "Suit yourself."

Cal asked Matthew to tell the story about discovering Ben over and over again. "Are you sure he didn't recognize you, Matthew?"

"Not at first. Then, when I realized he was our Ben and talked to him in Deitsch, he got real upset and the doctor told me to leave. I was so shaken I didn't even know what to do next. I thought I'd better just get word to you, Cal, so I hitchhiked from the Vet Hospital all the way to Stoney Ridge." He took off his hat. "But I really couldn't tell for sure if he recognized me."

"Matthew's changed an awful lot since Ben's been gone," Bud said quietly. "He's gone from being a boy to a man. And with that fancy haircut, he doesn't look Amish anymore."

Cal turned his head slightly. "Yes. So much has changed since he left us."

Maggie looked up at Cal. "Dad, I don't hardly remember Ben."

Cal rested a hand on her small head. "Two years is a long time when you're seven years old. But now you'll have plenty of time to get reacquainted."

At the Veterans Hospital, Matthew led them to the psychiatric floor and started to head into Ben's room, everyone following behind, until the doctor stopped them.

"Matthew, you can't just waltz in there—" Dr. Doyle started.

"Nobody's waltzing," Cal said. "We just want to see our brother."

"And you certainly can't bring children onto this ward," Dr. Doyle said, frowning at Maggie and Ephraim. He turned to Lottie, who was watching, with wide eyes, from the nurses' station. "Maybe you could take them to the cafeteria and get them something to eat."

Lottie wiggled her finger toward Ephraim and Maggie, who looked to Cal for permission. He nodded, so they followed her down the hall.

"Let's find someplace to talk," the doctor said. "Follow me to the waiting room. You'll overwhelm your brother if you all charge in there, claiming him. If he really is your family member, let's do this in a way that is best for him."

Cal, Bud, and Matthew followed the doctor into the waiting room and sat on stiff plastic chairs. The doctor looked through a chart and told them what he knew about this patient's history. "He was a conscientious objector doing nonmilitary assignments but got involved in an offensive. Within a few weeks of the incident, he started to show signs of instability. He was sent to Bangkok for psychiatric evaluation, his breakdown continued to escalate, and was sent here for long-term care."

"When will my brother be able to come home?" Cal asked.

The doctor held up a hand in warning. "Whoa. Slow down. Let's get an identification on him first."

Cal stood to go.

"Look, Mr. Zook," the doctor said. "If he is your brother, he's not well. He's . . . he's going to need care."

"We can care for him at home," Cal said.

Dr. Doyle looked like he'd had a long day. "His wounds aren't physical. He's a little scrambled up."

Cal looked at him. "Speak plain."

Dr. Doyle stood to face Cal. "He's going to need psychiatric rehabilitation. He's very withdrawn. He has what we call a clinical depression. He suffered some kind of traumatic incident that has made him shut down."

"He needs to be home," Cal insisted. He was losing patience with this doctor who spoke of Ben like he was reading from a medical book. What did he really know about his brother? Or about being Amish? About God's strength that helped them heal?

"Well, let's take this one step at a time. Matthew can accompany you, Mr. Zook." The doctor turned, then spun around. "Stay calm. No big show of emotion."

Bud gave a short laugh. "Doc, you're preaching to the choir. These folks are Amish."

"Let's go," Cal said. "I want to welcome my brother home."

In the hospital room, Matthew walked quietly up to Ben, who was seated in the same chair, staring out the window, fingers drumming. Dr. Doyle stood protectively by the door. "Ben, I've brought someone to see you. It's Cal. Our big brother Cal."

Cal crouched down in front of Ben as his eyes studied his face. Ben was barely recognizable to him. The laughter in his eyes—so much a part of Ben—was gone. In its place was an emptiness. His face was thin and pale. His head was shaved. Different, broken, yet the same. This man was indeed his brother. "Zwaar?" Cal asked, his voice cracking with emotion. *Can this be true?* "The good Lord has seen fit to return our brother Ben to us."

Ben showed no sign of recognizing Cal; his eyes remained fixed on his right hand, drumming restlessly on the arm of the chair. Cal wasn't disappointed—Matthew had prepared him for such a lack of response. His heart, though, was overflowing with joy . . . just to be near his brother Ben.

200

In a soft, gentle voice, Cal started talking to Ben as if he'd seen him only last week and wanted to let him know what crops were going to be planted soon and which cows were due to calve. Too soon, he felt, the doctor interrupted, saying he thought Ben had enough excitement for one day.

Slowly, Cal stood. "Ben, the Lord God answered our prayers and protected you. He brought you home to us. I'm so glad you're back with us." He cleared his throat; it felt as if he had ground glass in there. "So very glad." He clasped Ben on the shoulder as if he was afraid he might disappear again.

Out by the nurses' station, Cal crossed his arms against his chest and locked eyes with Dr. Doyle. That little doctor couldn't be much older than Matthew, Cal thought, and acted as jumpy as a cricket. "He needs to be home with us. He won't get better here."

Dr. Doyle shook his head emphatically. "I'm sorry, Mr. Zook. He's still under evaluation. There are procedures we need to follow."

Cal threw up his arms. "I am tired of the government telling me about my brother. First, you tell me he's dead. Then, that his body has been *cremated*. Now, we find out—through no help from the government, mind you—that he's alive! I want to bring my brother home. He belongs at home."

Bud sidled up to the doctor. "Remember, Doc, these folks are Amish. They aren't gonna sue you. They just like to take care of their own."

The doctor looked curiously at Bud, standing there with his hands jammed into his overall pockets, his straw hat tilted back on his wispy gray hair, his heavy boots giving off a faint whiff of manure. "This patient is suffering from a severe clinical depression. It's given him dissociative symptoms." At the blank look on everyone's faces, he tried again. "Something like amnesia."

"Amnesia?" Matthew asked. "So he *has* forgotten us?"

"No," the doctor sighed, deeply and grievously. "He hasn't forgotten you. He's tried to suppress painful experiences that are too difficult to endure. It's like his mind has shut down as a way to cope. It's not unusual behavior in a veteran, but it's not understood very well. If he went home too soon, with expectations from all of you heaped on him, it might cause the opposite response. He might withdraw even further, because he can't fulfill your expectations of him."

Cal spun the brim of his black hat around and around in his hands. "We don't want to cause him any more pain."

"That's why I want you folks to go home, let the professionals evaluate your brother, and let us decide what the best course of action to take will be," the doctor said.

"Could we come back to see him soon?" Cal asked. When the doctor hesitated, Cal quickly added, "We thought he was dead. For months now, we thought my brother was dead."

The doctor's face relaxed slightly. "Of course. Of course you can visit him. Look, we all want the same thing. We want your brother to get well. Matthew will be here every day and can call you with updates."

Bud made a snorting sound. "These folks don't have phones, Doc."

"How soon?" Cal asked. "How soon can we come and visit?"

"Next weekend," the doctor said. With visible relief, he noticed Lottie approaching from the elevator with Maggie and Ephraim. "Lottie has some paperwork for you to fill out about your brother. You have information we need."

He hustled away as if there was a fire on the ward.

Lottie had a large file folder in her hands and plunked it on the counter of the nurses' station. "The government loves its paperwork," she said to Cal, as if that explained everything.

Matthew offered to keep Maggie and Ephraim busy, so Cal began the process of filling out forms. When he was drafted in the Korean War, there was one simple form to sign. Why would it be so much more complicated to declare someone alive? he wondered, after filling out the sixth form. Thirty minutes later, Cal found Matthew, Ephraim, and Bud in the waiting room.

"Where's Maggie?" he asked.

"I thought she was with you," Matthew said, suddenly alarmed. "I was showing them around the hospital and Maggie said she needed to go to the bathroom. When she didn't come back to us, I figured she had found you."

"Matthew," Cal said, frowning, "you know Maggie's tendency to wander off."

They spent time retracing their steps, going floor to floor. They finally split up and each took a floor, until Lottie waved to Cal down at the elevator. "Come look what I found." She took him back to Ben's hospital room. There was Maggie, sitting on Ben's bed. Maggie was reading out loud from a comic book she had found in the waiting room. Cal watched them for a while.

"Well, well, look at that," Lottie whispered.

"What?" Cal asked. To him, Ben hadn't changed a wit. He was still in the chair, staring out the window.

"See his hands? They're still. First time I've seen his fingers not drumming a beat."

Cal's eyes shifted to Ben's hand, resting calmly on the armchair. Maggie looked up and noticed her father at the door. Gently, she laid the comic book in Ben's lap. "Next time we come, we'll finish up the story and see whether Archie ends up with Veronica or Betty." She patted her uncle on the shoulder. "See you soon, Ben."

Bud drove Matthew to the house where he was renting a room. "I wish we could stay and take you to dinner, Matthew," Cal said. "But the dairy . . ."

Matthew waved him off. "I understand. I'm kind of beat anyway." After he got out of the car, he shut the door and leaned through the window. "Maggie, what made you think to read to Ben?"

She pushed her glasses up on the bridge of her small nose. "Jorie told us to read whenever we got the chance. When I saw the comic book in the waiting room, I just thought Ben might like it."

Matthew reached in to give her a big wet noisy kiss on her cheek. "You did good, little Magpie."

Cal loved his dairy, but there were days, like today, when the relentless demands of thirty cows waiting to be milked felt like a ball and chain around his leg. They had left the hospital so late that he knew they wouldn't be back to Beacon Hollow in time for the milking. A whole set of problems could be waiting for him back home, the least of which would be the noise of thirty bawling cows with bursting udders. He kept glancing at the speedometer, wishing Bud would pick up his pace.

Bud scowled at him. "Stop staring at me. I'm driving the speed limit and that's all there is to it!"

"Aw, Bud," Cal said. "Little old ladies are passing us by!"

"So much for the slow life of the Amish, is all I got to say," Bud said, but he did speed up a little.

When Bud finally turned the station wagon up Beacon Hollow's long driveway, nearly two hours late for the milking, Cal was about to leap out of the car. He tossed a thank-you back to Bud and rushed into the barn, expecting to hear a chorus of thirty unhappy cows. Instead, the cows were quietly eating, udders emptied, manure shoveled off behind them in their stanchions, and the barn had been swept clean. Maggie and Ephraim skidded to a halt behind him.

"Wer hen schunn die K-Kieh g-gemolke?!" Ephraim said, looking around the tidy barn in amazement. *Who milked the cows?!*

Cal turned around in a circle, amazed. "Our good friends and neighbors. That's who milked our cows. They knew we needed help and they just stepped in." He sighed, deeply satisfied with this day of many miracles. "And *that*, Maggie and Ephraim, is what being Amish is all about."

In the kitchen, they found the table set for supper, the smell of a casserole baking in the oven. On the table was a bowl of pickled cucumbers, sliced tomatoes, and a basket of sliced bread, covered with a napkin.

As Ephraim made a lunge for the bread basket, Cal grabbed his wrist. "First, we wash up. Then, we thank the Lord for a day such as this. Then, we eat."

"Who do you think made us dinner?" Maggie asked, scrubbing her hands at the kitchen sink. "Same folks that milked our cows?"

Cal laughed. "I hope not. I think it was a female who made us this fine dinner. Maybe two. She didn't leave us a note. I'm guessing she didn't feel the need to be thanked. But we can sure thank the good Lord for this meal and the hands that provided it." He tucked his chin to his chest and offered a prayer, filled with gratitude, to God for this day's events, including a request for healing for Ben. *And dear Lord,* he added silently to his prayer, *please help me know what to do about Jorie.*

On Monday afternoon, as soon as school let out, Cal was waiting on the steps of the schoolhouse. The scholars poured out, scarcely noticing him, but Maggie and Ephraim stopped in their tracks.

"You both head on home before the rain starts up," he told them. "I'll be there soon."

Cal waited until the last scholar left, then went into the schoolhouse and stood by the door, awkwardly. He was hoping Jorie would say something. She sat at her desk, engrossed in writing on a paper. She didn't acknowledge him in any way.

He cleared his throat. "We went to see Ben yesterday." He took a tentative step inside and took off his hat.

"I heard," she said, without looking up.

So she did know he was here. Cal took a step closer. "He isn't . . . well. The doctor said he's suffering from a type of stress brought on by trauma. A depression. He's sort of in his own world." He took another step. "But there was a bright spot. Maggie read to him and it seemed to calm him. We thought that was a real good sign."

Jorie gave a slight nod. He noticed her hand was clasping the pen so tightly that her knuckles were white.

Cal rambled on for a while, trying to remember the details that the doctor had told him. "Matthew is going to call over to Bud's each night, a little after five when the long-distance rates go down, and tell us how Ben is doing. If there's some improvement, we're hoping we can bring him home soon. That doctor, though, he might take some persuading."

Jorie stood and went to the window that overlooked the playground. Rain had begun and it hit with a fury.

"Jorie," Cal said in a soft voice, coming close behind her.

She spun around. "You know what really makes me mad? You took Maggie! You took a little girl to a *psychiatric ward* of the Veterans Hospital. Yet you didn't take me! You left church yesterday with no intention of asking me to come. I saw you leave!"

"But—"

Her eyes were fiery. "I care about him too."

He tossed his hat on a nearby desk and raised his hands. "Jorie, please try and understand. I couldn't handle . . . having both . . ." He sighed. "We may as well have this out now as later. We've got a problem that's going to need some working out."

"I realize we've got a problem! But for you to exclude me yesterday, well, that's hard for me to understand. You're the one who's always saying that men need to listen to women, that a woman's point of view is like a gift." She lifted her chin a notch. "Well, yesterday, you had a chance to practice what you preach, and instead you just went off, without a thought for me. It hurt me to be left out. As if I didn't matter to Ben. As if I didn't matter to you."

"Of course you matter," Cal said, a strange roughness to his voice. "Why else would this whole thing feel so complicated?"

But Jorie had arrived at some conclusions of her own. "Let me uncomplicate this whole thing," she said, too calmly. "Ben needs you right now. Nothing else is as important as helping Ben get better."

"You're right," Cal said.

She turned back to the window. "Maybe the timing of this is a blessing. No one needs to know that a courtship has been broken."

Cal walked up to her and reached out a hand as if he was going to touch her, then thought better of it. He had a little trouble with his voice when he asked, "Are we broken, Jorie?"

She turned to him. Cal stared at her, his face settling into deep lines, and Jorie stared back, her head held high, erect. A silence drew out between them, underscored by the drumroll of rain hitting the roof above their heads.

Cal was the first to drop his eyes. "On Sunday, Bud said he'd drive us over to see Ben. If you want to see him. But I can't promise the doctor will let you into his room. He's a little protective, that doctor. Doesn't understand how important family is. I'm anxious to get Ben home as soon as possible. I know he'll get better if he can just come home."

Jorie gave a firm nod. "I'll be there on Sunday."

Cal picked up his hat and walked to the door. As he reached the doorjamb, he turned around. "It's a miracle, really. Like Lazarus, raised from the dead." He put his hat on and adjusted the brim, before walking out in the rain.

"But Lazarus came back whole," Jorie said, so softly Cal wasn't sure if she actually said it or if he had just thought it himself.

13

The following Sunday afternoon, Dr. Doyle led Matthew, Cal, and Jorie to Ben's door while Bud took Maggie and Ephraim to the cafeteria. The doctor explained that they shouldn't expect any response, that they should not cry or put any emotional pressure on Ben. "I recommend that you, Matthew, or you, Mr. Zook, go in first and talk to him for a few minutes. Prepare him for meeting someone else. Matthew said you're his girlfriend, right?" He looked to Jorie to respond, but she didn't answer.

Matthew cringed. Why did he ever tell the doctor that? And he didn't *say* "girlfriend," he said "girl."

"We're his family," Cal said. "We're all family. I'll go in first."

After Cal went into Ben's room, the doctor turned to Matthew. "What, is he like the patriarch of the clan?"

Matthew rolled his eyes at Jorie, as if to say, "English." Then he grinned. "Well, yeah, I guess you could say that. Cal is the head of our family."

A few minutes later, Cal came out and motioned to Jorie to go in. She put her hand on the doorknob and paused. Her heart was racing, part excitement, part dread. She still couldn't believe Ben—her Ben with his laughing eyes and teasing ways—was alive, right behind that door. And as happy as she was that he was alive, she worried terribly about what kind of condition he was in. Cal sounded so confident about Ben getting well, but she wasn't so sure. She'd heard stories of soldiers coming home, forever changed.

Cal placed a reassuring hand on her shoulder and squeezed gently. "It will be good medicine for him to see you, Jorie."

She closed the door behind her and looked across the room at Ben, seated in a chair facing the window. He didn't notice that she had come in. His chin was tucked to his chest and his eyes were closed, but his fingers were tapping the arm of the chair. He looked thin, terribly thin. His skin, normally tanned from the sun, was milk pale. His head—that beautiful head of dark, wavy hair—was nearly shaved, just a bristle remained like the bits of an old broom. She felt a fist tighten around her heart and hot tears sting her eyes. She wiped them away, took a deep breath, and went to his side.

When she spoke, her voice was hoarse. "It's really you. It's really our Ben."

As soon as she said the words, something cold seemed to shiver across his face. She had the impression that, in his mind, he had just seen something, or thought something, that hurt him terribly. The tension was too much and she felt her eyes well up with tears again. She fought them back. She wanted to touch him, just touch him. Just lay her hand against his cheek.

Instead, she pulled up a chair and tried to think of something to say—something that would speak to his heart. All week long,

Jorie thought up a dozen things to tell him, but now, none of them made it past the end of her tongue. Finally, she decided to talk to him as if she were writing a letter to him. She had written often while he was in Vietnam, though he seldom wrote back. She told him about her teaching job and about the foals they were expecting at Stoney Creek. She explained that they had a new veterinarian, one who actually knew about horses. "He's been such a help. Knows horses better than Atlee." She smiled. "You always said that once I got started on my Percherons, I could talk the ears off of a donkey."

Ben kept his head down, but she had a sense that he was listening.

"My grandmother still thinks she can heal anyone and everyone. She gave Fannie Byler a remedy to lose weight and Fannie promptly gained ten pounds. Why, Mammi is working on something for you, right now—" Jorie caught herself. She sighed. She really didn't know what else to say. "That Dr. Doyle, he warned me not to stay too long, so I'll say goodbye. For now."

She rested her hand on his forearm, but he flinched, so she took her hand away. At that, he lifted his eyes and looked at her, briefly, before closing them again.

"God is watching over you, bringing you back to us, Ben," she said, answering him as if he had asked her a question. "A sparrow doesn't fall from the sky without God knowing of it. Even you, Benjamin Zook."

While Jorie was in Ben's room, Cal remained in the hallway, pressing Dr. Doyle to release Ben.

"Why?" the doctor asked. "You can see for yourself that he's barely functioning."

"With all the pills you keep tossing down his throat, how could any man function?" Cal asked. As soon as the words left his mouth, he knew he shouldn't have said them. It wasn't like him to be sarcastic, but he and this doctor were on opposite ends.

Narrowing his eyes slightly, the doctor said, "The medications help stabilize him." He looked as if he was trying hard to keep his temper under control.

"You've had him more than a week now. There's been no real improvement to speak of."

"That's not true," Dr. Doyle said, squaring his shoulders. "He's speaking now. Says a few words when he wants something. And he's taking long walks each day."

"His nightmares are getting worse, according to Matthew."

"Those are called flashbacks and they're to be expected." The doctor put his pen back in his coat pocket. "You've got to give us time." He turned to go but then spun around. "Look, Mr. Zook, your brother is psychologically damaged. He may never get well. You need to keep your expectations in line with reality."

"I do, I do." Cal patted the doctor on the back. "I call it faith."

Later that day, when Bud dropped Jorie off at Stoney Creek, Marge and Atlee met her at the door.

"How did Ben seem to you?" Marge asked, concerned.

"He didn't seem to recognize me, if that's what you meant." Jorie hung her bonnet on the peg. "But he looked better than I expected." She sat in a chair. "It was his eyes that worried me the most. He was Ben, but not Ben."

Her grandmother was bustling around the kitchen, gathering ingredients to prepare biscuits. "That Caleb, the firstborn, he's the pick of that Zook litter. Always the serious one, deliberate and thoughtful, even as a boy." Marge scooped flour into a wooden bowl. "Well, if I were you, I'd be sweet-talking that Caleb into romancing you before Ben snaps out of his funk."

Atlee sighed. "I'd hardly call it a funk, Marge. Our Jorie knows what she's doing. Leave her be."

Jorie was watching her grandmother mix ingredients for the biscuits with a growing spike of concern. Marge made biscuits once or twice a week from a family recipe that she knew by heart. Today, after measuring the dry ingredients—flour, baking soda, and salt—she grabbed a can of tuna fish and started to open it. She was just about to dump the can into the flour when Jorie jumped up and held her wrist.

"I don't think tuna fish is supposed to go in the biscuits," she said gently.

Marge blinked a few times at the can of tuna fish in her hand, as if she didn't know how it got there. "Oh my," she said, flustered. "Oh my. I can't talk and cook anymore." She put the can down. "Maybe you could finish those biscuits, Jorie, while I go take down the laundry before it rains." Marge washed her hands in the sink, dried them on her apron, and hurried outside, avoiding Atlee and Jorie's eyes.

Atlee watched Marge go and Jorie wondered what was going through his head. Her grandfather wasn't one for sharing his thoughts. Quietly, she asked, "Do you think she should see a doctor?"

Atlee jerked his head back toward Jorie. "No. She's just a little overtired lately, is all." He got up and went to the barn, his place of refuge.

Jorie turned her attention back to the wooden bowl and added the liquid ingredients to the flour to make dough. As she gently kneaded, she set aside her worries of her grandmother and picked up her worries about Ben. Cal had prepared her well. She didn't expect much of a response from Ben and she didn't get one. She felt a twinge of sorrow for Matthew, that first day, seeing Ben without being prepared for what he was like. Ben didn't really seem to recognize her, not at first, anyway. When it was time to leave, she squeezed his hands in hers and she felt a squeeze in return, ever so slightly. But, maybe not. Maybe she was just wishing for some glimmer of recognition.

She thought back to one of the last times she had seen him. He had just returned from the Armed Forces Recruiting Office with the news that he was being sent to Vietnam as a stretcher bearer.

"You have to go back and make them change it, Ben!" she had said when he told her.

"No," he said, too calmly. "I want to go, Jorie. It's my only chance to see the world."

"You did this on purpose, didn't you? You signed up to go!" She was furious with him.

Ben gave her a cat-in-the-cream smile. "Aw, Jorie, you won't tell, will you?"

She was silent for a long moment, gathering her thoughts. It was so like Ben, to act on impulse before the fire in his belly had time to cool down. "I won't tell, but I won't be waiting for you either. You put yourself in this situation. You'll be sorry for it one day."

Now, those words seemed prophetic.

At the time, though, Ben only laughed and slipped his arms around her waist to pull her close for a kiss to say goodbye. "If you marry some hapless farmer while I'm gone, then you'll be the sorry one, Jorie King."

But she wasn't going to marry some hapless farmer. She was going to marry Caleb Zook, a fine man. A wonderful man. At least, she *was* going to marry him until Ben returned.

Now, she didn't know what was going to become of them.

Later that week, Matthew slid open the barn door at Beacon Hollow and shouted, "Cal! Cal! Where are you?"

Cal and Ephraim came out of the tack room, surprised to see Matthew. "What are you doing here? How did you get here?"

"Hitchhiked," he said, still out of breath. "You're not going to like what I have to tell you."

Cal pointed to a hay bale. "Sit down and catch your breath."

Matthew sat down, his hands on his knees. "They're giving treatments to Ben. Twice, now. It's making him seem weird too. He's back to just staring out the window."

"What kind of treatments?"

"It's called electroshock therapy. The doctor zaps Ben's brain with electric jolts to make him forget things."

Ephraim's eyes went wide. "L-like a l-lightning bolt?"

Cal took a deep breath and looked at the clock in the barn. "Let's go get Bud." He turned to Ephraim. "Can you handle the milking, Ephraim? I may not be back in time. You can ask Amos Esh or Samuel Riehl for help."

Ephraim nodded. "I c-can handle it."

"You can't forget and get to them late. You know they'll try to step on your feet when they see you coming with the milking pump." Cal's face filled with worry. "Maybe you should stay here, Matthew."

"I can't, Cal," Matthew said. "I need to work in the morning."

"I said I c-can handle it, C-Cal," Ephraim said more forcefully. "I've done M-Matthew's j-job since he l-left."

Matthew looked at the earnest face on his little brother's face. It seemed that every time he came home, Ephraim had grown another couple of inches. He wasn't a little boy anymore. "He can do it, Cal."

Cal nodded. "Of course you can. It's a big job, though, thirty cows. Keep Maggie in the house while you're milking." He squeezed Ephraim's shoulder. "Just don't be late for them and you shouldn't have any problem."

Cal told Bud and Matthew to wait in the car in the parking lot of the Veterans Hospital, he would only be a few moments. The truth was, he wanted to keep Matthew out of this and not jeopardize his job. Cal walked past Lottie at the nurses' station and went straight to Ben's room, scooped him up from the chair in his large arms, and carried him out like a rag doll.

Lottie must have alerted Dr. Doyle because he appeared out of nowhere and stopped Cal in the hallway. "Hold on there, Mr. Zook. You can't just take a patient out without being released."

"Yes, I can," Cal said, shifting Ben's featherlight body for a standoff.

"No, you can't," Dr. Doyle insisted. "There are procedures!"

"You didn't ask me about any procedures before you gave my brother this electric therapy."

"It's part of our treatment here. We've been doing ECT for two decades now with remarkable results. It helps the patients forget unpleasant memories."

Cal peered seriously at the doctor. "We are shaped by our life experiences, both good and bad."

The doctor blanched. "ECT is not a moral issue. It's a medical treatment."

"It isn't right to play God and suppress a man's memory."

"We're just trying to help these men live as normal a life as they possibly can."

Cal shook his head. "Now, Doctor, I do appreciate that you are trying to help Ben. I really do. But if I don't even have electricity in my home, why would I let you put it into my brother's head?"

The doctor held his breath for a long moment, then gave a loud exhale. "Mr. Zook, you remind me at times of a granite wall. An unmovable granite wall."

"'They that trust in the Lord shall be as mount Zion, which cannot be removed.'"

The doctor gave Cal a look as if he thought he might belong on the ward too. Then he shook his head and looked through Ben's file, scanning pages until he found what he was looking for. "Fine!" He slammed the folder shut. "Your brother's service date was officially over a few weeks ago, anyway. If you want him, he's yours."

"Just like that?" Cal asked, a broad smile covering his face.

"Sign off on paperwork and he's all yours." The doctor brushed the palms of his hands. "I wash my hands of him." He sighed. "Would you at least put him in a wheelchair when you take him out of here."

After signing release papers, Lottie handed Cal a white paper bag filled with amber-colored bottles. "These are all of his medications," she said. "They're clearly labeled. Little orange ones are sleeping pills. Blue ones are antidepressants. Big pink ones are tranquilizers."

Cal thanked her for her kindness to Ben. Lottie leaned down, planted a kiss on Ben's forehead, and disappeared down the hallway, her rubber soles squeaking on the tiled floor.

As they passed through the front door of the hospital, Cal tossed the bag of pills in the nearest garbage can.

Dusk set in early on that late winter afternoon. It was nearly dark when Bud drove back into the drive at Beacon Hollow. Maggie had heard the car and ran out to greet them. Cal jumped out of the passenger side and opened the back door, helping Ben ease out of the car the way he helped the aunties step down from the buggy. Then Cal picked him up and carried him to the house. He smiled when he saw the wide-eyed look on Maggie's small face.

"This is your uncle, Maggie, come home."

14

These last few days Ben had spent a good part of the time in bed. Maggie and Ephraim took turns reading to him, which, Cal thought, seemed to comfort him. Lizzie made all kinds of tempting treats to coax him to eat and he did try to oblige her, though Cal knew he didn't have much appetite. He hadn't come downstairs for meals yet, nor did he participate in evening prayers. But there was a little improvement, Cal noticed, with each passing day. He thought it had to do with getting Ben off of all of those drugs. Ben didn't say much, but he was starting to answer questions, as long as they weren't too penetrating. Cal had the feeling that he just didn't remember much. But once, Cal made the mistake of referring to Vietnam, and he could see Ben recoil and close himself off, as real as if he had blown out the light in a lantern. In that instant, though, Cal caught a glimpse of the horror that lived within him.

After Ben had been at Beacon Hollow over a week, Cal heard him get up and go downstairs in the middle of the night, then the kitchen door—a stubborn door to close—was pulled shut. Cal looked out his window and saw Ben, in the bright moonlight,

219

walk down the long drive of Beacon Hollow toward the road. He watched him for a long while, unsure if he should go after him or leave him be. He finally decided to let Ben have this time to heal. He had to trust in the Lord to take care of him, to take care of them all.

Every day after school, Jorie stopped by Beacon Hollow to see Ben, but he was always upstairs, sleeping. He had been back well over a week now. Ephraim had told her that he stayed mostly in bed, though he was starting to take meals with the family.

During breakfast one morning, Marge said she was planning to pay a call to Ben. She had been brewing up a curative for him and was eager to try it out.

"Please, Jorie, go with her," Atlee whispered when Marge was out of earshot. "It makes her happy to think she can doctor him."

As soon as school let out, Jorie walked her grandmother over to Beacon Hollow. She was relieved that she didn't see Cal anywhere, though she hadn't really expected to. She knew he was busy plowing the fields for spring planting. They hadn't spoken much in the last few weeks, and the silence that was wedged between them felt like it was stretching them further and further apart.

Jorie and Marge had just climbed the kitchen steps when Lizzie threw open the door, welcoming them in. "You're just in time!" she called out. "Freshly made doughnuts! Made from my secret recipe. I call them 'Sleeper, Awake! Doughnuts.'"

Jorie and Marge took off their bonnets and capes and handed them to Lizzie.

"I've been pulling out all the stops, making the most tempting, best-smelling food I can think of, trying to lure that Ben downstairs." Lizzie smiled, conspiratorially. "And it's been working! For two days now, he's been coming down, about this time of day." She glanced up the stairs. "Just see if it doesn't work!"

"Have you been having many visitors?" Marge asked, raising an eyebrow at Jorie, who had told her grandmother that no one was visiting Ben yet.

"Gobs! Of course, Cal's been real protective of Ben and doesn't let anybody go upstairs poking their nose at him. That Ben, he's as skittish as a newborn lamb. But yesterday, he was down here and didn't even skedaddle when the aunties came calling." Lizzie poured the coffee into three cups. She stopped and got a fourth. "You just wait and see. He'll be down. No one can resist my doughnuts." She took a dishrag and whirled it around the kitchen, fanning the smell up the stairs.

Jorie had to hold back a laugh as Ephraim and Maggie came galloping up the basement stairs, following their noses. They were all talking together at the kitchen table, dipping the doughnuts in coffee or milk, when suddenly Jorie felt someone's eyes on her. She glanced toward the stairs.

There was Ben. She almost gasped at the sight of him: he looked thin, so thin, and pale, with dark circles under his eyes. And his eyes—usually so bright, filled with mischief—they looked flat and empty. Jorie put down her doughnut and went to him.

"Jorie," he said so softly she thought she might have imagined it.

She reached out a hand for his. "I saw you in the hospital awhile ago, but I don't know if you remember that I came."

"I remember," he said. His voice cracked a little, rusty from lack of use. They held each others' gaze for a long while, when suddenly the kitchen door opened and Cal walked in. He stopped abruptly when he saw Jorie. A look of unspeakable sadness came over his face, but then he recovered almost instantly and the look vanished, replaced with a gentle smile.

"Marge, Jorie, glad you came," Cal said, but avoided their eyes when he spoke. "Those doughnuts can be smelled in the next town over, Lizzie. They drive a man to distraction." He washed up at the kitchen sink. "Please, sit down, ladies. Ben, have a doughnut before they get cold." He tossed a doughnut to Ben, who caught it, then grabbed one for himself and went to the door.

"Cal, stay and join us," Jorie said.

"Can't," he said, stopping at the doorjamb. "Time to start the milking."

Automatically, Ephraim scraped the chair back as he rose to join Cal.

"I'll come too," Maggie said.

Cal warded them off. "Ephraim, finish your doughnuts first. And Maggie, you stay. Practice being a host."

Maggie rolled her eyes and plopped back in the chair as her father closed the door behind him.

Ben sat at the table as Lizzie poured a cup of coffee for him. His hands were restless, drawing circles in the oilcloth. Everyone else was distracted by Ephraim, stuffing his mouth full of doughnuts, washing them down with milk, wiping his mouth with his sleeve before bolting out the door. Maggie watched him go, looking like she'd rather be in the barn.

An awkward silence fell over the table, until Marge opened the bag she brought with her. "Now Ben, I've been working on some remedies for you." She pulled out bottles of mixed dried herbs. "Steep them, like a tea. One fourth teaspoon to one cup of hot water should do. This one is to help you sleep. And this one is to give you energy. And this one will cure fever, stomach pain, and diarrhea. It's a mixture of cayenne pepper and salt. In fact, it'll cure constipation too."

Ben's eyes went wide at that and Jorie nearly laughed out loud.

"Uh, thank you, Marge. Valuable stuff," he said and wiggled his eyebrows at Jorie. She did laugh then. It was something Ben used to do at her during church meetings when the preacher said something very serious that he thought was ridiculous.

Marge continued to pull out bottles of herbs, describing the contents, until Jorie could see a wave of exhaustion roll over Ben. His face suddenly seemed haggard, almost gray. "If you'll excuse me, ladies, I'm a little worn out." He went back upstairs, holding on to the rail as if he didn't quite trust his own balance.

After he left, Lizzie looked at Jorie's face. "Now don't go feeling too badly. The aunties wore him out in just a few minutes. And that was the most words I've heard out of him all week."

Jorie smiled and plucked their bonnets and capes off of the wall pegs. "We should be going too, Lizzie. My grandfather likes his dinner at the same time, every night."

As she helped her grandmother down the steps on the front lawn, she glanced up at the second story of the farmhouse and saw Ben at the window. She waved to him. When she turned back, there was Cal, standing at the open barn door, watching her. When their eyes met, he dropped his head and turned to go into the barn.

"How does he seem to you?" Cal asked Jorie two weeks later when he stopped by the schoolhouse late one afternoon on a cold, wet day. "Ben, I mean. I was just wondering what you thought. How does he seem?"

Jorie was surprised to see him. Cal had been studiously avoiding being alone with her since Ben returned home. Any conversation between them was drawn and tight, carefully guarded. She saw him from a distance when she stopped by Beacon Hollow to see Ben, which was often. It was hard to see Cal but not be able to chat like they used to, laugh like they used to, and share private smiles like they used to.

"At times he seems like the old Ben." She hesitated. "But . . ."

"But other times, he seems like a stranger."

She nodded.

"He has terrible nightmares. I wake him up but he can't remember a thing. Or he doesn't want to tell me." Cal paced up and down the aisle. "Then he goes out walking in the night. I have no idea where he goes . . . just walking. When he comes back, he sleeps away most of the day."

"He's certainly getting better each time I see him. He's gaining weight and his color is better. His eyes seem brighter too."

"He seems angry," Cal said. He looked so discouraged.

"Maybe. But underneath the anger, I think he's wounded."

Cal took his hat off and spun it around in his hands. "Do you think it was a mistake, taking him out of the hospital?"

Jorie shrugged. "I'm not sure the hospital was going to ever be able to fix him." She wasn't sure any of them could. She picked up her books and headed to the door.

Cal followed her outside, waiting while she locked up.

"How could this have happened, Jorie? How could Ben have veered so far off course? I spend more time worrying about Ben than I do Maggie and Ephraim and Matthew altogether." He started to say something else, then stopped and looked away.

She wondered what he was about to say. Was he going to say

that he worried about her too? That he missed her? Did he ever wonder whether they would be able to find their way to each other? Did he even want her anymore? But she didn't say anything. She let the silence between them lay there. Silence that was heavy and full of words that weren't being said.

He looked up at the sky, then right back at her, and she saw all she needed to see.

Spring weather was always unsettled. One day in mid-April, the rain came in waves, beating down all morning. Just as the first grade finished reciting addition facts, Maggie asked if she could go to the outhouse.

Jorie glanced out the window. It was like someone was pouring an ocean's worth of water on the ground. "Maggie, you need to wait until the rain has passed. You'll get as soaked as if you'd jumped in the creek."

"But I can't wait!" Maggie had one leg crossed over the other and was squeezing tight.

"Try thinking about something else," Jorie said firmly. She gathered the second grade to the front of the classroom, when suddenly the room became dim. She lit a lantern and hung it from the ceiling—something she only did on the darkest of winter days. Thunder rumbled in the distance, then a blazing white light pierced the sky.

One of the boys called out, "One one thousand, two one thousand, three one thousand," until a great clap of thunder shocked him silent. Jorie went to the window and studied the clouds. To the north, the sky had an eerie greenish-blue glow. To the east, heavy, low clouds were scudding over the fields. The boys had noticed the strange-looking sky, too, and were hanging by the window. "Let's get back to work," she told them. She gave them a look that meant no kidding around. She was accustomed to thunder and lightning storms, but something felt portentous to her.

"It's going to be a wild one," Eli Schlabach said with a grin.

The sky split with a resounding crash of thunder, so loud it shook the lantern. "That's it," Jorie said. "Down we go."

The basement stairs were on the back porch. As she herded the children down the concrete steps, she spotted Cal running toward her at full speed. "Get in there. Fast. Bud heard on the news that four storms are coming in from different directions."

"It's miles away. Not at all dangerous," Eli said with great authority, as if he could predict where storms would collide.

"I think it's heading north," Ray added, suddenly another expert weatherman.

Once inside, they squinted at the clouds through the dusty basement transom windows as Cal latched the basement doors shut.

"Where's Maggie?" Cal asked, eyes sweeping over the frightened children.

For an instant, Jorie froze in a sick panic. "Outhouse!"

She leaped forward, unlatched the door, and dashed up the concrete steps, Cal racing behind her. It was hard to walk in a straight line because of the wind, and they held hands for stability, fighting their way across the schoolyard. When they reached the outhouse, Cal yanked open the door and found Maggie huddled in the corner, terrified.

When Maggie saw her father, she flew into his arms. He snatched her up and held her tight to his chest as he carried her to the basement steps.

Cal handed Maggie to Jorie and yanked the basement doors

shut. It took numerous times, fighting the gusts of wind. "Jorie! Jorie! I need your help."

While he held the doors, she jerked the latch shut. Satisfied, they went back down into the basement. The rain fell heavy and loud, drowning out conversation. Jorie made all of the children sit down in the corner, supposedly the safest place to be. Everyone sat but Cal. He stood looking out the transom window. There was a blue-white flash, dazzlingly bright, and what sounded like a bomb going off. Then they heard a loud crack and the sound of splitting timber, followed by a crash.

He turned to look at Jorie at the exact moment that she looked at him. "Lightning struck the elm tree."

The wind continued to blow, not in fits and gusts, but with sustained howls that made her wonder if the schoolhouse windows might shatter from the pressure. Jorie didn't know how much time had passed until the wind died down and the rain slowed its pounding. When sunlight streaked through the transom window, Cal still made them wait. He kept peering out the window to see as far as he could see, making sure they weren't getting fooled by the eye of the storm, that it had truly passed them by. Then he gave a nod and the boys jumped up to unlatch the basement doors.

"That was a doozy!" Eli hollered, leaping outside to survey the destruction.

Jorie walked around the sides of the schoolhouse, picking her way carefully over the broken glass of the windows. When she came to the far side, she gasped. An enormous branch of the elm tree had dropped directly onto the outhouse, destroying it. The roof was torn off, the sides were split apart. She stood there for a moment, gripping her elbows, heart pounding.

Cal came around the corner, holding Maggie by the hand, and stopped abruptly when he saw the obliterated outhouse. He looked at Jorie with a stunned expression and then turned to the children. "All of you, get your coats and lunch pails and go straight home so your parents know you're safe."

As soon as the children were gone, all but Maggie, he turned to Jorie. "How could you have let Maggie go outside with that weather brewing?"

Jorie looked at Maggie, who tucked her chin to her chest.

Ephraim came running around the corner and skidded to a stop when he saw the outhouse. "Cal, that c-could have b-been our Maggie!"

"But it wasn't," Cal said sharply. "The good Lord protected her. Ephraim, take Maggie and get started home. I'll catch up."

He handed Maggie off to Ephraim. She kept her head low as she passed Jorie.

When Jorie and Cal were left alone, he turned to her with angry eyes. "How could you be so careless? What kind of teacher sends a child out in that weather and then *forgets* about her?" His glance shifted over Jorie's shoulder. "Esther, quit your eavesdropping and get home. Now!"

Esther gasped at Cal's sharp scolding, burst into tears, then turned and ran.

"Jorie!" Cal barked in a cold, steely voice that made her flinch. "Have you nothing to say for yourself?"

Words felt stuck in Jorie's throat. She couldn't stop staring at the outhouse. What if the lightning strike had happened a few minutes earlier? What if Maggie *had* been in it? She felt as if she was stuck in a bad dream. She couldn't even think to defend herself; her heart was pounding so loud she could hear it in the quiet. She only closed her eyes, aware that Cal was waiting for an answer. A ragged silence fell between them and the crack that had started with Ben's return split into a chasm.

"Cal!" Ephraim burst around the corner, panting. "Cal, you've g-got to come! Lizzie is d-down the road. She says to t-tell you to c-come q-quick. Ben is acting as c-crazy as a M-March hare. He's hollering at the s-sky and c-cussing at it."

Cal ran back to Beacon Hollow and found Ben outside, down by the willow tree, soaked to the skin, but no longer shaking his fist at the sky like Lizzie described. Instead, he was on his knees, tears streaming down his face, breathing hard. Cal told Ephraim and Maggie and Lizzie to go in the house and leave them alone, and he just sat down next to Ben. Waiting, just waiting. He was waiting for Ben to spill out whatever it was that was eating at him.

After a time, Ben's breathing returned to normal and he seemed calmer. He eased back to sit on his feet. Finally, he wiped his face with the back of his sleeve. "That thunder, it just . . . it sounded like gunshots," was all he offered as an explanation.

"That Dr. Doyle mentioned something about how noises could trigger flashbacks," Cal said quietly. "But it was just a bad storm." He knew not to ask anything, that it could cause Ben to clam up, but he hoped he might elaborate.

He didn't. Ben gazed out at the field. "Your wheat's ruined."

Cal groaned as he took in the sight. Just this morning he had thanked God for the fields that were greening with the first shoots of spring. Those green shoots were now flattened. The center of the field, always a low spot, looked like a muddy pond.

Ben slowly eased himself to a stand.

Well, Cal thought, as they walked back to the house, *I can thank God for Maggie's narrow escape in spite of the storm. And because of the storm, I can thank God that Ben is out of bed and talking. Two miracles in one day.*

As Cal finished milking the last cow that afternoon, he was grateful for the routine of work in his life. It gave him deep satisfaction, to end each day caring for his dairy. As he looked over each cow, checking each one to make sure she was settled for the night, he realized that work was the best medicine God could give a man. He had a sense, maybe an answer to a prayer he hadn't yet asked, that it was time to ask more of Ben. He decided that he would give Ben and Ephraim the job of building a new outhouse and repairing the windows to the schoolhouse.

When Cal came inside, he found Ben seated at the kitchen table. Maggie was setting the table for dinner. Ephraim was still out in the barn, sweeping up, and Lizzie was stirring the stew she had made.

Washing his hands at the sink, Cal felt such gratitude to the Lord for the comforts of a home. "Ben, I could sure use your help building a new outhouse for the school. You and Ephraim could take it on tomorrow. I can get the lumber from town in the morning and get you set up." He turned around, drying his hands on a rag. "You were always the best carpenter of us all."

Ben had been drawing circles in the tablecloth with his fingers. Cal wondered how he could live with such restlessness inside himself. It would, he thought, be like trying to stare into the sun. But after Cal asked him the question, Ben's hands stopped.

"Remember when you broke your thumb?" Ben asked.

Cal tilted his head, stunned. "I hadn't thought about that in years." He lifted his hand and spread out his fingers. His thumb remained slightly bent; it hadn't healed properly and he couldn't straighten it fully. They had been young boys when it happened, younger than Ephraim. They were at a barn raising and were given

230

the job of pounding in nails that men had started. Ben tried to turn it into a race, like always, and Cal had ended up hitting his hand so hard it broke his thumb.

Laughter burst out of Cal, surprising him. It stemmed from the memory, and from the joy that Ben was finally rejoining the human race. Once started, Cal couldn't stop. He laughed so hard he buckled at the waist. Ben couldn't help but laugh in return, which got Maggie giggling, and soon, Lizzie joined in. When Ephraim came inside, he looked at all of them as if they had lost their senses, which only got them laughing more.

Wiping his face with his hands, Cal realized he hadn't laughed so hard in a long, long time, and it felt good, so good.

Sylvia had never seen her daughter in such a state. As soon as Esther arrived home from school, she explained—between sobs—all that had gone on that afternoon, claiming it had given her a horrendous headache. Sylvia made a cup of chamomile tea for her and sent her straight to bed to rest. Esther was such a delicate child and not only did she have to endure a terrifying electrical storm, but then she was unjustly snapped at by Caleb Zook! In all the years Sylvia had known him, she had never heard a harsh word out of that man's mouth. Until today. It grieved her, because she knew he was under terrible stress. How close they came to losing Maggie today! All because of Jorie King's poor judgment. She whispered a quick word of thanks to the Lord Almighty that he protected Maggie.

She glanced at the kitchen clock on the wall and plucked her bonnet off the hook. There was just enough time before dinner to go speak to the deacon about this troubling situation. Something *had* to be done.

Early the next morning, Cal drove the wagon to the school-house and dropped Ben and Ephraim off to dismantle what re-mained of the outhouse. He hadn't expected to see Jorie there so early. When she heard the wagon, she came outside to see what was going on.

"We'll have this outhouse rebuilt today and the windows replaced," Cal told her, "so school won't be disrupted. And if it's all right with you, Ephraim will help Ben with the building today."

She nodded but didn't say anything more to him. There was a hardness between them, he knew, from yesterday. He should be quick to forgive, but he wasn't quite ready to overlook what a close call Maggie had experienced. And Jorie wasn't exactly feeling too friendly with him, he could tell. She avoided him. In fact, her eyes, he noticed, were on Ben, as if she still couldn't believe he was here, among them. He couldn't blame her; he felt the same way.

By the time Cal returned from the hardware store with lumber and supplies, the school day was under way. The boys kept pop-ping their heads out the window to catch sight of the legendary Benjamin Zook, the Amish man who had gone to Vietnam and died, only to be back among the living. He was pleased to see how effectively Jorie reeled them back in. From what he could observe, the scholars went through their day with routine, giving Jorie respect.

During lunch, Ben pitched softball to the children in the schoolyard while Jorie watched and cheered. Once, the ball landed near her and she lobbed it overhead to Ben at the pitcher's mound, laughing in that soft way she had, like honey pouring out of a jar.

Cal tried to concentrate on measuring a board, but his eyes kept riveting toward Jorie. The wind lifted a stray lock of her copper-colored hair and laid it across her cheek. Absently she coiled it and tucked it back beneath her prayer cap.

Cal continued working during the softball game until Maggie ran up to him and pulled him by the hand to come pinch hit for her team. When Cal went up to bat, he swung the bat a few times to warm up.

"Take all the warm-up swings you need, Cal," Ben said in his teasing voice. "You still can't touch my pitch." Ben wound up and fired, frowning when Cal hit a foul ball. "Strike one!" Ben called out.

The second ball went past Cal so hard and fast that he swung and missed. Jorie clapped her hands together like a young girl.

Cal looked at Jorie and thought her eyes were shining bright and soft as spring sunshine. He knew she was trying hard not to laugh at him.

A look of boyish mischievousness flashed across Ben's face. He rubbed the ball in his hands, eyed Cal carefully, and threw a pitch that nailed him on the forehead, knocking him down. There was a moment of stunned silence before Jorie raced to Cal's side and knelt beside him.

"Cal, are you all right?" Concern covered her face.

Cal was flat on his back, dazed, looking up at the sky, seeing stars. He wasn't sure what stung more, the bruise on his forehead or the one on his foolish pride.

"Ben, how could you do such a thing?" Jorie accused when he came over to examine Cal.

Cal pushed himself up as far as his knees. "It was an accident, that's all," he said.

Ben helped Cal to his feet and patted him on his back. "See?

He's fine." He turned to Ephraim. "Let's go finish building that outhouse."

Even though Cal wouldn't have admitted so to Jorie, he was pretty sure that Ben aimed that softball to intentionally hit him. Ben always had flawless aim.

As long as Cal could remember, Ben turned everything into contests between them. He seemed determined to one-up Cal, and Cal always obliged him, content to let Ben triumph. He didn't feel a rivalry toward Ben, which only seemed to exacerbate the situation. Ben was like that, quick to anger. Usually, just as quick to get over it.

But Cal sensed that Ben had been changed, altered deep, by whatever had happened to him in Vietnam, and in some way that he didn't understand. Ben couldn't concentrate on a task. He was never still or calm, as if he was trying to distract himself from letting his mind settle on something disturbing. He was constantly on edge. During evening prayers, Ben acted bored or fidgety, uncomfortable.

It worried Cal, because even though Ben was acting more like himself every day, something about him remained more lost. Lost to their family, lost to the church. Cal hoped and prayed that he wasn't lost to God.

15

Late one evening, a couple of weeks after the great storm, Jorie woke to the sound of someone pounding on the kitchen door. She threw on a robe and hurried downstairs. Standing outside was Ben. Next to him was Marge, in her nightgown and bare feet, wrapped in Ben's coat.

"Missing someone?" Ben asked, as casually as if he had found a stray cat.

"Mammi! *What* are you doing?" Jorie asked, pulling her grandmother inside.

"I thought I heard the rooster crow, so I went to get the eggs from the henhouse," Marge said. She held up an empty basket. "But then I got a little turned around."

"She was down by her roadside stand, setting up for the day," Ben added.

Marge handed Ben back his coat, scowling at him. "So I was a little early for the day's business."

"I'll say!" Ben laughed. "About two months early."

Marge put her hands on her hips and glared at him, annoyed. Then her face softened. "Oh, you still look positively wrung out,

235

Ben." She brightened. "I have just the thing for you. A spring tonic that thins the blood and will have you fit as a fiddle in no time. It's made of sassafras tea, from the inner bark of the root that makes the finest tea. The very best flavor is stored in the root when the tree is dormant. And . . ." Her voice trailed off, as if she couldn't remember what she was talking about. She was silent uncomfortably long, almost as though she had forgotten Ben and Jorie were there. Then she remembered herself with a start. She lifted a finger in the air. "And I've got some new remedies too. I'll go get them." She went to the stairwell and slowly walked up the steps.

Jorie turned to Ben, feeling thoroughly bewildered by her grandmother's odd behavior.

Ben, though, was amused. "She told me about a pinworm cure she named Devil's Bait." He wiggled his eyebrows. "I pray I'll never need it."

Jorie plopped down on a kitchen chair. "I don't know what's wrong with her lately."

Ben sat down next to her. "Aw, Jorie. She's always been a bit of a . . . character."

Jorie winced. "This is different. She's never been like this."

"Haven't you taken her to a doctor?"

"My grandfather doesn't think it's necessary."

Ben's eyes went up the stairwell. "Well, sure. He slept through her night sojourn."

The wind pushed the door open, blowing in a gust of cold air before Jorie jumped up to shut it. "The hinges on this door are practically falling off."

Ben stared at the door for a long moment, mesmerized.

The strange look on his face puzzled her. "What is it, Ben?"

Still staring at the door, he said, "I'm starting to remember things, more and more. It's like a fog, lifting slowly."

Softly, she asked, "What are you remembering right now?"

It was awhile before he answered her. "When I was in the looney bin, the first one, the one in Bangkok, there was a row of doors right by my bed. The doors barely hung on these old rusty hinges. All day long, I stared at those doors, all hanging on those fragile hinges. That's what my mind was like. Hanging on a fragile hinge. Still clinging, still holding on, but with a big gust of wind . . . *whoosh!* Anything could happen." He turned his gaze from the door back to her, looking directly into Jorie's eyes with a hint of pity.

He held her gaze until the truth of what he said hit her. Her grandmother's mind was coming unhinged.

Ben reached over and covered her hand with his.

A spring storm came through in the middle of the night. Lightning flashed through the sky and thunder rattled the glass in the windows. In the morning, the storm had lapsed into slow, even sheets of rain that paused for a minute or an hour, but soon returned. Cal took out his list of chores and divided them up among Ephraim and Ben. The two went out to the barn to muck out the horse stalls and the stanchions of the dairy cows.

Ben took the nine-tine pitchfork off the wall and handed the four-tine pitchfork to Ephraim. "Some things just never change."

Ephraim looked around for the wheelbarrow.

"Seems like I've been doing this my whole life," Ben said, sliding open the door to a horse stall.

Ephraim snorted. "L-long as we k-keep f-feeding them, we'll k-keep c-cleaning up after 'em."

"And just what is Cal doing while we're doing this work?"

Ephraim gave him a sharp look. Ben's hostile tone caught him off-guard. "He's p-paying bills. S-So?"

"Just seems like he gives us a laundry list of hard things to do while he does the easy stuff."

Ephraim never thought about chores like that, like they had a value assigned to them. There were just things that had to get done and they all had to do them. He'd seen Cal muck out the stalls plenty of times.

Bud walked in as they were just about to get started. "Hello, boys. Ben, you're looking more like yourself every time I see you." He walked over to the workbench. "I wonder if I could borrow Cal's split maul?"

Ben opened up a drawer at the workbench and pulled out the maul. "Here it is. Let me sharpen the edge for you." He went to the grind wheel and poured some water on it. "Bud, why would you call it Cal's split maul?"

Bud watched as Ben started the wheel rolling and ran the maul's edge along it. "What *should* I call it?"

"Why not Beacon Hollow's split maul? Why does it have to be Cal's?"

Bud gave Ben a strange look. "What does it matter?"

Ben finished sharpening the edge, wiped it with a rag, and handed it to Bud. "Just wondered, that's all."

"I suppose I call it Cal's because he's the one who's been taking care of this place since your dad passed."

"Now, that's my point," Ben said. "If Dad hadn't passed when he did, Beacon Hollow wouldn't be Cal's." He turned to Ephraim. "Rightly so, it should be Ephraim's one day. The Amish pass the farm to the youngest son."

Ephraim looked at Ben. "Cal always s-says we'll d-divide it or f-figure it out when the t-time comes."

Ben shrugged. "Maybe so. Maybe not."

Bud raised an eyebrow. "Like I said, Ben, you're more like your old self every time I see you."

A perfect fingernail moon shone down from the midnight sky onto the Kings' dark farmhouse. Jorie woke with a start, knowing that something was stirring in the barn. She dressed quickly, grabbed a flashlight and a blanket, and hurried to the barn. As soon as she slid open the barn door, she knew what sound had woken her: a horse was set to foal. All of the horses were shuffling nervously in their stalls. She walked down the corridor to the foaling stalls, past each pregnant mare—with their enormously swollen bellies—and stopped when she came to Fancy. The horse was pawing almost frantically in the straw with her forefeet to make a nest. Fancy was a maiden mare and Jorie knew it could be a long night ahead, but she didn't mind. She loved the barn at night. She loved the barn during the day too, but at night, it felt like a different world. The sweet scent of hay and oats, the sour tang of manure, the richness of leather harnesses, the gentle sounds of the horses, shuffling and snorting.

She lit a lantern and hung it on a hook, then checked and re-checked the foaling basket stuffed with all sorts of useful birthing objects—towels, scissors, iodine, rubbing alcohol, garbage bags, thermometer, twine, clamps. Her concentration was interrupted by the rumble of the barn door sliding open. She slipped the lantern off its hook and walked to the center of the barn.

"Daadi?" she called out, sure that Atlee had come.

"It's me, Jorie. It's Ben."

At the sound of Ben's deep voice, her heart missed a beat. She waved the lantern in front of her, casting a light over him. "Why, Ben! What on earth are you doing here?"

"I was out walking and saw the light in your barn. Thought maybe something was wrong."

She pointed toward Fancy's stall. "A mare is set to foal."

"Want me to go get the vet?" he asked.

"I don't see any signs of trouble so far." Jorie walked back to Fancy's stall and put the lantern on the hook. Ben followed her. "As long as things seem to be progressing, I'd rather let nature be her midwife."

She leaned her arms against the top of the stall railing as she watched Fancy lay down on her side, her hind legs stiffen and start to quiver. Signs that hard labor had begun. Standing behind Jorie, Ben raised his arm and leaned against the post. As focused on Fancy as Jorie was, she was aware of how close Ben was to her. He smelled of laurel soap and the crisp night air.

A thin white bubble—the amniotic sac—appeared in the opening under Fancy's tail, then disappeared. She lifted her head as a contraction hit. Her neck stretched out, her upper lip peeled back, her whole body strained, her eyes bulged. When the contraction ended, Fancy groaned and dropped her head into the straw. Yet for all of her laboring, the mare was silent, except for a grunt deep in her throat.

"Why doesn't she just let loose a whinny?" Ben asked quietly.

Jorie lifted her head to look at him and was surprised to see he appeared to be suffering right alongside the mare. "Probably just an instinct, so that wild animals won't know she's given birth."

Fancy's opening widened, and more of the white membrane appeared. Jorie could see the emerging foal's front hooves, then a small nose. Relief flooded through her. This foal knew how to make a proper appearance. A loud *whoosh* broke the quiet, and the black mass slid out of the womb like a chute, landing in the nest of hay that Fancy had prepared. Jorie grabbed a towel, slipped quietly into the stall, and rubbed the foal's head and body roughly, trying to wipe the amnion away from its nostrils. She laughed as the foal came to life, lifting its head and gasping for air.

Fancy turned her long neck, stretched her nose out toward her baby, sniffed, snorted, and rumbled in recognition. Then she came to life, heaving and shuddering and scrambling to her feet, eager to nuzzle and lick her baby.

"A filly," Ben said quietly. "Solid black. You should name her Indigo." His eyes were riveted to the sight. "It's the most beautiful thing I've ever seen."

Jorie glanced at Ben, who was watching Fancy try to nudge her foal to its feet by pushing up on its little rump. A gentleness came over his face, softening his features. This was how she loved him best, with tenderness in his eyes. He could be kind, so kind.

As soon as the filly was on her feet, nursing, Jorie went to get a bucket of fresh water and some oats for Fancy while Ben cleaned up the stall. Afterward, they watched the mother and foal for a long time. The barn had quieted down and the animals had gone back to sleep.

She let her gaze roam lovingly over the interior of the barn. "I love this quiet."

Ben blanched, as if she had said something profane. "I can't stand it," he said, surprising her with its sharp, bitter tone. "The quiet makes me crazy. And I can't stand how time goes so slowly. Everything is always the same. Every day like the one before. Every year looks just like the one before."

That was exactly what Jorie loved about her life. The days, how they could flow one into the other the way a river flowed into an ocean. The slow, steady passing of time was a sweet comfort to her.

A barn owl, high in the rafters, hooted. Another hooted back. Jorie lifted her eyes to try and see where they were perched. "Give yourself time, Ben."

"For what?" he asked with a sharp bite of a laugh. "For wanting to be a farmer so I can spend the rest of my days looking at the wrong end of a horse?"

A sickening jolt rocked through Jorie. After all Ben had been through these last two years, all he had seen of the outside world, he hadn't changed. Not really. These were the same endless loops of conversations that she had with him before he left. She would try to convince him of all that was right and good about their life, and he would dismiss her thoughts with a careless shrug.

She remembered one time, after Communion, when he was as cranky as a bear with a toothache. "Ritual! That's all it is," he had complained. "Year in, year out, wash somebody's stinking feet and you're good to go for another year."

"But that's not it at all," she tried to explain. "The foot washing is meant to show our humility toward each other. We stoop—we don't even kneel for it. It's to remind us of when the Lord washed his disciples' feet—even Judas Iscariot's feet. Think about it, Ben. Our God is a *foot washing God*."

But Ben wouldn't listen to her and eventually she gave up trying to convince him. Besides, it wouldn't do any good. It never did. Ben's mind, once made up, was hard to change. He was like Cal in that way. But Cal's way of thinking was solid and reliable, like a straightly plowed furrow. Ben's thoughts zigged and zagged, first one direction, then another, as if he couldn't quite make up his mind which direction he was heading but he was definitely in motion.

There were so many things she could say to Ben in this moment. She chose what seemed the easiest, the safest. "Well, morning will be here soon. Wouldn't be right to have the teacher nodding off during a spelling bee." She took the lantern down off of its hook and blew it out. "Do you need my flashlight to find your way home?" She held it out to him.

He leaned toward her, taking care not to touch her. She stared up into his face, a face that was so dear to her.

Then he looked down at the flashlight in her hand. "Jorie, I feel like I'm suffocating."

She took a step closer to him. "Ben, what's troubling you?"

He cupped her face with his hands and his gaze wandered all over her face—eyes, cheeks, mouth—as if he was memorizing every feature. She thought he was going to kiss her, but he released her, passed around her, and slid open the door, waiting for her to follow him before he closed it behind her.

Then, without a word, he simply walked away under a sliver of a new moon.

"Uh-oh, looks like trouble just arrived," Lizzie said as she peered out the kitchen window of Beacon Hollow.

When Cal saw who climbed out of the buggy, he braced himself. Sylvia and Jonas, Samuel, and Isaac were heading to the door, somber looks on their faces. He asked Lizzie if she could get some coffee brewing and went out to welcome his company.

A few moments later, seated around the kitchen table with steaming cups of coffee, Samuel and Isaac launched into a long discussion about the weather and what the *Farmer's Almanac* predicted for the next few months. Cal knew they hadn't come to discuss the weather, but he also knew that Isaac needed time to get to his point. It concerned him that Sylvia was a part of this. It occurred to him that Isaac, in his own polite way, was waiting until Lizzie left the room.

Cal went over to the sink, where Lizzie was washing breakfast dishes, to quietly ask if she'd mind getting the laundry in before it rained. "There's not a cloud in the sky!" she objected. Then, her eyes went wide as silver dollars as she grasped what he meant. "But you never can tell about Pennsylvania springtimes, can you?"

After Lizzie went outside, Isaac sat back in his chair and spoke. "Sylvia told me about what happened in the schoolhouse. During the big storm."

"Oh?" Cal asked, lifting his eyebrows. "Because I'm pretty sure Sylvia wasn't there. I was, though."

Sylvia's face tightened. "Esther told me all about it, about how Jorie let Maggie go to the outhouse in the middle of a raging storm."

"That's not the way it went, Sylvia," Cal said. "Maggie went out before the big storm hit."

"Esther said she completely forgot about Maggie," Sylvia continued as if such a detail was minor. "According to Esther, you said so yourself. She said you called Jorie careless."

And what could Cal say to that? He wanted to defend Jorie, but the truth was, it bothered him greatly that she had been so neglectful with his daughter.

"This is just *another* reason why Maggie should be living with me," Sylvia said. "I owe it to my sister to see that her daughter is growing up well cared for."

For a moment Cal looked as if he was about to say something unpleasant—he was clearly fairly angry himself—but finally his face relaxed and he said, "Maggie is growing up just fine, Sylvia."

Isaac raised his hand. "Sylvia, you agreed to not say a word if you came this morning."

"Then why are you here, Isaac?" Cal asked frankly. "Why are you all here this morning?"

Jonas spoke up first. "We have decided that, come the end of May, Jorie King will not be asked to return to teach next year."

Cal leaned back in his chair. "All because of a big storm."

"Not at all," Jonas said. "That was just the last straw. We have had complaints all year long."

"From Esther?" Cal said with more sarcasm than he should have allowed himself.

Sylvia's eyebrows lifted.

Jonas leaned forward in his chair and pointed a finger at the table. "Let's start with renting a cottage to Dr. Robinson without consulting Isaac first."

"She spoke to me about it," Cal said. "And what she did was the right thing. We've all benefited from the doctor. You have, in particular, Jonas, when your prize cow had a nasty case of mastitis recently." He turned to Samuel, hoping he could count on him to reason with Jonas, but Samuel avoided his eyes. "So what else?"

"They haven't gotten through a single textbook yet!" Sylvia said. "Last week she sent the entire eighth grade outside on the porch with books and told them to read, read, read!"

"Thank you, Sylvia," Isaac said in a longsuffering voice. He turned to Cal. "Now Caleb, you have admitted yourself that she spends more time out of the classroom than in it."

"I might do the same thing if I had a classroom made up of seventeen boys." He folded his arms against his chest. "So, Isaac, do you agree with this?"

Isaac placed his hands on the table. "I have a doubt or two

about whether those scholars are being well prepared to pass the state exam."

"There's still a month to go," Jonas said. "There's time for a new teacher to bring them up to speed."

Isaac lifted his hands. "We will allow Jorie King to finish what she started this year. But then, Caleb, after the exam, you need to tell her that she won't be coming back next year."

"Me? Why me?" Cal asked.

"You're on the school board. And you were the one so doggoned determined to hire her," Jonas said, eyes narrowed. "So you need to finish what you started."

"That's enough," Isaac said in a dismissive tone. "We've said what we came to say." He stood. "It's time we went on our way."

16

$\mathcal{M}$atthew couldn't believe the improvement in Ben in the last week. He could hardly wait to tell Lottie and Dr. Doyle when he went back to work on Monday. *Especially* Dr. Doyle. He had the gall to call Cal "selfish and ir-responsible" for taking Ben away like he did, but that just showed how little the doctor knew. Cal was the most responsible, most unselfish person on this earth.

Sometimes, Matthew thought, a little too responsible and a little too unselfish.

At lunch on Sunday following church, Matthew could see that something was definitely amiss between Jorie and Cal. Jorie served the men at the table seated far away from Cal. More than a few times that day, Matthew caught Cal watching her with sorrow in his eyes.

At rare moments, Matthew thought, you could catch a person in an unguarded moment. What he thought and how he felt showed on his face for a brief second, before passing away.

It hurt him to see Cal suffering. First he lost Mary Ann, now he was losing Jorie. Not that Matthew knew that for sure, but he knew Ben's effect on others, especially women. It had always been that way. Ben had an easy, charming way about him that drew women to him like bees to a flower. Even Lizzie seemed to light up like a firefly when Ben was around. And she was still making every sweet and cake and pie she knew how to make, just to entice Ben to eat.

Lizzie had never baked Matthew a thing. Not one blessed thing.

That evening, at the singing for the young folks, Matthew made a point of getting on Lizzie's volleyball team. He tried to be thoughtful and set up shots for her, but she never seemed to notice that he was going out of his way for her. In fact, she seemed to be going out of her way to ignore him. He was getting tired of being treated as if he was nearly invisible.

Afterward, he saw Mose Riehl head toward Lizzie, probably to ask her if she wanted a ride home. He made a quick beeline for Lizzie and reached her side just as she was opening her mouth to answer Mose.

"She can't. She's going home with me," Matthew said firmly.

"Oh I am, am I?" Lizzie said, eyes narrowed, hands hooked on her hips.

"Yes," Matthew said, trying to look as cool as a cucumber even though his heart was pounding. "You are."

Lizzie stared defiantly at Matthew, then turned to Mose's befuddled look, then back to Matthew. "Well." She lifted her chin a notch. "I guess I am, then."

Matthew smiled. Things were looking up.

Cal woke earlier than usual and slipped outside. The morning air was crisp and clear, like pure water from a spring. It

248

would be a warm, sunny day, a good day for plowing the north field and getting it ready to plant corn. After a substantial breakfast, Cal and Ben hitched up their large draft horses to the metal plows and led them out to the field. Cal started on one end of the field, Ben on the other. They could have plowed separate fields, but this was the way their father had taught them. Working together made the work go faster, Samuel Zook had often said.

When the horses met in the middle, Cal and Ben stopped to rest the teams. They sat against the fence that separated Bud's property from Beacon Hollow's. The hum of Bud's tractor plowing a nearby field underscored the quiet.

Cal drew in the scent of the early morning. The distant whiff of manure from a neighboring farm drifted his way, mingling with the aroma of thawing earth. Of spring. He lifted his face to the sun and reveled in it. "Smell that, Ben? *What* a fragrance. Freshly plowed dirt." He handed Ben the water jug.

Ben rolled his eyes. "I'd like it a whole lot more if I were sitting on Bud's tractor." He took a long drink of water. "Those English have a way of making easy work out of hard things." He gave a sideways glance to Cal. "Have you given any more thought to no-till farming? Sure beats plowing."

"I enjoy plowing," Cal said, stretching out his long legs. "No matter which angle I look from, I fail to see the benefits of using chemicals on fields."

A few days ago a salesman from a large chemical company had paid a call at Beacon Hollow, trying to convince Cal and Ben of the merits of no-till farming. "I know you Amish have unscientific minds," the salesman had said, "so you need to rely on outside experts to understand proper soil management."

Kindly overlooking the salesman's patronizing remark about

his intelligence, Cal listened patiently to a lecture on the virtues of no-till farming.

"You can get twice the output from half the work," the salesman explained. "It will free you up to get off the farm and go work in a factory. You'll make extra income."

When Cal asked the salesman why he assumed extra income would improve the quality of life, the man had no answer and soon left.

But ever since Ben heard the salesman's pitch, he kept badgering Cal to consider no-till farming. "Why can't you just give something new a try?" Ben asked, tipping his straw hat over his eyes to shade them. "Just because generations of Amish have farmed one way, it doesn't mean there isn't something new to learn."

"Generations of Amish have developed a way of farming that is proven, that is excellent. And our way doesn't harm the environment, either." Cal rose to his feet, looking out to the edges of his fields. He waved his arm in a large arc. "There's the Kings' farm, and Bud's, and along the treetops you can see the barn roofs of other neighbors. Many of those herbicides that the salesman was trying to sell are suspected carcinogens. If I used those herbicides on my fields, every time it rained, those chemicals would leach into the streams and creeks that run into our neighbors' properties." He turned to Ben. "Tell me this: how can we love our neighbor and do such a thing?"

Ben closed his eyes and lifted one shoulder in a careless shrug. "Beats the drudgery of plowing."

One fine sunny morning, Jorie had just finished first and second grade arithmetic recitation when the door opened and in walked

Cal. Behind him was a short, slight, unhappy man who seemed to have the weight of the world's troubles on his bony shoulders. Cal motioned to Jorie to come to the door.

"Jorie, this is Harry Whitehall." As they shook hands, Cal added, "The public school superintendent."

The scholars, especially the eighth graders, turned toward Mr. Whitehall with wide, worried eyes.

Mr. Whitehall, ignoring the dramatic effect his appearance created, merely walked to the front of the classroom and started unloading the contents of his dark leather bulging briefcase, filled with whatever a public school superintendent carried with him. He started to unpack reams of paper and peered at the back of the classroom, toward the large eighth grade, who sat stiffly at their desks, like cottontails caught in the glare of a lantern. "Are you ready, class, for your exam?"

Jorie glared at Cal and hurried to the front of the class to talk to Mr. Whitehall. "Perhaps if we had some notice . . ."

"Were you not informed that your class would be tested, come May?" Mr. Whitehall asked her.

"Yes, I knew." Jorie lifted her eyebrows at Cal, hoping he would intervene, but he raised the palms of his hands, helpless.

Unconcerned, Mr. Whitehall continued unpacking. "Well, then. Is it not the month of May?"

"Yes, but it's only May 2nd!" Jorie said. "I expected the test to be closer to the end of the month—"

Mr. Whitehall held up a hand to stop her. "We've agreed that it is, indeed, the month of May. So let's stop wasting time and begin."

Jorie turned to the row of eighth grade boys, who stared back at her with blank looks. She felt a great sinking feeling in her stomach. She exhaled, resigned. "Perhaps I should take the other classes out so that you can have the classroom to yourself."

Mr. Whitehall waved her away. "Do with them whatever you want."

"How long will you need?" she asked.

He managed a thin smile for her. "As long as it takes."

Jorie told the rest of the scholars to take their tablets and lunches and go sit under the large maple tree. She gathered some books and walked past the eighth grade, giving them encouraging looks.

When she passed Ephraim's desk, she stopped and leaned over to whisper, "I'm counting on you, Ephraim, to boost the average for the rest of the class."

He whipped his head up in alarm.

She squeezed his shoulder. "You can do it. The Lord gave you a good mind and he will not fail you."

Ephraim dropped his head on the desk with a clunk. She patted him on the back and went outside. Waiting outside the door, Cal intercepted her.

"You could have warned me," she hissed at Cal.

"I didn't know he was coming!" Cal said, clearly uncomfortable. "He just showed up at the house, not thirty minutes ago."

Cal took a step toward Jorie and she took a step back but hit the porch railing. She was stuck. He was so close that Jorie saw the darker blue flecks in his eyes and the lines around his mouth and a few gray hairs at his temple that she hadn't noticed before. Had those gray hairs just sprouted in the last few months, brought on by all of the burdens he had been carrying? The sight of those gray hairs made her resolve weaken. She felt that same tenderness for him begin to melt her heart. She wanted to reach out and touch him, to let him know that everything was going to turn out all right.

But it wasn't.

The superintendent was here and her eighth graders were probably going to flunk the test and . . . then . . . there was Ben. She didn't even want to get started on Ben—her feelings for him were as tangled up inside as one of Marge's balls of yarn. She didn't even know where to find a loose end to start unraveling the snarled mess, and she was even more uncertain about where it would end.

She lifted her eyes and looked right at Cal. His light blue eyes were searching her face and they were soft, so soft. So very soft.

She had to remind herself to breathe.

A shout from the playground distracted them and Jorie used the moment to slip around Cal. Before she stepped off the porch, she turned back to him. "Have you asked Maggie what's been troubling her lately?"

Cal looked surprised by the question. His eyes searched out Maggie on the playground. He found her crouched under the elm tree, playing tic-tac-toe in the dirt, alone. "Well, no. What makes you ask?"

Jorie looked at him as if it was the most obvious thing in the world. "Haven't you noticed? She's stopped humming."

In the middle of May, spring weather finally arrived. One warm evening, Atlee noticed Marge walking across the driveway from the barn to the house. "What were you doing out there at this time of night?" Atlee asked her, holding the kitchen door open for her.

"I just wanted to see little Indigo," Marge answered. "She might be the prettiest foal we've ever had."

Atlee looked worried. "You locked up, didn't you?"

"Of course I did," Marge said, clearly annoyed.

Atlee glanced at Jorie and she gave a slight nod of her head. When it came to horses, she could read her grandfather so well that he didn't even need to utter a word. As she watched her grandmother climb the stairs to go to bed, Jorie got up to go check that the barn had, indeed, been locked up. Just as she put her hand on the kitchen door, she heard strange noises coming from the barn. Something was wrong with the horses. She could hear neighing and stamping, much more than was normal at night.

Alarmed, Atlee grabbed his gun and followed Jorie outside. She reached the barn first and found the door wide open. The horses were in their stalls, pacing and huffing in alarm. At the end of the dark corridor was Fancy, out of her stall, rearing and kicking out at something in the shadows. Jorie aimed the flashlight at the end of the corridor and felt her heart skip a beat. There was a cougar with its mouth around Indigo's head. Atlee pushed Jorie into Fancy's stall and shot his rifle into the rafters, shocking the cougar. It dropped Indigo and darted past them, disappearing out the open barn door and into the woods.

Atlee grabbed Fancy's enormous-sized halter to get her back in her stall so that Jorie was able to get to Indigo. The foal lay quivering on the ground, panting quick short breaths. Blood was everywhere. Jorie worried the foal was going into shock. Telling herself over and over not to panic, she found some blankets in the tack room and covered Indigo.

"Stay here by her and I'll run to get Dr. Robinson," she told her grandfather, who looked as if he might be going into shock himself.

The story of the cougar attack spread quickly throughout the neighborhood.

"Dr. Robinson was able to save Indigo's life," Jorie told Ephraim when he came to see the injured foal the next day. "She's probably going to be blind in one eye, and we have to watch her carefully for infection in the next few weeks, but if all goes well, she might still be able to be a broodmare."

"It's all m-my fault," Ephraim told Jorie, when he saw the foal's eye, covered in a white bandage.

"How could it possibly be your fault, Ephraim?" Jorie asked. "It was my grandmother's doing. She opened Fancy's stall to pat the foal and forgot to close it—the barn door too. She wasn't thinking straight." Marge had slept soundly through the entire night's drama.

And what a heartbreaking drama, for so many reasons. Dr. Robinson sedated Indigo to sew and bandage her wounds, gave her a shot of an antibiotic, and explained to Jorie and Atlee that the foal would be blind in one eye. The cougar's teeth had punctured the sclera. But even more upsetting than the foal's injury was the reason that it had happened. Jorie and Atlee sat at the kitchen table until nearly dawn, still in shock over what had occurred and all that it meant. She would never forget the defeated look on her grandfather's face, or the way his voice broke when he finally admitted, "My darling is losing her mind."

Indigo sneezed, shaking Jorie to the present. Ephraim had opened the bag he had brought with him and was handing her his sketch pad. Jorie flipped the cover and slowly went through the pages. On page after page were sketches of the cougar, caught in different poses. In flight, crouching before pouncing, standing at the top of a rock ledge, peering over the ridge. Jorie didn't say a word. Toward the end, the pages included two kits.

"I'm the one who's b-been f-feeding the c-cougar. I thought if I c-could f-feed her, she wouldn't be t-taking our livestock. But L-Lizzie started to n-notice that our f-freezer was emptying out and I c-couldn't t-tell Cal what I was d-doing b-because he would m-make me stop. So I tried g-getting the cougar squirrels and c-cottontails with my slingshot. But then she had her k-kits. She m-must b-be so hungry that she needs m-more than I c-could hunt for her."

Confused, Jorie told him to slow down. "Take a deep breath and start at the beginning."

The entire story spilled out, starting with the circus, including the day that Cal was beaten. When he was finally finished, Jorie put her arm around his shoulder. "Aw, Ephraim. She's a wild creature. You'll never be able to change the nature of a wild animal, no matter how kind or loving you are. She was just born to be wild and free."

Matthew practically ran from the bus stop to Beacon Hollow but slowed as he reached the rise. He couldn't wait to see Lizzie again but didn't want to seem too eager. He took the kitchen steps two at a time, opened the door, and worked to keep a grin off of his face when he saw her standing by the stove. He dropped his sack off with a thud, hoping she would turn to look at him. Instead, she slammed the spatula on the counter and turned her attention to chopping tomatoes.

"Lizzie, I'm home."

She ignored him and kept chopping.

He took a step toward her. "Uh, is everything all right?"

She spun toward him with the sharp edge of the knife pointed right at him. "*You* tell *me*, Matthew Zook!"

He took a step back. "Did I do something to make you mad?" He couldn't imagine what he could have done. They had fun on the way home from the volleyball game, laughing and teasing each other. When he said goodbye, everything was fine between them. More than fine. She even let him hold her hand when he walked her to the house.

She took a step toward him; the knife was still in her hand. "After you dropped me at home from the volleyball game last week, did you or did you not take Sarah Bender home in your buggy?"

He gave a faint, guilty smile and took another step back, for safety's sake. "I did."

She turned back to the counter and started chopping the tomatoes with a vengeance.

Matthew watched her for a moment. She finished the tomatoes and turned her attention to cracking eggs in a bowl. She cracked an egg against a bowl so hard that half of it landed on the counter. Matthew grinned. *Well, what do you know? Lizzie is jealous—of a girl like horse-faced Sarah!* "I was heading home and passed Sarah's buggy. Her horse had gone lame, so I tied her horse to the back of my buggy and took her home." He took a step closer. "That's all."

With one arm, Lizzie held the bowl of eggs against her body; with the other hand, she was whipping them senseless. "Sarah told . . . everybody! They're all teasing her, saying you're sweet on her."

Matthew took one step closer to Lizzie. No one might ever call her pretty, but she was a girl full of strength: a high forehead, a strong jaw, wide cheekbones, large brown eyes. Why did he once think her eyes were too big for her face? Those eyes were wonderful: large and luminous. And it shamed him to think he

257

used to call her Fat Lizzie. She wasn't fat—not fat at all. As far as he could tell, she had curves in all the right places. He gazed at her fondly.

When he spoke, his voice was hoarse. "I'm not sweet on anybody but you, Lizzie Glick."

Lizzie stopped stirring and was still for a long moment. She put the egg bowl down and turned to face Matthew. They stared at one another in silence for a long moment. Matthew leaned forward to kiss her, but she deftly picked up a plate of freshly baked cookies, putting it between them. He looked down at the plate, picked up a cookie, and took a bite.

"So, do you like it?" she asked, eyes dancing. "It's a recipe I made up this morning. I call it my Green-Eyed Monster Cookies."

"Very nice," Matthew said, his voice quiet, his eyes locked on Lizzie's. "Very, very nice."

Jorie sat on the porch steps, her arms wrapped around her bent legs, her eyes turned up to the sky, to the lovely, wispy cirrus clouds that looked like the flowing tails of running horses. Mares' tails. The sunshine felt so good after such a long, gray winter. Slowly, she tipped her head back and let herself be drawn, up, up, up into the periwinkle blue of the sky.

Suddenly a deep and familiar voice broke the silence. "Thoreau once said a cloudless sky is like a meadow without flowers and a sea without sails."

Jorie had to squint against the sun to see Ben. He stood leaning against the white picket fencing that surrounded the farmhouse, one booted foot crossed over the other, his straw hat dangling from his fingers. In his hand was a book to lend to her. It was one of their favorite things to do—share books and discuss them. Oh, the arguments they would have over plots and themes! It made her smile to think of those times.

She watched Ben carefully. There was something in his expression: a longing? Sadness? Something else too. She wished she could tell what was going on in that head of his. And what a head—despite being too thin, he had an arresting face. Angular cheekbones, dark eyebrows rimming those penetrating eyes. Those eyes ... Her grandmother said recently that Ben had cold eyes. Those eyes weren't cold, certainly not when they were looking at her. Not cold at all.

Jorie smiled. "I'd have to agree with Mr. Thoreau. Cloud watching can be addictive."

He walked over and handed her the book *To Kill a Mockingbird* by Harper Lee, then sat down beside her, stretched out his long legs, and leaned back on his elbows.

"What do you think about when you look up at that big sky?" she asked him.

"Truth be told, I think about what a fool I am," he said. "Before I went away, I looked up at that sky and felt desperate to see the edge of the world." He glanced at her. "So I did. And the sky looks just as blue and welcoming and innocent over there as it does here." He scraped a hand over his jaw. "But it isn't."

She wondered what kinds of things he *did* see over there, in Vietnam, but didn't dare ask. He could be like a skittish sheep if asked too many questions. They used to be able to talk about all kinds of things, but that was long ago. She didn't even know if she knew him anymore. There were complexities to Ben that she just couldn't seem to puzzle out. His experience in Vietnam had left a taint on him, wounds and scars that couldn't be seen but were just as real as if they were on the flesh. Yet there was still laughter in him, and unexpected wells of gentleness. She let the silence lay between them. Sometimes, she thought, silence was the only thing that could bring two people together.

"Have you ever seen a Greyhound track, Jorie?" He gave a short laugh. "No, of course not. I saw one once. These witless greyhound dogs go around and around a track, trying to catch this rabbit running along the fence line. A mechanical rabbit!" He paused. "That's what I feel like, like one of those stupid dogs. I get so close, but I never seem to catch the prize."

For a moment Jorie stared at him in wonder. "But Ben, they're not *meant* to catch it."

The easy charm had vanished. He looked aloof and formidable, eyes narrowed in a silent accusation. Then he pushed himself upright, his boots hitting the porch step with a soft thud. He stood and walked away without a word to her.

Ephraim was cleaning out the buggy by the back of the barn one afternoon when a car pulled into Beacon Hollow's drive. It was driving fast and came to a sharp stop by the farmhouse. He dropped the sponge in the bucket with a splash and walked to the car curiously, surprised to see his brother Ben jump out and wave to him.

"Ephraim, come with me! I need you to show us where the new vet's office is." Ben's voice grew impatient, frustrated that Ephraim wasn't hurrying. "Come on—we've got an emergency."

Ephraim had skidded to a halt when he saw the driver of the car: Jerry Gingerich. Ben pulled Ephraim's arm and practically pushed him in the backseat of the car.

Jerry turned the car around to head back to the road. "Which way, kid?"

Ephraim didn't answer until Ben turned to him. "Over at the K-Kings' old c-cottage on the m-main r-road."

Jerry turned right and gunned the engine, causing Ephraim to slide against the door. He heard an odd moaning sound and peered over the front seat. There was Rex, covered with a bloody towel, his tongue lolling out of his mouth.

"At his house?" Ben asked.

"No one will r-rent him office s-space," Ephraim said, glaring at Jerry. "What happened to R-Rex?"

"Jerry's dog took a slug in its leg when we were hunting," Ben said.

As they approached the cottage, he pointed to the drive. Jerry pulled in, parked the car, and scooped up Rex in his arms. He ran to the door and knocked until Mrs. Robinson opened it and let him in.

Ben turned to Ephraim in the backseat. "Poor Jerry. Not sure that dog can be saved. That bullet chewed up its leg pretty bad."

"W-what were you h-hunting?" Ephraim asked.

Ben motioned to him to get out of the car. He pointed, proudly, to the rack on top. He pulled back a covering and there, roped down, was the beautiful cougar, dead. "We got that big cat," Ben said with evident pride. "Shot it myself. It won't be going after anybody else's livestock this summer, that's for sure."

Ephraim whirled around and exploded in rage. "H-how c-could you?"

Ben looked surprised. "How could I? Easily. I talked Jerry Gingerich into going with me. He's the best tracker in town. After hearing about Jorie's foal, I had to do something." He pulled the cloth back over the cougar and tied the edge to the rack. "She'll be pretty darn pleased about this kill."

"You d-did this to impress Jorie?" Ephraim asked.

"Well, sure. I guess that was part of it. But Stoney Creek is close to Beacon Hollow, Ephraim. It wouldn't be long until we started losing stock too. If anybody would know how to track a cat, it would be Jerry Gingerich."

Ephraim wiped his eyes with his sleeves. He hated tears, they made him feel weak.

"Aw, Ephraim," Ben started, "I know you got a soft spot for critters, but someone needed to get rid of that cat."

"W-why did you ever come back? Why didn't you j-just s-stay away? You ruin everything!" The words had startled Ephraim coming out of his own mouth, and they just kept coming. "You d-don't understand how th-things are, but you c-come here and you act l-like you own the p-place and you own everybody."

A tight look came over Ben's face, as if he were suffering a hurt somewhere. "What are you talking about?"

"How c-could you b-be friends with Jerry? He tried to b-beat the l-living t-tar out of Cal! You d-don't care about C-Cal. You're always trying to hurt him. You even threw that s-softball right at his head on p-purpose. I know you d-did. You're even t-taking Jorie away from him! And you d-don't even care about her! If you d-did, you would have m-married her years ago! You just d-don't want C-Cal to have her."

Ben grabbed Ephraim's shirt in one hand. "What do you mean by that?"

"Excuse me?" Mrs. Robinson asked. Her eyes darted anxiously between the two of them. "We need a little help in here. Would you mind coming in to be with your friend while my husband is examining the dog's injuries? He's a little . . . distraught."

Ben released Ephraim; they eyed each other warily but followed Mrs. Robinson into the cottage. There, huddled in the corner of the room, was Jerry, weeping.

17

A few days later, Ben and Cal were alone, having lunch in the kitchen. Lizzie was upstairs changing linens on beds.

"Cal," Ben said. "How difficult would it be to get at my share of Beacon Hollow? In cash?"

Cal looked at him, startled. "Very difficult."

"I need the cash to start a business."

Cal leaned back in his chair. "What kind of business?"

"A friend and I were talking about taking folks out during deer hunting season."

"For the sport of it?"

"Yeah, I guess."

Cal shook his head. "That's not our way. We don't kill for the sport of it."

Ben took in a deep breath, as if he expected as much from Cal.

"Why would you need money for that, anyway?"

"In the off season, we thought we'd lease land for a rifle range."

"Who is this 'we'?"

"Jerry Gingerich." Ben frowned. "Look—I don't know what went on between you and Jerry, but he's been a friend to me. A real good friend."

Cal had to work hard not to make a disparaging comment about Jerry. If he even started . . . no, he checked himself. He shouldn't even go down that path. He had to trust in God's justice. "We Plain folk don't start businesses with the English. You know that."

"Well, I'm *not* planning on being a farmer," Ben said. "So you can get that notion out of your mind right now."

"If you want a business, then do something that's truly needed. Something you're skilled at. You're an able carpenter."

"Maybe. Maybe I'll think about it. But I still need the money now."

"Why?"

"I'm thinking to buy a house in town, for me and Jorie to live in."

Cal kept his eyes down. "You aren't even a church member yet, Ben. Aren't you getting a little ahead of yourself?"

Ben flashed him a dazzling smile. "Gotta start somewhere, brother Cal."

"What makes you think Jorie would leave her grandparents and her Percherons?"

Ben lifted a dark eyebrow. "Because . . . it's *me* doing the asking."

Cal looked straight at Ben. Sometimes he had the feeling that Ben really didn't know Jorie at all. He leaned toward him, placing his elbows on the table. "Ben, you're in a tremendous hurry to do everything but sit down and face your demons."

Ben rose to his feet so abruptly that his chair tipped over backward. He glared at Cal. "You'd do anything to keep me down, wouldn't you?"

"What?"

"You know what your problem is, Cal? Just because you had to step into Dad's shoes when he died, you resent the rest of us for having time to be young." Ben turned and left, slamming the door behind him.

Cal got up to pick up Ben's chair, exasperated. Ben had always been one to flirt with the wild side. His mother used to say Ben was born looking for a rule to break. When their parents were killed, Ben went even further on the precipice. It was Jorie who seemed to temper him and keep him from going too far. Now, it seemed that as Ben's body grew healthy, his mind grew dark and anxious. There were times when Cal thought Ben seemed as tightly wound as a coiled spring.

Standing at the kitchen window, Cal watched Ben storm off down the drive, hands jammed in his pockets, head down. Cal felt a little sorry he hadn't kept those prescription drugs from the Veterans Hospital. He thought maybe Ben could use a sedative or two. He rubbed his knotted fist against his stomach. Or maybe he would take one himself. Dealing with his brother's moodiness was starting to give him an ulcer. He offered a quick apology to the Lord for such an ungrateful heart. Just a few months ago, he had been praising the Lord for bringing Ben home.

Later that week, after giving the matter considerable prayer, Cal drove the buggy into town and stopped by the bank to empty out his savings account. The amount wasn't entirely a quarter of what Beacon Hollow was worth, but it was close. If this would be a way to keep Ben in Stoney Ridge, close to his Amish roots, then Cal would gladly hand it over. He had always known Ben wouldn't be a farmer; his brother just didn't have the patience for it. It made him heartsick to think of Ben going into business with the likes of Jerry Gingerich, but Cal believed a man had to make his own decisions. And mistakes.

When Cal returned to Beacon Hollow, he put the cash in an envelope and laid it on Ben's pillow. Not much later, he heard a loud whoop of happiness coming from Ben's room. Ben burst downstairs and found him at his desk. "Thank you, brother Caleb! You won't be sorry." Ben pulled on his hat and coat and hurried out the door.

"Ben!" Cal called after him.

Ben stopped and turned.

"Ask Jorie about being the keeper of the song."

Ben looked confused.

"Just . . . just ask her."

As Jorie stepped out the side door with an empty laundry basket anchored on her hip, she drew in the scent of the late May afternoon. The fragrance of the grape arbor that wrapped around the back porch drifted her way. She folded the dry laundry as she took it off the line and was about to bend over to lift the basket when she spotted Ben ambling toward her. She smiled.

"A day like this is so good, don't you find it so?" she asked when he reached her. She looked up at the puffy white clouds that danced in the sky. "It just sings with the promise of summer. It makes a person want to praise God, and thank him for giving you the life to enjoy it."

When he didn't answer her, she turned to face him. The gentle wind fluttered her cap strings. He took one in each hand and pulled them down until they were stretched taut, then flashed her a dazzling half-smile that made her weak in the knees.

"Cal said to ask you about being the keeper of the song. What does that mean?"

She studied him for a long moment, puzzled. Why *that* question? Cal's telling me something, Jorie thought: something has happened with Ben. "It means that we are carrying on for those we love. Caring for Beacon Hollow is the keeper of your folks' song. I'm the keeper of my grandfather's song."

Ben stared at her with such fierce intensity that she could almost feel it, like a warm gust of breath on her flesh. "Let's get married, Jorie." There was a strange gravelly sound to his voice.

She was shocked silent. That was the *last* thing she expected to come out of Ben's mouth. She had been waiting for years for this moment, and now that it was here, she didn't know what to do with it.

He took her hands in his. "I've been working on a plan. It's all figured out. I'm going to start a business."

"You're what?" She was stunned.

"I've got the money from Cal. My partner and I—we're just finalizing details now."

She shook her head. "Wait a minute. Cal knows about this?"

"Yeah."

"And he supports you in this . . . this business?"

An annoyed look crossed through his eyes. "I don't need Cal's approval, if that's what you mean."

"Why would Cal give you money?"

"He just gave me what's due me. My quarter of Beacon Hollow."

She cocked her head. "Who is your business partner?"

He looked past her to the horse in the pasture. "Jerry Gingerich."

She yanked her hands away as if he had blasphemed. She

couldn't believe what she was hearing. "How could you do such a thing to Cal? To Matthew and Ephraim?"

"I'm not doing anything *to* them! I'm trying to make a life for *us*."

"You can't go into business with the English."

Ben's eyes grew unnaturally hard, set above a stern mouth. She suddenly realized that he didn't consider himself an Amish man.

"You know I would never consider marrying someone who isn't a church member. You know what that would mean."

His eyebrows slammed together. "That was *your* doing! I *told* you not to get baptized, but you went ahead and did it while I was gone! You made this so much harder for us!"

"For us?" She tried to draw in a breath, but it caught in her throat. "For us? You mean, harder for you." She splayed her hand against her heart. "I know what I want, I know who I am."

"Jorie," he said again, impatient now. "I'm finally ready to get married." His face went soft and his voice grew sweet. "You want this too. I know you do."

Did she? She had known him all her life, had loved him for years, almost like a habit, and yet she had no idea at all whether or not she loved him anymore.

She wasn't looking at him, but she could feel his gaze hard on her, as if he could will the words into being. He never expected her to turn him down. Ben was used to getting what he wanted.

She fumbled to find the words for a long moment. When she found them, she risked a look at him. "Oh Ben, I can't fix what's ailing you."

Ben's face clouded over. At first, his eyes flashed with anger. Then they grew soft again. "Yes, Jorie, you can." He bent over and took her face in his hands, his thumbs lightly tracing the hollows in her cheeks. "You *can* fix me. You're the only one who can. Marry me, Jorie. I count on you. I always have. I don't know what I would do . . . if I didn't have you by my side. I *need* you." His voice broke on those last three words. He still had her face cupped in his hands. He leaned closer now and kissed her, a kiss from his heart that said so much more than words could ever tell her.

But it only told her what she didn't want to hear.

Sylvia pounded the bread dough again and again, trying to get it to that point when it would be smooth and elastic, ready for its final rising. She supposed it was a silly thing to be doing so late in the afternoon—it wouldn't be ready to bake until midnight—but she needed something to occupy her head and hands. If she slowed down, her prickling conscience caught up with her.

When the lump of dough finally passed inspection, she put it into a greased bowl and covered it with a damp towel. She looked around the room for a place for it to rise, deciding on the tabletop by the window where sunlight streamed in. It was a small kitchen for such a big house—barely large enough to hold the rectangular oak table with eight ladder-back chairs. Plenty of seats for the children she was going to have with Noah . . . until he died so unexpectedly on that dreadful winter day, at the young age of thirty-eight. It still irked her that no doctor could figure out what killed Noah. She knew *someone*—she was pretty sure it was Benjamin Zook—had started a nasty rumor that Noah was henpecked to death.

For four long years, that big table held only two people: Esther and her. Thank God for her daughter, her Esther.

But it wasn't too late to give Esther a sister or brother. Sylvia was still a young woman, only thirty-four, still beautiful. She was aware of the approving looks of men, Plain or English, though she knew it was vain to derive pleasure from those looks.

She had finally decided that she was ready to marry again, but he had to be somebody worthy, a man she could look up to. Someone who would hold the Word of God high in their home.

Someone like Caleb Zook.

Of course, she had never thought of Caleb in *that* way before her sister passed. The day that she saw Maggie dressed as . . . a *boy*! It still galled her. In that instant, she knew what had to happen. It was her God-given duty: her role in life was to take care of people. She was born to it. She was at her best in that role.

If she and Cal married, Maggie would have a mother, Esther would have a father. It just made perfect sense. Why, she could probably put an end to Ephraim's annoying habit of stammering too.

She knew she suited Caleb better than any one of those spinsters who signed up for the aunties' Saturday Night Supper List. Even though she disapproved of that ridiculous form of matchmaking, she had recently decided that she would add her name to the list in the next available opening. It would be a way to let Caleb know she would be willing to consider him as a husband.

But first . . . she needed to make sure that Jorie King would keep her attention on Benjamin Zook where it belonged.

Earlier today, Sylvia drove past Beacon Hollow and happened to see Benjamin out by the barn. Impulsively, she turned her horse into the drive. She thought it to be high time that someone let Benjamin know what had been going on while he was serving his country in Vietnam: Jorie had been working her wiles on his eldest brother.

She told Benjamin all about the way Jorie was trying to tempt

Caleb—sending him special smiles in church, taking him on picnics. Oh, Jorie thought no one knew she was trying to snare Caleb, but Sylvia was wise to it. She had seen the two of them, more than a few times, walking together. Talking together. Laughing together.

Benjamin didn't even look at her as she spoke, didn't ask a single question. But she knew he was listening, because she could see he was shifting his weight restlessly and his facial expression set like concrete. Those were signs of a man trying to hold his temper, she remembered that from her Noah.

"I wouldn't put it past her if she let her hair down for him too."

At least, that was what she *meant* to say. What came out was more like, "She let her hair down for him too." She felt just the tiniest pang of guilt over stretching the truth like that— she had never lied before in her entire life—but every time that guilty twinge poked her conscience, she dismissed it. After all, she wouldn't put it past Jorie to flaunt that flaming red hair. And besides, that tiny piece of information set Benjamin off. His eyes glowed edgy and wild and his big hands clenched and unclenched.

Oh, it was definitely the right thing to do.

Sylvia went outside to wait for Esther's arrival from school. As she sat on the porch chair, she closed her eyes, sorely aware of the emptiness, the loneliness in her heart.

Jorie couldn't shake the feeling that something about this day felt different. She sensed a strange restlessness, as if something was about to happen that would change things forever. She was glad when four o'clock finally came and all of the scholars ran home, even Maggie, who usually stayed to help her clean up. She had just finished wiping down the blackboard when she heard the door click shut. She turned to see who was there. It was Cal, standing in the middle of the aisle, looking so big and tall next to the small desks.

And sad.

Cal looked so sad. She couldn't bear to see him looking like that. They stared at one another in silence for a moment. Then she took a step toward him, and then another. She reached out her hand to him, and he met it halfway with his own, entwining their fingers. They stayed that way awhile, touching in silence. Then he gave a little tug, pulling her closer, and she came toward him.

He brushed his knuckles along her jaw, so lightly it was as if he'd only thought about touching her. "Jorie," he said again, so softly it was as if he'd only imagined saying it.

She heard in his whisper, she saw on his face, the same longings that cried from her heart.

But she knew why Cal was here. She could read it on his face. He had come to tell her goodbye.

She shook her head and the tears splattered. She squeezed her eyes tightly shut, trying to hold them back. He still had her face cupped in his hands. He leaned closer now and brushed his mouth across hers, almost with reverence. He started to pull away, but she reached up and wrapped her arms around his neck, holding him, holding him as tight as she could until his arms folded around her. She laid her head on his shoulder, and he rested his chin on her head. She didn't know how long they stayed that way.

It was the sound of a shout that pulled them apart. "Ich mache dich dod!" *I'll kill you!* Ben had come into the schoolhouse and witnessed their embrace. He lunged toward Cal, grabbed him by the shoulder, and spun him around to hit him in the jaw.

Cal fell backward against a desk.

"Get up! Get up and fight like a man!"

Cal struggled to his feet as Ben kicked him down again.

"Halt! Halt jetzt!" *Stop it! Stop it this instant!* Jorie tried to put herself between Ben and Cal, but Ben pushed her off. "Was is loss mit dir?" *What is wrong with you?*

Ben's eyes were as black as thunder. "Me? Me?! My brother and my girl, kissing behind my back! Du settscht dich scheme!" *You ought to be ashamed!*

"We were doing nothing of the sort!" Jorie said. "We were . . . we were saying goodbye."

"Why should I believe that?" Ben yelled, his voice tinged with the deepest betrayal. "You *always* wanted him. You wanted *me* to be him. You're probably thrilled that Mary Ann made this easy for you and died."

"Don't you say those terrible things!" Jorie shouted.

"I thought I *knew* you." His voice whipped around Jorie like an arctic blast. "I thought I understood *us.* Sylvia told me! She said you let down your *hair* for him!"

"That's enough, Ben!" Cal said, wiping blood from his mouth. "You're talking crazy."

He whirled around to face his brother. "And you! You don't care about Jorie! You're just trying to take her because Mary Ann told you to. I know that, for a fact! I read her letter! It was in that box of Mary Ann's things. The one you gave to Maggie."

Cal's fists clenched at his side, as if he was barely holding himself back from throttling Ben.

Ben whirled back toward Jorie. "He was only courting you because Mary Ann told him to. And because Sylvia threatened to take Maggie." He pointed a finger at Cal, as if he were a child that needed scolding. "I heard! I heard it all! Right after the big storm, when the bishop came to tell you to fire Jorie from her teaching job." He spun around to Jorie. "Did Cal tell you that yet? That you're fired? The bishop is willing to let you finish the term but then"—he drew an imaginary line across his throat—"you're axed." He spun around to Cal. "Tell her, Cal. Tell her the truth."

Cal's face went still. Tension prickled the air.

Jorie's eyes darted between Cal's and Ben's. The fact that Cal didn't deny it told her that Ben was speaking the truth. She shook her head, not understanding, not knowing them. She backed up a few steps, nearly tripping over something, then made herself walk out slowly with her head up. At the doorway she looked back at them as though she were about to add one last thing, then she thought better of it and turned and walked down the road.

She walked all the way to Stoney Creek, into the barn, all the way into the middle of it, and just stood, gripping her elbows as if she was trying to hold herself in one piece. Dust motes danced in the shaft of sunlight that shot through the open doorway. She swallowed and drew in a deep breath, taking in the comforting smell of animals and hay. She told herself not to cry, but in the next instant, scalding tears pushed against her eyes. Soon, she was sobbing.

When she was done, a huge sigh from her heart escaped her body, a sigh so deep and long she felt it as a breath she had been holding for years.

Ever since she first loved Ben.

"For such a peaceable man, you sure get the bejesus walloped out of you on a regular basis," Matthew said as he prepared an ice pack for Cal's swollen eye.

"Matthew," Cal said wearily, "don't blaspheme." Cal was sitting at the kitchen table at Beacon Hollow, staring at the salt and pepper shakers on the center of the table.

"You might need some stitches for that cut on your eyebrow," Matthew said as he handed Cal the ice pack. "You gonna let me know why your face came to look like a side of butchered beef?"

Cal sighed. "Ben and I had a . . . misunderstanding."

"Ben did this to you?" Matthew whistled. "Guess the Army taught him a few things." He leaned back in the chair. "I suppose Ben isn't looking any worse for the wear."

"I didn't hit him back, if that's what you're implying."

"It is," Matthew said. "Any idea where Ben went off to?"

"No," Cal said. "I don't even know if he's coming back." But surely he would. They were bound, he and his brothers, with ties strengthened by life and love and God, too strong to break. Surely, surely, they were bound too tightly to be broken apart.

Matthew leaned forward on his elbows. "I'm guessing that this had something to do with our Jorie."

"It's a long story," Cal said, shifting the ice pack to the cut on his eyebrow.

"I've got time, at least until the cows start bawling like they're fit to be tied and need me to ease their misery."

Cal didn't tell Matthew everything, but he did tell him about the big storm and that he was told to fire Jorie. "The look on Jorie's face when Ben told her she had been fired . . . I'll never forget it." He shuddered. "Wouldn't surprise me if she never wants anything to do with a Zook—any of us Zooks—ever again." Cal saw Matthew wince. It felt so wrong, hurting people like this. Every morning, Cal prayed to God that he would be a blessing to others. Instead, he was causing pain.

"So what are you going to do?"

"I'm going to do the right thing."

"Well, sure. But what is that?"

Cal sighed. "That's what I don't know yet."

Matthew dropped his chin to his chest. "Must be hard, caring about them both."

Cal was surprised by his younger brother's sensitivity—a characteristic with which Matthew wasn't overly endowed. The thought pleased Cal. Maybe his brother was turning into a man. "You're in the same spot, though, aren't you? Wanting the best for both Ben and me."

"I guess I am." Matthew looked up. "The thing is, I want you and Jorie to end up together because she's so right for you. She's smart enough and she speaks her mind and, well, she'd be a good wife to you. And Maggie and Ephraim are crazy about her. But there's a part of me that wants Ben to have her too, because . . ."

"Because he needs her," Cal said with a heavy heart.

"Yeah. I guess there's the rub. He needs her more."

18

That night, Ben still hadn't returned. After everyone had gone to bed, Cal opened his Bible at the kitchen table, hoping God's Word could provide some guidance through this mess. Communion would be coming in a few weeks. This was a season of making amends, of setting things right between people. He had always loved Communion for that very reason. But this spring, he would need to set things right with a long list of people: Sylvia, Ben, smooth over that nettlesome tension with Jonas, and now Jorie. He wondered if things would ever be right again with Ben or with Jorie. Two people he cared about deeply and yet he didn't know what to do. Loving Ben meant not loving Jorie. And loving Jorie meant not loving Ben.

He heard a scuffling noise and turned around to see Ephraim and Maggie standing at the bottom of the steps in their night-clothes. Ephraim was holding Maggie's hand, but she was hidden behind him.

"Cal," Ephraim said. "We got something to t-tell you."

Cal turned his chair to face them. "Something that's troubling you?"

Ephraim pulled Maggie forward to stand side by side. "Matthew t-told us. He said Jorie was g-going to be f-fired. Cuz of the b-big storm."

Cal rolled his eyes. "Is nothing private in this household?"

Ephraim looked at Maggie, who kept her gaze on her bare feet. "Jorie t-told her not to go."

"Who?"

Ephraim waited.

Maggie pushed her glasses up on her nose. "Me," she answered, as her eyes welled up with tears. "Jorie told me not to go. To wait until the storm was over. But I couldn't wait. I slipped out when she wasn't looking."

Cal raked a hand through his hair.

"I didn't mean to get Jorie fired," Maggie said. "I just had to go to the outhouse, real bad."

Cal grimaced and rubbed his forehead. "Maggie, in the morning you're going to tell this story to the bishop. He needs to hear this. We have to put things right."

She cringed, scrunching her small shoulders, then gave a nod.

"I'll c-come too," Ephraim whispered to her.

Cal had just finished mixing feed in the barn when he heard the familiar clip-clop of a horse driving a buggy. He wiped his hands on a rag and went out the side door to see Isaac's mare slow her gait as she reached the steep incline of Beacon Hollow's long drive. Seated next to Isaac in the buggy was the superintendent of public schools, Mr. Whitehall. Cal wrapped the mare's reins around the hitching post and helped Isaac climb down from the buggy.

Isaac's sparse eyebrows shot up when he saw Cal's black eye. "Looks like you met up with a grizzly bear, Caleb," he said in his quiet, slow way.

"Something like that," Cal said.

The superintendent didn't even notice Cal's eye. He had a big smile on his face. "I thought that buggy ride would rattle my bones, but it was smooth as molasses." He shook Cal's hand. "I'm learning that it's high time I unlearned some assumptions."

Cal gave Isaac a questioning glance. The superintendent looked the same but acted like a different man entirely than the one who gave the eighth graders their exam just a few weeks ago.

Isaac's face was unreadable. "Caleb, Mr. Whitehall has some news to tell you."

Mr. Whitehall lifted a knee to prop open his briefcase and pulled out some papers. "We just received the scoring from the state exam."

Cal straightened his back, bracing himself for bad news.

Mr. Whitehall practically burst forth with the news. "The eighth grade at the one-room schoolhouse at Stoney Ridge earned the top marks in the state!"

Cal thought he hadn't heard correctly. He looked to Isaac for confirmation and noticed his pleased look.

"You don't say," Cal said, working to keep a grin off of his face.

Mr. Whitehall thrust the report at him. "Not only top marks, but a full five percentage points higher than any other public school. In the entire state of Pennsylvania!" He laughed glee-fully, as if he had been a proponent of one-room schoolhouses all along. "In fact, you've got one pupil who beat out everyone, in every subject! A perfect score! Reading comprehension, mathematics, science!" He slapped his knee. "Imagine, nearly

100 percent on the *science* exam from a boy in an *Amish* school-house!"

Isaac leaned over toward Cal. "Ephraim," he said quietly. "It was our Ephraim who earned those high marks."

Cal didn't know what to say. He let the news soak over him. He felt so pleased for Ephraim, and for Jorie too, who had brought the best out of Ephraim. Even his stuttering had improved lately. It was just what Mary Ann had said would happen: Jorie would be the best choice. For Ephraim, for Maggie. For him too, though that prospect seemed markedly dim.

"The bishop and I are stopping by to see that schoolteacher of yours next. I want her to speak at a conference in Harrisburg and give suggestions to the public school teachers about making improvements."

Cal exchanged a look with Isaac, sharing a thought. They wouldn't stop Mr. Whitehall from asking, but they knew Jorie would never agree to such a prideful thing.

Isaac took off his hat and scratched his head. "Uh, Caleb, have you already spoken to Jorie about the teaching job for next year?"

"In a manner of speaking, yes, she knows," Cal said.

"Oh dear," Isaac said, looking worried. "I suppose I have a little smoothing over to do."

"Speaking of that, Isaac," Cal said, "if you have a minute to spare, Maggie would like to speak to you. She's in the kitchen, waiting." Peering out the kitchen window with wide, worried eyes were Maggie and Ephraim.

Cal knew Jorie well enough to know that she would be in the barn after sunset, checking on each horse one last time before locking things up for the night. He found her in the stall of a mother and new foal. He couldn't help but smile when he saw her standing by her feather-footed Percherons. She looked tiny next to the giant horses. Even the foal—only a few days old—was nearly as tall as she was.

"So school is over for another year."

She glanced up when she heard his voice. It was getting dark, too dark now to see her face, and he was glad for it. Maybe, without realizing it, he had even planned it that way.

"Maggie and Ephraim were both down in the mouth the day after school let out. Ephraim, in particular. He's done with his formal schooling."

It was more than the last day of school that had Maggie and Ephraim upset. Esther had told everyone that Jorie had been fired. Some—even Ray Smucker, Maggie said—had tears rolling down their cheeks as they helped clean out the schoolhouse on the last day and pack up Jorie's belongings.

Jorie continued to handle the foal, brushing it gently, stroking its back, lifting its hooves one at a time. He knew it was part of a daily ritual she had, to make sure the foal was comfortable with a human touch.

"I owe you an apology, Jorie."

Finally, she spoke. "For what in particular?"

He was surprised that she didn't sound mad, for she had every right to be. "Accusing you of neglecting Maggie. Last night she told me what really happened." He looked embarrassed. "It's why she stopped humming. She was feeling guilty."

"I don't deny that it hurt me you wouldn't have more faith in me than that," Jorie said. "But . . . apology accepted." She slid the stall open to slip out, then shut it and locked it tight. She stood and looked at him, knowing he had more to say.

He wondered what she was thinking; he knew there was a deep hurting behind those blue eyes. "Maybe you shouldn't forgive me so easily. I've made quite a few mistakes lately."

She walked past each stall, checking its lock to make sure each was tightly hitched. "Was everything Ben said true?"

He fell into step beside her. "He got things mixed up, but there was some truth in it. It's true that Mary Ann had chosen you for my wife. But that wasn't why I asked you to marry me." He stopped himself. "That's not really the whole truth. At first, I didn't want to even consider you because of the very reason that people were telling me I ought to. But then Sylvia started talking about taking Maggie from me and I panicked. That was the first time I asked you to marry me."

She finished checking the last latch and turned toward him, listening. He couldn't read what she was thinking; her face remained expressionless.

"The second time I asked you, I really believed that you were the right one for us. For Maggie, for Ephraim, for me."

She just kept looking at him with mild interest.

"The third time, that was when I asked you for me, Jorie. Just for me." His voice broke a little as he added, "To be the wife of my heart." He walked up to her. "I'm sorry that I hurt you, especially what I said to you after the storm. I knew better. Look how each horse gets tended to every night—I don't know why I didn't think you'd do the same for your scholars. For Maggie, in particular."

He saw her expression soften, ever so slightly, and took a step closer to her. "I think I just wanted a reason to be angry with you. It felt easier to be angry with you than . . . to try and stop loving you. Knowing it's really Ben you love."

There, he said it. And she didn't deny it. It pained him to even say it aloud, that she loved Ben, but at least the truth was out in the open. He turned to go and stopped when he heard her speak.

"You're not the only one who's been making mistakes."

He spun around to face her, but she avoided his eyes, fixing her gaze down on her clasped hands.

"Ben was right, Cal." Her voice broke over the words. "He was right about me wanting him to be more like you." She lifted her eyes to meet his. "Don't misunderstand. I never coveted my friend's husband. I never, ever wanted Mary Ann to be gone. Never that." She looked away. "But I can't deny that I've always thought . . . highly of you. And then, this winter, that feeling grew into something else." She tucked her chin to her chest. "But feelings can't be the only thing that guides us, can they?" She lifted her face, her expression strong and clear.

She was so strong, his Jorie, the strongest person he had ever known. But he reminded himself that she wasn't his Jorie . . . she was Ben's Jorie. He wiped the tears off of her cheeks with a gentle brush of his hands—not the touch of a lover but that of a friend.

On an unseasonably hot afternoon in early June, Jorie led two mares and their foals out to pasture. As she closed the gate behind her, she stopped to watch the foals chase each other in play. It was a sight that never failed to pull at her heart. What was it about being young that brought such joy and abandon, even to animals?

She heard someone call her name and turned to see Ben standing there. She hadn't seen him since that awful day at the schoolhouse, when he raised his fists against Cal. He looked like he hadn't slept in a few days; his beard was scruffy and his eyes were rimmed with dark circles. He looked so hurt, so frightened and broken, and she found she couldn't bear it. She knew she should be angry with him, but it was no use. She felt her anger slip away, like an ocean wave from a shoreline.

Ben stared at her for what seemed like forever.

She came up to him, her gaze moving over his troubled face.

"Don't," he said. "Don't come any closer, Jorie."

She took a step toward him and he flinched, backing away again, lifting his palms to stop her.

"I lost all of my inheritance—every cent of Cal's savings—in a card game. Every blasted dollar."

She took his hand in hers as if she were cradling a wounded bird.

"Please, Jorie. Please. Don't touch me. I'm filthy," he said. He tried to pull his hand free, but she tightened her grip. She wanted to comfort him and he made it so hard.

She took a step closer and wrapped her arms around his waist and pressed her face against his chest. He started to cry then and let her hold him until he stopped. After she released him, she struggled to find words to fill the silence and break the uneasiness that lay between them.

All that she could think to say was, "Please. Go to Cal. Talk to him."

It was so hot that the thick air shimmered in waves before Cal's eyes. Sweat dripped off his hair and down his neck. He was planting a section of the vegetable garden to cultivate for fall vegetables when he looked up and saw Ben. It had been more than a week since Ben had disappeared. Cal dropped the shovel, wiped his forehead with a rag, and walked up to his brother.

"A garden's the sign that life keeps going on, that people are home and happy to be there," Ben said, his hat brim covering his eyes. "Isn't that what Mom always said?"

Cal nodded.

Ben lifted his head and peered at Cal's eye. "You did more damage to my hand than I did to your eye." He held out his hand. His knuckles were still bruised and scabbed.

Such a terrible thing, Cal thought, an Amish man bearing marks of violence on his hands. "Oh, you gave me a shiner. Folks at church wanted to ask but didn't dare."

A smile tugged at the corners of Ben's mouth.

"Have you seen Jorie yet?"

"Yes." Ben's smile faded. "I'm sorry, Cal. Sorry for all of the trouble I've brought on you. I've just been so . . ."

"Angry."

"Yes. Angry. Since the war."

"It's not just the war, Ben. You've been angry a long time. You've been clinging to your anger with every ounce of humanity left in your body."

Ben's chin lifted a notch. "It wasn't easy following you, Cal. You cast a deep shadow for me. For Matthew and Ephraim too."

Cal choked down a retaliation, which would have been futile. "Don't go making me an excuse for your choices."

"What's that supposed to mean?" Ben said, his voice tinged with irritation.

Cal took off his hat and spun it around in his hands. He was trying to remain calm, but he had some things to say to Ben, things that would be hard for him to hear. "You're always looking for a shortcut. You lead Jorie into thinking you'll marry her, but never quite get around to it. You stay as close to being Amish as you can, but never choose to baptize. You find the one loophole to being a conscientious objector and make the rest of us think you've been cuckolded."

Ben looked away. "So Jorie told you," he said, his voice flat.

"Es macht nix aus," Cal said, frustration in his voice. *It doesn't matter.* "You've *got* to stop blaming others. Blaming me, blaming Jorie, blaming the Army."

Cal saw something shift over Ben's face. It looked as if he wanted those secrets spilled, like it would be a relief to spew it all out.

Ben let out a deep breath. "Have you ever found yourself in a situation when you did one thing that led to another? And that led to another thing? Until suddenly you find yourself at a place where there is no going back, and no escaping."

Now, *finally*, Ben was talking from the heart. Cal pointed to a tree with a large canopy. "Let's get out of this hot sun and sit."

After they sat under the shade of the tree, Cal waited patiently for Ben to start talking.

"I had a friend in Vietnam. Another Amish guy like me, a stretcher bearer." Ben's voice was rough, as if his throat kept tightening up, choking off the words.

The humidity of the warm day was oppressive, even in the shade, but Cal thought Ben looked as if he felt cold. His face had grown pale and his hands were trembling.

"We nearly had the same name too. Benjamin S. Zook. His 'S' was for Simeon, mine was Samuel. We had been put together in the same company because of our last names. One day, this Ben and I were taking supplies to the field medic. There'd been sniper activity in the area, so the captain insisted we carry weapons. Small guns. My friend and I talked about it, what to do. He said he wouldn't carry a gun, no matter what. But I slipped the gun into my pocket." Ben sat forward, elbows resting on his knees, eyes fastened on the garden. "We got a little lost on the trail, the overgrowth was so dense. Suddenly, we were face-to-face with an NVC—a North Viet Cong—holding a rifle to our faces. Ben— the other Ben—started saying the Lord's Prayer, like a chant, especially the part about loving our enemies. And that sniper, he walked around Ben, as if he was listening to him, then he gave him a big smile—I'll never forget that smile—and shot him dead. One bullet to the forehead. By the time he turned toward me, I had slipped my hand into my pocket, pulled out the gun, and fired it. I did it without thinking, like it was a survival instinct. Like I was hunting in the woods with you and Dad. I killed him, Cal. I . . . *killed* . . . a man." He covered his face with his hands.

Cal felt shock jolt through him, to think his brother—for that matter, to think *any* Amish man—took the life of another . . . he felt sick with disgust. But he worked to keep his face empty of judgment. This was why his people avoided war, for just such a thing as this. Who knew how he would have reacted had he been in the same situation?

Ben dropped his hands and lifted his head to the sky. "I was stunned by what I had done. I just stood there, watching blood pour out of that sniper's neck . . . like a kitchen faucet. A soldier heard the gun shots and came to help. He found me with those two dead bodies around me. He saw the dead sniper and congratu- lated me. He *congratulated* me! Told me I'd be getting a medal. For *killing*. He ran back to get the captain and that was when I switched dog tags with my friend. I knew I would be viewed as a hero and I couldn't stomach it." He gave Cal a sideways glance. "I wasn't thinking straight. I didn't even consider that folks back home would be told I was dead. I only thought about getting a medal for *killing* a man. I tried to put it out of my mind, that killing, but it kept coming back at me. I couldn't sleep, and pretty soon I was acting like a nutcase. Couldn't even get out of bed one morning. That was when I got shipped off to the looney bin in Thailand. The doctors kept slapping me with different diagnoses, different labels. First it was a nervous breakdown, then combat trauma, then a clinical depression."

He rubbed his face with his hands, wiping away tears. "They were all wrong. It was dread and fear and guilt—most of all, the guilt—that was churning around inside my belly for so long I just couldn't take it anymore." Emptied of words now, he rubbed his eyes with the arm of his shirt. "So tell me, Cal. *How* do I get rid of this crushing guilt?" His voice broke on the words.

Cal spun his straw hat in his hands around and around, thinking hard. He took his time answering. "God doesn't convict us of sin just to make us feel guilty. Conviction is meant to move us to confession and repentance. After confession comes forgiveness. It's like the sun shining after a summer storm. There is peace and joy to be found in God. And there is forgiveness and eternal life. It's never too late to make your soul whole. You've been dwelling on your sin and forgetting that we have a gracious God who loves to forgive the repentant sinner."

Ben dropped his head, hiding his eyes beneath the brim of his hat. "So you think it was a sin, killing that sniper?" His voice turned hard and cold again. "He would have killed me, you know. Is that what you preferred?"

Cal's gaze shifted to the road to watch a buggy with a high-stepping gelding drive by. He felt as if he was on the edge of a precipice—one wrong move and the conversation could slip down the wrong path. "I don't judge you, if that's what you're asking. But I don't think killing that sniper is all that's troubling you."

Ben looked away.

"Somewhere there is a family who doesn't know what has

happened to their son. You need to find them and tell them all that happened. I think Matthew would know how to track them down."

Ben fell silent, but Cal didn't mind. Silence was good. When Ben finally glanced over at him, a question in his eyes, Cal added, "I don't know what's the cause of the hardness between you and Ephraim, but you need to make things right. He's a sensitive boy, Ben. You've done something that has made him feel betrayed."

Ben gave a quick nod but didn't explain. "What else? Go on. I know you've got something else you're itching to say."

Cal nearly smiled. They knew each other so well. "It's high time you start being the man God created you to be." He leaned his elbows on his knees. "Think about all of the experiences God gave you—the good ones and the bad ones—and let God *use* them, Ben. Stop trying to hide from your past. Give your past to God."

He stood, put his hat on his head, and adjusted the brim. "Ben, this time in Vietnam, all that happened over there—it's a chapter, not the whole book."

Ephraim had gotten in the habit of stopping by Dr. Robinson's office when he was passing by the cottage and saw his car. Mrs. Robinson said she appreciated his help, cleaning out the animal cages—their patients, she called them. Dr. Robinson even let Ephraim sew a couple of stitches on an ear of an anesthetized cat that had gotten into a fight. Not too bad for a first time, the doctor had said, but he took out the stitches and redid them.

Today, when he was at the Robinsons' feeding the cat with the sewn-up ear, Jerry Gingerich dropped by to pick up Rex. He couldn't believe how Jerry practically gushed over Dr. Robinson, shaking his hand, thanking him again and again for saving Rex's leg. It made Ephraim feel uncomfortable. It was easier to hate Jerry than to see something good in him.

On the way back to Beacon Hollow, Ephraim was coming up the drive as Ben was walking down. Ephraim scowled when he saw him and crossed to the other side of the drive, ignoring him, but Ben blocked his path.

"Ephraim, I'm sorry about the cougar," Ben said. "I really am. I wish I could make it up to you somehow."

Ephraim gave him a suspicious look, wondering how sincere he was. He actually looked quite contrite. "Then help me k-keep the c-cougar k-kits safe from Jerry Gingerich. He's going out t-tonight to trap them and k-kill them, I heard him say s-so himself, just now, over at Dr. Robinson's."

Ben tilted his head. "You know where the kits are?"

Ephraim nodded. "I've been f-feeding them every d-day since you murdered their mother."

Ben winced. "Sheesh, you put it like that, Ephraim, it makes me sound heartless." He folded his arms across his chest. "Even if we built a cage for them, they're going to grow. They're not pets. They need to be free and wild."

Ephraim turned away. "You s-said you wanted to help m-make things right."

Ben sighed. "But I can't help you do something stupid." He leaned his elbows against the fence with one boot heel resting on the low railing. He was quiet for a while, then slapped his hat against his knees. "Why not? I've done plenty of stupid things." He pushed himself up with his foot. His hand fell on Ephraim's head, propelling him up the drive. "Let's go trap us some cougar babies."

Before sundown, Ephraim and Ben had two cougar kits, safe

and sound and mewling in a burlap sack, and headed back to Beacon Hollow through the Deep Woods. When they emerged at the opening of the woods, Ben said, "Ephraim, go to Jorie's with this sack and tell her what's happened. She'll know what to do."

"Aren't you c-coming with me?"

"I can't, little brother. There are a few things I need to take care of." He patted Ephraim on the back. "Jorie will know what to do." He looked out at the setting sun. "I have no idea what that will be, but she'll figure it out. She's always had a sense of knowing what to do."

He started down the road, then spun around as if he'd just remembered something. He reached in his pocket and handed Ephraim a folded piece of paper. "Give her this."

Ten minutes later, when Ephraim knocked on Jorie's door and showed her the wiggling sack, she couldn't believe her eyes. "Oh, the poor darlings, they must be hungry."

As soon as Ephraim heard her call them darlings, he knew that Ben, for once, had given him good advice. These kits weren't darlings, they were monsters. He had cuts and scratches all over his hands and face to prove it.

"What do you think we should feed them?" she asked.

"They l-like p-peanut butter sandwiches."

Jorie looked at him as if he were crazy. "How about milk?"

Ephraim shrugged.

"I'll be right back," Jorie said. She came back a few minutes later with two large bottles used for foals, filled with cow's milk. "Let's go down to the barn and find an empty stall so you can let them out of this sack."

In the barn, the horses sniffed the air—detecting the smell of an enemy—and started making nervous sounds but settled down as Jorie called to them in her soothing voice. She pointed to an empty corner stall. Ephraim slid it open and closed it behind them, setting the sack on the floor so the kits could scramble out.

After watching them explore the stall for a few minutes, Jorie handed him a bottle and said, "You grab one, I'll take the other." She picked up a kit like she'd been doing it her whole life, cradled it in her arms, and tipped the bottle into the gaping, eager mouth. "Drink up, little one, drink up," she crooned, tickling it under its little mouth.

Ephraim was amazed at Jorie's gentle way with animals, even a wild cougar kit. But then again, Jorie always seemed to amaze him. In his mind, there was nothing she couldn't do. He picked up the other kit and tried to imitate her. They sat there, quietly letting the kits drink from their bottles, until the sucking slowed and the kits fell asleep, milk dribbling down their chins.

Softly, Jorie said, "Maybe Dr. Robinson knows of a zoo that might like two baby cougars."

Ephraim shook his head. "Please, n-not a zoo. No c-cages. They n-need to be free."

"Maybe a wildlife reserve then. Someplace where they could roam but be protected too."

He thought that sounded like a good idea.

"We need to do this right away, Ephraim. As long as you can stay here in the stall, the horses won't get anxious. I'll run over to Dr. Robinson and tell him the situation. I'm hoping he'll be willing to come and get them before my grandparents get back from town. If my grandfather catches wind of these cougars, he'll have their hides tanned and hanging on the walls by breakfast." She carefully tucked the sleeping kit into a nest made of hay.

If Jerry Gingerich found out what I've done, Ephraim thought, *he would probably tan my hide.* The thought made him smile.

Dr. Robinson made a few phone calls and found a place for the kits to live. He and Jorie returned an hour later with two crates in the back of his station wagon.

"Tomorrow, Ephraim, I'm going to meet with a friend of mine with the Audubon Society of Western Pennsylvania. They have a nature reserve in Butler County where the kits might be able to live."

"You're s-sure?" Ephraim asked. "They won't end up in a z-zoo?"

"I give you my promise," Dr. Robinson said. "I kind of feel responsible, anyway. I'm the one who started this by giving you those circus tickets."

Ephraim went to the back of the station wagon to say goodbye to the kits. Jorie saw him wipe his eyes with his sleeve. After Dr. Robinson left, Ephraim handed her a note. "It's from B-Ben."

Ephraim waited expectantly, so Jorie read it aloud:

> Dear Jorie,
>   I'm going away for a while to sort a few things out. I'm going to get my head fixed.
>   Love, Ben

"That would be g-good, w-wouldn't it?" he asked, but she didn't answer.

19

Communion was held late that year because the bishop's spring cold turned into a bout of pneumonia, and both Samuel and Cal knew they needed to wait for Isaac. The preparation service, the Attnungsgemee, held two weeks before Communion, was quite strenuous and physically draining for the ministers, who not only preached long sermons but needed to give emotional support to the members as well. The Attnungsgemee was an all-day meeting, filled with importance. The Ordnung, the rules and practices of their district, was presented by the ministers, and each member was asked if he was in agreement with it, at peace in the brotherhood, and whether anything "stood in the way" of entering into the Communion service. Great emphasis was placed on the importance of preparing one's heart for this holy service. Sins were confessed, and grudges—less obvious but just as dangerous—were settled between members. It was this *intention* that Cal loved. A reminder that folks should be keeping short accounts with each other, to not let bitter feelings take root. Mary Ann used to call it internal spring cleaning, and she was right, in a way. It was a cleansing ritual.

Communion would be scheduled two weeks' hence, but only if the members were in full agreement. Maggie and Ephraim always looked forward to Communion because they would be left at home without any adult supervision. Lizzie, having joined the church last fall, planned to attend too.

Cal loved the day of Communion. It occurred twice a year, after a day of fasting. To him, it was layered with symbolism. By starting the day hungry and weak, aware of his humble state, he felt he entered into the suffering and death of Jesus Christ. The long day ended in joy, with a full stomach, and with vivid gratitude and remembrance for Christ's death on the cross. The Communion service always reinforced the unity and commitment of the church members, binding them together.

Toward the end of the day, Cal read John 13, about Jesus washing the disciples' feet, while Jonas and a few helpers carried in towels and pails of water. Isaac announced a hymn and the men began to remove their shoes and stockings, to wash each other's feet. The women, in the next room, followed the same pattern. They worked in pairs and were reminded by Isaac to wash the feet of the person sitting next to them. But from the corner of his eye, Cal saw Jorie purposefully make her way around two rows of benches to reach Sylvia. Jorie stooped down low, and gently washed Sylvia's feet.

And he fell in love with Jorie all over again.

One July morning, Cal asked Ephraim and Maggie to run over to Bud's and call Dr. Robinson to see if he could drop by to check on one of the dairy cows later today.

"Bud? We're here!" Maggie started into the kitchen, but Ephraim held her back, waiting for Bud to invite them in.

No answer returned except an odd blurping sound.

A chill ran through Ephraim. "Bud?" he ventured. "C-can we c-come in?"

Ephraim told Maggie to stay there and approached the doorway with slow, unsteady steps. He quickly found the reason Bud hadn't answered him. Bud was collapsed forward in his chair, his strong arms outstretched across the table, his head turned toward the door and his lifeless eyes opened wide. It took Ephraim a moment to recognize the blurping sound as coffee percolating in its pot. Cold toast had popped out of the toaster.

Ephraim gulped so hard he practically choked. He went back outside and told Maggie in a clear, calm voice, "Go get Cal."

Bud's son was notified and he swooped in to take care of his father's effects. Cal met with Bud's son right away and offered him full price for the farm. He had always hoped to buy that property for his brothers' sake, but there was more to it than that. Keeping Bud's farm intact was his way of honoring his good friend. He'd known Bud all his life; he was nearly like family to him.

At the hardware store, when they heard Ron Harding say that Bud's son had sold off the Deep Woods, Cal saw Ephraim wipe hot tears from his eyes with the back of his coat sleeve.

"I couldn't afford anything more, Ephraim," Cal said on the ride home. "Those woods can't be farmed. I had to take out a loan for Bud's farm as it was, and I had never wanted to take a loan out for anything." He balked at the notion of a mortgage. He had been saving his money to buy farms for his brothers ever since his folks passed—but now that money was gone. He had no choice but to take on a mortgage. He knew Bud's son had wanted to sell the land to a housing developer. But he couldn't rationalize the debt he would take on if he tried to buy up the Deep Woods.

Still, Cal had the same gut-wrenching sense of loss as Ephraim. Those woods meant something special to each one of them. When he heard that the timber had been sold, he felt a stab of concern. He knew their Deep Woods was doomed.

"Everything keeps changing, in ways I don't like," Maggie complained to Cal and Ephraim. "Ben's gone, Matthew doesn't come home, Jorie doesn't come around." She lowered her voice so her father wouldn't hear her. "Only that Elsie lady."

Everyone in the district was talking about Elsie Lapp, the aunties' newest find. Elsie had come to Stoney Ridge from Somerset County for the summer, staying with her brother Jonas and his family. "She's 'the one' for you," Ada told Cal.

"The very one," Florence echoed.

So convinced were they, Elsie was automatically signed up for four Saturday nights, which meant all of June and July. "She's supposed to head home by the end of July," Ada explained to Cal. "If you're going to court her, you need to hop to it."

"Try harder," Florence added, more firmly. "We're running clean out of prospects."

Late Friday afternoon, Ephraim saw a row of trucks carrying bulldozers as they drove past Bud's farm.

Cal came up behind him, watching the parade. "Come Monday morning, our Deep Woods will be history," he said solemnly, as much to himself as to Ephraim.

After milking the cows the next afternoon, Cal promised Ephraim and Maggie a hike through the woods, their last. Just as they walked out of the farmhouse, the aunties and Elsie drove up.

"Oh no," Maggie groaned. "Does this mean we can't go on our hike?"

Ephraim looked up at Cal.

"I'd forgotten . . . ," Cal said, swallowing hard. "I forgot it was a Supper Night."

"Aw, Cal," Ephraim said.

"We're still going on our hike," Cal said, squaring his shoulders. "We need to admire those woods for the last time." He walked out to meet the buggy and help the ladies down. "I promised Ephraim and Maggie a hike into the woods before dinner. Would you mind, Elsie, if we put off dinner for another hour or so?"

"No," Elsie said. "In fact, I'd like to join you."

Surprised, Cal handed the basket of food to Ephraim to take inside. "Tell Lizzie that she's going to be in charge of the aunties for a while," he whispered.

After getting the aunties settled in the living room with Lizzie hovering around them like a bee over a field of flowers, they set off on their hike. When they came to the edge of the woods, they followed the flow of the stream. It led them to a stand of sugar maples, along with a few oak and hickory trees. At the east edge of the grove was a small cemetery where a pioneer family had been buried. Ephraim had forgotten about that cemetery; he hadn't ventured to that part of the Deep Woods for a long time. He had only been in the area where his cougar lived.

"Look, Maggie." Ephraim pointed out two small graves of children who had died of scarlet fever, one day apart.

"I can almost see the grieving family," Cal said quietly as he brushed off the moss on the graves.

Elsie gave Cal a strange look. "So can I."

Ephraim decided, at that moment, that maybe Elsie wasn't so bad. Maybe the aunties had finally stumbled on someone who would be good for Cal. They rested for a while in the cool shade of the cemetery trees.

"D-do you think they'll s-spare these trees?" Ephraim asked Cal.

"Surely so," Cal said. "Surely they wouldn't take trees that were nourished on the pioneer family."

As they walked through the woods, Ephraim took the lead, blazing a trail to his favorite place, underneath the ancient beech tree where his father had carved his initials when he was a boy. When Ephraim pointed it out, they all stopped and stared for a long while. Ephraim eyes glistened a little, but so did Cal's, he noticed.

"Just the tree I wanted to say goodbye to," said a quiet voice.

"Jorie!" Maggie ran over to her and grabbed her hands.

Ephraim was so happy to see her that his hat slipped off when he nearly tripped over a tree root to get to her side. "W-what are you d-doing here?"

"Same as you, wanting to take one last walk in these woods," she said, tousling his hair.

It was so hot that his hair stuck straight up, making Maggie giggle. She interrupted the uncomfortable silence, dragging Jorie over to the beech tree to point out her grandfather's carving.

"I wish it could be saved," Jorie said.

"You must be that schoolteacher everyone talks about," Elsie said kindly. "Folks say you're a wonderful teacher."

"This is . . . I'm sorry . . . Jorie King . . . this is . . ." Cal turned to Elsie with a blank look on his face, his cheeks stained with red.

Elsie looked at Cal, a little nonplussed. "I'm Elsie Lapp, Jonas's sister."

Jorie stuck out her hand to shake Elsie's. "Pleased to meet you, Elsie," she said, sounding like she meant it.

Ephraim wondered what was running through Jorie's mind. She looked as pleased as could be to come across them in the woods. Cal, on the other hand, looked as if he had been caught with his fingers in the cookie jar.

Early Monday morning, the quiet of the countryside was shattered by the snarl of chain saws. Soon afterward came the whine of power log skidders. Throughout that week, Ephraim came to shudder when the sound of a saw shut off, knowing that what would follow would be the thunderous crash of a tree falling. At the end of each summer day, smoke-belching diesel trucks rumbled past Beacon Hollow laden with mammoth logs.

Last night, Cal had stood with Ephraim and watched the trucks go by. He said something that gave Ephraim an unforgettable twinge, a sense that something major was ending. "What nature had taken more than three centuries to create, man will undo in a few weeks' time."

Jorie couldn't stop thinking about Elsie Lapp. She had told her she was pleased to meet her, but she wasn't. She had watched Cal and Elsie in the Deep Woods, unobserved, for a long while before she made her presence known. Elsie was fine-boned, tall, and blond. She had a gentle voice, soft spoken and polite. She suited Cal well, that was plain to see. Jorie noticed that she even leaned slightly toward Cal as they stood side by side, staring at the beech tree. She fit against his side as neatly as a matched puzzle piece. Anyone watching them would think they were already a family. The sight of it nearly broke Jorie's heart, until she reminded herself that God always had a plan. For her too.

But for the life of her, she just didn't know what that plan might be.

Rain was coming. The clouds were low and dark and the wind had kicked up, mercifully cooling the air. Jorie went out to bring the horses in from the pasture before the rain began. Something had set the foals off and they were galloping around the pasture, all thundering legs and raised tails. She stopped to watch the impressive sight. The Lord had seen fit to bless them with five healthy foals this spring when one mare, Stella, delivered twins. Those five foals, including Indigo—who had healed up quickly from her eye injury—galloped from one end of the pasture to another, headed straight toward the fence. At the very last second, they would change direction as one, like a flock of starlings. It was when they galloped back toward the other end of the pasture that she noticed Ben, standing with one leg bent, leaning against the fence like he always did, with a book in his hand to loan. He was waiting for her.

The sight of him caught her breath and made her feel a little dizzy, the way she used to feel when he came calling. "Hello, stranger," she said, walking up to him.

He looked much better. Gone was that haunted look. His features—just a little too sharp when he was so underweight—had softened. His dark hair had grown in, full and thick and wavy, the way she loved it. A hundred memories rushed at her—the way his hair had always smelled of laurel soap, the small scar under one eye, the lazy way he leaned against a fence, as if he had all the time in the world.

"Hello, Jorie." He pushed himself off the fence and handed the book to her. She glanced down at the title—*The Winter of Our Discontent* by John Steinbeck. "Walk with me?"

He reached out a hand for hers as they walked down the long lane that led to the road.

"Where have you been?" she asked.

"Over in Lebanon, staying with Matthew. I've been having a bunch of tests from that shrink, Dr. Doyle. He pronounced me 'officially cured.'"

He gave her a dazzling smile. She had always liked his smile best of all. It had a touch of sweet whimsicality about it.

"Said he's going to send all of his worst nutcases out to Beacon Hollow."

At the end of the drive, he stopped, released her hand, and leaned his back against the fence.

He looked out over the green pastures where the Percherons were grazing. "I'm sorry for those terrible things I said to you. I shouldn't have said what I said. About you being glad Mary Ann passed. I know that wasn't true."

She looked away.

"I'm sorry, too, for telling you about getting fired. That wasn't my place."

She smiled at that. "The bishop wants to rehire me. Said he'd even give me a raise for doing such a good job."

Ben looked pleased. "You gonna take it?"

"I don't know."

"But . . . I thought you loved teaching."

"Oh, I do! It's been such a wonderful experience. I love it more than I could ever have imagined. Even some of the scholars who are hardest to love—Ray and Esther—they have grown dear to me." She sighed. "My grandmother needs more help. We took her to a doctor last week. He thinks she has . . . he thinks she has senile dementia. She's going to require more help. My grandfather . . . he needs me."

"You're the Keeper of Atlee's song, huh?"

She nodded.

Ben smiled a sad smile. "Ironic, isn't it? I've been trying so hard to forget my life while poor Marge is trying so hard to remember hers." He exhaled a deep sigh. "It's been hard, being back."

"I know. It's an adjustment."

Ben turned around and placed his hands on the top of the fence. "It's more than an adjustment, Jorie."

"You've got to give yourself time."

"Time isn't going to make a difference." He turned to her. "There's something I came to talk to you about. I've been thinking of going back to Vietnam. Still as a C.O. Maybe as a medic."

Jorie was shocked. "*What?* How could you even consider such a thing?"

"To finish what I started." He gave her a wry smile. "It's been pointed out to me by my wise older brother that I am not very good at that."

"Ben, give yourself some time to think that over."

"The thing is . . . the thing is, Jorie, I've already done it. I signed up to serve." He bit his lip. "I'm leaving today." He jerked his chin toward the road. "When the bus comes."

"Oh," she whispered, stunned. "Oh." She noticed a suitcase leaning against the mailbox and stared at it for a while. "Have you told Cal?"

"Yes. I've already said my goodbyes." He sighed. "I wish I were the kind of man you deserve, Jorie. The man you wanted me to be. I wish I wanted to be a farmer, an Amish farmer, and wanted to stay here at Beacon Hollow the rest of my life. But I can't be something I'm not." He took his hat off and raked his hand through his hair. "You don't have to say anything. I know it's a shock."

She peered into his face, searching it out. Something was different in him. A wound had healed. "I guess that's what surprises me. I'm shocked . . . but not shocked. I think, deep down, I always have known you weren't here to stay."

He risked a look at her. "Think you'll be able to forgive me?"

He didn't understand; he'd always had such trouble understanding her and her faith. She reached out her hand for his. "Oh, Ben. I already have."

They stood there for a long while, neither one wanting to let go. They heard the whine of the bus as it started to chug up the hill, and Ben's eyes started glistening, but he released her hand and bent down to pick up his suitcase.

"Jorie," he said, as the blunt nose of the bus appeared over the rise. "I hope I haven't messed things up so badly with Cal that you can't find your way back to each other." The bus slowed to a creaky stop.

She looked down at her shoes. "He and Elsie . . ."

"Jonas's sister? Nah." He gave a short laugh. "You know our Cal. Takes him awhile to make up his mind, but once he's done it, not even a stick of dynamite can budge him loose." He put his suitcase down again and faced her. "Cal loves you, better than I ever could."

Her eyes filled with tears. "May the Lord bless you and keep you safe, Ben Zook."

He reached his hand out to caress her cheek. "And may he do the same to you, Jorie King." He held her gaze for a long time, a look of settled peace, then picked up his suitcase and hopped up on the bus.

Jorie watched as Ben wound his way to a seat and waved at him until the bus disappeared around the bend. For a long time afterward, she stood watching the empty road, gripping her elbows, offering a prayer to the Lord over Ben and his future. To her, Ben seemed unfinished and rough-hewn, a man still waiting to happen.

Then she thought she heard someone call her name, just a gentle whisper on someone's lips. She thought she only imagined it, but then she heard it again and turned toward the sound. There she saw a man.

It was Cal, standing at the turnoff to Beacon Hollow with his broad shoulders squared straight, spinning the brim of his straw hat around and around in his hands, his eyes soft around the edges. He was waiting for her, like he had been doing for months now.

Her heart stood still.

He smiled.

She started walking to him, slowly at first, then faster and faster. Soon, she broke into a run.

And then she was in his arms.

The Waiting

Reading Group Questions and
Topics for Discussion

1. A theme in this novel is that our memories—good and bad—shape us. Instead of trying to forget painful memories, the characters learn to embrace their past. But Cal reminds Ben, "This is a chapter. Not the whole book." What is your response to that?

2. With which character do you most closely identify? Why?

3. Mary Ann wanted her family to see that her faith made a difference, even—no, especially—as she faced her death. In this scene, the family is drinking hot chocolate out on the front porch:

   "Maggie, how do your hands feel right now, holding on
   to that warm mug after playing in the cold?"

"Good."

"Really good?"

She nodded.

"But after a while, that good feeling fades away."

She nodded again.

"In heaven, that good feeling won't go away. That warm, good feeling is like the presence of God, and it will last for all eternity."

How do Mary Ann's words help you feel less fearful of death?

4. After Cal is beaten by Jerry Gingerich in the Deep Woods, Bud (the English neighbor) wants to inform the police and press charges. Jorie refuses, saying it isn't the Amish way. Who is right? Do you struggle with not fighting back?

5. This novel is set in 1965 and attitudes reflect that ethos: the town's reluctance to accept an African-American veterinarian (a true event in the author's childhood) is one example. Another is the kinds of therapy used by the Veterans Hospital to try to help Ben recover from combat trauma. Are we more enlightened or accepting now? Have things changed for the better?

6. Ben told Jorie that he felt as if he was suffocating. What made him feel that way?

7. After Ben tells Cal that he killed a sniper in Vietnam, these thoughts run through Cal's mind:

Cal felt shock jolt through him, to think his brother—for that matter, to think *any* Amish man—took the life of another . . . he felt sick with disgust. But he worked to keep his face empty of judgment. This was why his people avoided war, for just such a thing as this. Who knew how he would have reacted, had he been in the same situation?

Cal brings up two points of view before settling on the third. As you were reading, what were your reactions to his viewpoints?

8. What kind of a man is Ben? What do you see in his future? Do you think he will return to his Plain heritage?

9. Throughout this novel, Cal and Jorie never said aloud that they loved each other. Did they need to? Cite examples from the book that show their feelings.

10. What aspects of this novel particularly resonate with you?

11. What did you learn about Amish life while reading this novel?

Acknowledgments

I'd like to express my deep appreciation to my first draft readers—Lindsey Ciraulo, Wendy How, Nyna Dolby—who read the manuscript with tough and loving eyes and generously shared their insights.

As always, enormous gratitude to my agent, Joyce Hart of The Hartline Literary Agency, for being so helpful and steadfast.

A heartfelt thank-you to the entire staff of Revell Books, for making each book they publish the best it can possibly be. A book passes through many hands—editing and marketing and sales—before it ends up on a bookshelf: Erin Bartel, Michele Misiak, Deonne Beron, Claudia Marsh, Carmen Seachrist, Twila Brothers Bennett, Cheryl Van Andel . . . and so many others. Barb Barnes, whose deft, perceptive editorial touch was invaluable. And a special thank-you to my acquisitions editor, Andrea Doering, whose insightful questions helped craft the story more effectively. It is a privilege to work with all of you.

Above all, thanks and praise to the Lord God for giving me an opportunity to share the wonder of His reconciling love through story.

Suzanne Woods Fisher is the author of *The Choice*, the bestselling first book in the Lancaster County Secrets series. Her grandfather was raised in the Old Order German Baptist Brethren Church in Franklin County, Pennsylvania. Her interest in living a simple, faith-filled life began with her Dunkard cousins.

Suzanne is also the author of *Amish Peace: Simple Wisdom for a Complicated World*, a finalist for the ECPA Book of the Year award, and *Amish Proverbs: Words of Wisdom from the Simple Life*. She is the host of "Amish Wisdom," a weekly radio program on toginet.com. She lives with her family in the San Francisco Bay Area and raises puppies for Guide Dogs for the Blind. To Suzanne's way of thinking, you just can't take life too seriously when a puppy is tearing through your house with someone's underwear in its mouth.

Meet Suzanne online at

Suzanne Woods Fisher   suzannewfisher

www.SuzanneWoodsFisher.com

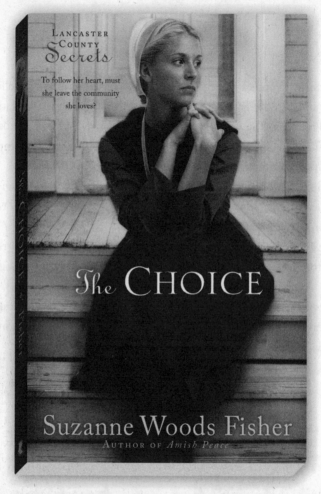

Make the Peace and Wisdom of the Amish a Reality in Your Life